PRAX

Nikki Auberkett

TALA EDITORIAL, LLC

ISBN-13: 9780578377735

ASIN: B09QK5GWB5

Cover design by: Benjamin Richard

Typography by: Kristy Lynae Moore

Interior design by: Deni Dessastra

Tala Editorial, LLC

www.TalaEditorial.com

Instagram: @TheTalaEditorial

TikTok: @TheTalaEditorial

Printed in the United States of America.

This book is dedicated to everyone who waited nearly 20 years for me to finally publish something.

Boom. I did it!

"The greatest trick the Devil ever pulled was convincing the world he didn't exist."

- Charles Baudelaire

S usan Cartwright couldn't decide if it was a good or bad thing that a single watermelon could render so many batches of pickled rinds.

She'd heard from her neighbors down the road that pickled watermelon rinds were delicious and easy to make, and finally, the season was here for the perfect thickness, the perfect juiciness, and the perfect amount of free time to cook them and can them. The spices were easy enough to gather. Lord knows she had more than enough jars and lids from last summer.

What she didn't figure on was just how long—or how much—cooking up one watermelon would actually take.

The sun had nearly set by the time the first jars were cool enough to take down to the pantry. Two at a time seemed the safest bet, so Susan cradled one in each arm as she carefully made her way down the basement stairs. Her neighbors all had furnished basements with expensive carpets and plush furniture, but she preferred to use the cold, damp darkness of her old cellar to store her treasured preserves. It was worth not having an extra lounge space; her spiced applesauce won the blue ribbon at the state fair three years in a row.

As she slid the heavy jars of pickled watermelon rinds onto a dusty shelf, her lips pursed and she wondered if there would actually be enough room for all the jars still cooling upstairs on the kitchen counters. If not, maybe she could "gift" a few extras to the neighbors and get some goodies in return.

Pop.

The sound was soft but unexpected in that silent basement, and Susan jumped a little with surprise. She laughed at herself and shook her head. At least the lid seals were working.

Pop.

Pop.

That was odd. There were only two newly canned jars down there; the others had sealed themselves months, even years, ago.

Pop.

Pop.

Pop.

Pop.

Susan took a step back from the old bookshelf, then another. The popping sound continued, lids on jars from floor to ceiling inverting without provocation. She couldn't feel any heat that might cause this, verified by the goosebumps rising on her arms.

Pop.

Pop.

Pop.

Pop. Pop. Pop.

Pop. Pop. Pop. Pop. Pop. Pop.

From upstairs came the sounds of more lids sealing—or unsealing—too many to reason with herself they were just the newly pressurized cans of watermelon rinds. In the distance, she could hear a train approach, and she let out a sigh of relief. It sounded like a heavy load, probably coal weighing down cars and shaking the ground enough to set her precious jars off balance. She felt the low tremble in the damp pavement of the cellar and nodded. That must be it.

And then she remembered.

She didn't live near the tracks.

Susan's knuckles grew white as she gripped the railing and climbed the stairs. The old wood steps trembled until they shook, and something deep in her soul whispered to only take one, quick peek through the doorway.

"Oh, my God."

He must have heard her whispered prayer - that was the only explanation as to how she was able to close the basement door in the split second before the windows shattered inward and the kitchen table flew across the room. She screamed when she felt it slam against the other side of the door, a pointless sound deafened by the freight train roar. Her fingers fumbled with the lock and she prayed, oh did she pray, the flimsy thing would hold.

It didn't.

"Hey, Babe, can you toss me another?"

Amy giggled and rolled her eyes with a dramatic flair. She happily handed her husband a cold can of beer from the cooler they'd brought out to the driveway earlier that evening. Warm summer nights like this were perfect for sitting on the hood of their car and enjoying a case of Austin's favorite brew after the kids were tucked into bed.

John and Nancy Sturgis lived in the house next door and

always made sure to bring an extra case of beer whenever they joined the Walcotts. Tonight was no exception, and John cracked his own can open almost perfectly in sync with Austin. The men laughed and tapped their beers together, "cheers," and chugged.

"Hey, Honey?" Amy squinted her eyes, blinking a few times. "Is...am I...is it just me, or is the night *moving*?"

"Whoa! Amy, Baby, maybe we should cut you off a little early!" Austin chuckled and playfully grabbed for her beer. "Gettin' tipsy already?"

"No, I mean..." She felt ridiculous for doing it in the night, but she cupped her hand over her eyes anyways and pointed at the horizon. "Look."

The men and Nancy cocked their brows and shared a humorous smile, but spared their beloved friend and wife the benefit of the doubt and followed her gaze, then her pointed finger. Austin quickly sobered up when he noticed the slight tremble in her hand. Now it was his turn to squint.

Beer splashed on his shoes, the can forgotten.

"EVERYONE INSIDE! *NOW!*"

Amy ran inside their house and into the rooms of their children with a speed only a mother's adrenaline could fuel. Their soft voices whimpered confusion, but the wild look of terror in her eyes woke them up and they nodded, each clinging to the thick quilts she wrapped around them as she ushered them down into the basement. Austin was not far behind, his voice barking into his cell phone for his parents to seek shelter immediately.

"Austin." Amy spun around halfway down the stairs and was nearly bowled over when he ran into her. She righted herself and grabbed him by the front of his shirt. "Where are the sirens?"

Austin held the phone away from his ear and listened with her.

Silence.

"Take the kids, get in the freezer." He kissed her firmly before she had a chance to protest. "I'll be right there, I promise."

Only once the door to their standing freezer sealed shut behind his wife and children did he run back outside to his car. Everyone gave him so much good-humored grief for being "one of those" guys, investing in an at-home meat locker so he could personally prepare and store his deer meat every hunting season. Now that he was about to have the last laugh, he didn't feel much like laughing.

His heart pounded in his ears and he used the rhythm like a metronome as he slammed his palm on his car horn over and over and over again. He revved the engine, flashed the brights, honked and honked and honked some more. Next door, John did the same, and soon so did their neighbor another house down. And then another.

When dawn broke over the Miskwa River Valley, it did so without the presence of three small towns.

The President of the United States declared a national emergency and immediately dispatched the National Guard to what remained of each town. Cities from across the state, even border states, lent their hospital staff to operate the medical tents erected to manage the overflow of victims.

No one judged the soldier who tossed his breakfast over

the side of the ditch when they tried to reach Mae Schmidt's farm. Three tours in Iraq still didn't prepare him for the sight of horses ripped in half, their limbs scattered across the bean fields. The small, oh so small relief when they finally reached Mae's farm was that no one had to break the news about her prized horses to her. What little remained of the former rodeo queen clutched the chains of the barn door - found in the woods three miles away.

Local officials scrambled to explain why the consistently tested tornado alarm system of the Portund township failed that fateful night. All anyone was able to figure out was the reason why emergency personnel gathered survivors instead of bodies: "the ungodly ruckus", as one woman huffed, of Austin Walcott and his car. No one gave him crap about his eccentricities ever again.

The director of the city morgue strongly considered retiring right there on the spot when he pulled his truck into the center of what used to be Stillwind. Not only were tombstones from the local graveyard split and scattered in the debris and rubble—entire caskets had been ripped from the ground and tossed around like ghoulish confetti. Ralph Coulter, so close to retirement age anyway, felt that final sip of coffee slide down his throat as he stared at the fractured marble marker of "Jim Bar-, Beloved..." lodged in the hood of someone's tractor engine. He sighed, then fished his outdated flip phone from his pocket to speed-dial an old friend.

"Heya, Phil? Yeah, it's a mess. An absolute mess. I've gotta handle the fresh ones but there's more than just - yup, you heard me right. Straight outta the ground. If I'm lyin', I'm dyin'." He winced at the ill-timed joke that tumbled from his lips before he could stop himself, but his friend either didn't mind or didn't care. "Thanks, Phil. I'll keep an eye out for 'im."

Ralph slid out of his truck and immediately thanked his good sense for wearing steel-toed boots to the site. The ground was nothing but shattered brick and twisted rebar, with old wood beams and only-God-knows-what scattered amongst the debris. His mouth pressed into a firm line when he saw one of the local rescue workers wave him over, and he gave them a quick nod.

He felt his phone buzz in his pocket and he snapped it open, not stopping his careful trek across the rubble. "Yeah? No, that's fine, I understand. Take care of you and yours first, we can meet up when you're done there. Thank God you weren't turned away, right? I heard the overflow is insane. Yeah, alright."

They were going to have to figure out some sort of organizational pattern for the grim job he was here to do. It was only 6 am and this was going to be the first of many, many bodies Ralph would have to identify so the police could notify the next of kin. His heart sank into his stomach when he thought of the estimated population of the three towns that, in literal minutes, were wiped from the map forever.

One small blessing, if he could call it that, was that he already knew who this first body belonged to. They attended church together. She always brought a fresh jar of her spiced applesauce to the potlucks.

There wasn't enough room in the car for Prax, and she was the one who needed the ride. Dozens upon dozens of flowers, most of them roses and lilies, many more she didn't recognize, were packed inside the small vehicle. Very beautiful, to be sure, but it made for a very tight-fitting squeeze into the front seat. "Mom, really...."

Her mother blushed and laughed it off as she helped Prax settle into the seat and find the buckle. "Hey, I can't help it if you're popular! These are just the traveling flowers; wait until we get home."

"Oh no." Prax laughed and brushed a stargazer lily from her face, careful to not let pollen fall on her clean shirt. After spending over a week in a hospital gown hooked up to monitors, she wanted to enjoy the new freedom and new clothes without staining either one.

No one knew how Prax was even alive.

They said it was some random storm chaser who found her unconscious in one of the cornfields ravaged by the deadly tornado. The path of destruction left by the record-breaking F6 vortex was staggering. Scientists both certified and amateur immediately swarmed the region prowling for data, quickly joined by storm chasers of similar variety who bemoaned missing this titanic twister and began searching the clouds for signs of another. That's the only explanation any of the medical staff could muster as to who the Good Samaritan might have been.

The media storm that ensued nearly rivaled that of the tornado itself—no one could believe that amidst such carnage, such record-shattering damage, this young woman was found alive. All other survivors were found locked inside shelters, makeshift safe holds, or deep underground in century-old root cellars in forgotten fields.

Prax was found naked, covered in mud and debris, and breathing. Her injuries healed well, quickly enough for the hospital stay to wrap up without much fuss from her doctors. When she first awoke from her coma, there was significant concern over her memory loss and she heard the physicians murmur frightening words like "amnesia" and "keep under observation". It was terrifying enough to wake up with endless tubes and large machinery attached to her body. Her red-haired doctor kept saying a name she didn't recognize, kept talking to her as if she were someone else, and frowned while furiously scribbling notes onto a clipboard when the only response was confusion and fear.

But the moment Demi Sadeh entered the room, relief washed over both their faces. She recognized her, even if not on a logical level—something deeply innate, intrinsically primal, confirmed this serene, older version of herself was, without a doubt, her mother. Concern flickered in the eyes of her nurses when she didn't respond to the name her mother used, the same name her doctor kept trying. Or another, shorter word that made the doctor pause mid-scribble while her mother looked at her expectantly.

Still nothing. No flicker of recognition. If everyone in the room hadn't been staring at her so expectantly with bated breath, she wouldn't have even bothered to look up.

It was with a heavy sigh, one laden with resignation as her mother pinched the bridge of her nose and rubbed, that Demi tried one other name. "Prax—"

She sat up immediately, whipped her gaze from the bland gelatin on her lunch tray to grin at her mother. "Yes! Prax! That sounds right!"

The fiery-haired doctor lifted a brow and peered curiously at her mother, whose face showed signs of an internal war between trepidation, irritation, and sheer relief. "Prax it is, then," was all she said before she turned to the doctor and asked for a prognosis.

No broken bones, according to the multiple imaging tests they ran immediately upon her arrival. With only a few bumps and scrapes, a few bruises, the main concern was more about any potential damage to her brain. They all initially thought her sleep was due to exhaustion, but when she remained asleep for several days, unresponsive to any stimuli, that's when the worry sank in. When the word "coma" was used.

Now she was wide awake and happy to go home.

Wherever that was.

Another media storm threatened to brew, all with the good intention of welcoming this "Miracle In the Mud" back to the realm of the living, but the hospital staff supported Demi's formidable insistence that they be left alone.

"Remember—" Demi stopped herself with a small laugh. "Sorry. I meant to just say, to remind you, that the doctors said it's okay if you don't remember everything right away. As long as it comes back to you eventually, even if it's piece by piece."

"I know." Prax offered her mom a genuine smile and relaxed as they drove.

Bogarten wasn't a large city by way of Chicago or New York, but it was sizable enough for the rural peoples of the American Midwest. The town-city boasted its own hospital, a feature that turned into a benefit and relief for Demi when they found her daughter. Somehow, for reasons literally no one possessed, the tornado had completely skipped over Bogarten and resumed its journey towards the smaller towns only a few miles away. No one wanted to imagine the true devastation that might have been, had the tornado touched down sooner than it did.

The Miskwa River flowed through the center of town and was the source of most of the founding industry, which evolved into more of a tourist attraction over the decades as new technology replaced the need for water power. Being the Midwest, Bogarten's residents didn't see a need for "total facelifts", as Planning and Zoning called it, so many of the buildings retained the historic beauty of their handcrafted brick and chiseled moldings.

They also proudly hosted a small university near the center of town, where Professor Demi Sadeh taught biology and supervised the botanical center alongside aspiring graduate students specializing in botany. She pointed out the buildings which housed her office, her classrooms, and several other features as they drove through campus on a "mini-tour", as she called it, the final leg of their purposefully slow drive through Bogarten. Prax held a loving suspicion that at least half of the fragrant bouquets tightly packed inside the car were grown, picked, and arranged by her mother's students from the botanical center to welcome her home.

"Home", apparently, was only a few blocks away from campus—and what a building! As the car pulled into the driveway, Prax marveled at the glass dome framed with wrought iron through which she could see the tops of ferns, ficus, and the blossoms of even more flowers she didn't recognize. The sharp angles of the brick and stone combined with elegant curves in the iron mimicked several of the buildings they drove past through the campus, leading Prax to wonder if "home" once belonged to the university. Letters faded by time and the elements confirmed her hypothesis when she stepped to the front door; the words "Department of Biology" were etched into the stone. Given the way her mother packed every nook and cranny with foliage, even on the front doorstep, it might as well be.

"Honey, we're home!" Demi called out as they walked in through the foyer, and Prax winced. Her mom had a boyfriend? A husband? No memory of a father came to mind.

A head of amber curls poked around the corner, quickly followed by bright hazel eyes and a lopsided grin. "Prax!" the girl squealed, and she practically leaped into her arms. "You're home! You're here!" She stepped back and let out a scoff of disbelief, her eyes doing a once-over. "You're here! Oh wow, it's so good to see you!"

Prax swallowed hard and mustered a shy, apologetic smile. "I'm...sorry...I don't...."

"Mya." She grinned and squeezed her hand. "It's okay, Mom told me all about your condition."

Prax's eyes widened. "Mom?"

Demi let out a soft sigh and nodded. "Mya is my younger daughter, your sister."

"We have different fathers, but it's okay, it doesn't matter to me." Mya's eyes sparkled. "We're sisters, and that's all that matters."

Guilt filled Prax for not remembering such a loving and beautiful girl, her own sister, who did resemble their mother the more she looked. All three of them had thick curly manes threaded with strands of amber and gold among the richer chocolate tones, Demi's hair pinned up in an elegant chignon while Mya's hung loose down to her waist. Prax felt like braiding her own hair was a natural thing to do while they drove around in the car, and now the thick plait hung over one shoulder—no less wild and rebellious even in this restrained state. The three of them each had bright eyes of hazels and greens under dark arched brows all set over plump, curvaceous mouths which seemed to naturally curl upwards in a blend of mirth and mischief.

Maybe it was best that there seemed to be no men in this household, as it was filled with incredibly beautiful women. Of course, Prax had to admit, she may have just felt a natural bias towards her family. "Where is your father, if...if I may ask?"

Demi's face fell and she looked away. "He left."

Mya nodded, a sadness, even darkness, touching her sweet face—but it was quickly replaced with another beaming grin.

"Come on! I wanna show you your room!"

With a laugh, the girl tugged her sister's hand and led her into the house where, Prax noted with no small amount of amusement and love, flowers bloomed and leaves glowed in various shades of green absolutely everywhere. The kitchen, the living room, the dining room, the laundry room, the hallways... Demi Sadeh was a "plant mom" with zero limits.

Prax's room was spacious but cozy, and the potted plants weren't quite as numerous here, allowing her to settle in and make it her own. The bed was made with beautiful quilts of hand-stitched greens and golds, ambers and okras, all swirling in patterns she didn't outright recognize but wholeheartedly found beautiful. Soft, decorative pillows were propped near the wall, a desk to one side, and a reading nook nestled in the far corner of the room. Mya wasted no time plopping down on the bed with a giggle. "What do you think?"

"It's perfect." Prax tucked a window curtain to the side and smiled when she saw the view overlooked the private garden out back. "Where's your room?"

"Down the hall. I can show you later, if you want."

She nodded. "Definitely!"

In the warm afternoon sunlight, Prax noticed one difference between their mother and Mya: their skin tones. Demi's was a warm caramel that boasted of years basking in the sunlight, and great genetics, while Mya's was distinctly paler in comparison. She still had that charm, that glow that radiated from within, and Prax glanced at her own arm as she wondered if her days in the hospital had made her just as pale. Sure enough, her skin was much closer to Mya's alabaster with just a hint of Demi's golden glow.

Why was she so obsessed, even if for a moment, about their skin? Maybe it was her subconscious fighting to put pieces together—for instance, had she ever met Mya's father? Was he particularly pale? If she pulled enough differences from Mya's appearance, would memories start to stitch back together about the people who were in her life before the coma?

Her head began to throb and she sighed. One step at a time, her mother encouraged. Don't push it, the doctors had said. Prax was fixated on that itch she so desperately wanted to scratch, but a headache was enough to dissuade her from scratching that itch just yet.

Mya must have noticed because she tucked her head with a sheepish smile. "I'm so sorry, you're probably exhausted. I can leave you be."

Prax didn't want her "newfound" sister to leave, but she also couldn't deny the headache or the weariness that settled over her after arriving home. "It's okay, really. I'm just going to take a nap, and then we can hang out later, if you want."

The smile reached her ears, and Mya quickly stood and hugged her. "I'm so glad you're home! Really, I've been waiting for today for what feels like forever." She kissed her cheek and ducked out of the room, flitting away with the kind of energy Prax envied and hoped to regain soon, once she found her footing.

Her bedroom was dark when she awoke, and Prax inwardly groaned at herself for sleeping the day away. She knew her family wouldn't mind, but she minded. After days of doing nothing but sleep, Prax was more than ready to enjoy being awake.

From the smells drifting down the hall, that enjoyment was going to start with a delicious meal—and she was not disappointed. Demi and Mya beamed as they finished setting the dining table with a veritable feast of all the comfort foods she could ever want, from pot-roasted beef to buttery potatoes and crisp asparagus spears, and somehow she just knew the tea towel draped over a bowl concealed a pile of warm biscuits. There were other dishes that she couldn't quite remember the names for, but the smells were familiar enough to make her stomach rumble with excitement.

Mya poured glasses of ice water for them and grinned as she sat down across the table from Prax. "Mom thought it'd be best to just make all your favorites so you wouldn't have to pick from memory."

"You know, literally anything beats whatever that horrid green blob they kept giving me was!" Prax eagerly accepted the bowl of biscuits Demi handed to her and felt her eyes sting with gratitude. "Thank you. Really, Mom, thank you. And you, Mya," she quickly added, returning her sister's grin. "I feel terrible for having such a selective memory, but I won't forget this!"

They dug into their meal with comfortable silence, occasionally complimenting each other over a particular dish or flavor. Prax felt an interesting unease between enjoying how natural it felt to sit here with her family—they were absolutely, without a doubt, her family—and yet remembering so little about everything…including herself.

Demi noticed the worried look on her face and offered another warm biscuit while she asked, "What's on your mind, Darling?"

Prax did recognize the signs of bribery for information, but happily accepted the food and shrugged. "I'm just trying to sort things out, bit by bit. Like myself, for one. How old am I?"

"Mya, would you like another biscuit?" When the youngest Sadeh politely shook her head, Demi traded the plate of bread for a bowl of wild rice and passed it to Prax. "You should definitely try some of this. Minnesota, up north, is known for their long grain wild rice and I am particularly in love with this season's crop."

"Mom." Prax did take the rice, and quietly agreed it was pretty darn good, but she narrowed her eyes with suspicion at the attempted misdirect. "How old am I?"

Demi dabbed at her mouth with a cloth napkin and seemed to consider it for a very careful moment. That playful mischief always hinting at the corner of their mouths grew in hers, and she tilted her head to one side. "Let's see if you can remember. How old do you feel?"

At that, Prax snorted. "After what I've been through? I feel freaking ancient." She sighed and stared at her fingers as they held her fork poised over the mound of rice, almost as if the answer could be embedded in the whorls of her fingerprints. It was true: her muscles constantly needed stretching, her bones creaked in places she didn't know existed, and a deep weariness in her soul she couldn't identify all made her feel like huddling over one of the walkers she'd seen at the hospital.

"It'll come back to you, gradually and in time. Don't try to rush things before they're ready to reveal themselves." Her mother offered a warm, comforting smile. "If I gave you all the answers right away, do you think that would help jog your memories?"

Prax wasn't sure if a simple number would ruin all her chances of regaining her memories, or her identity, but she did see the logic. "No, I guess not."

"Well, ancient or not, you look fabulous." Mya's bright smile was infectious, which added all the more guilt to Prax's heart that she could not remember such a sweet sibling. She kept chanting to herself that it was a miracle she even remembered her own mother, that her sister had already forgiven her, that the even bigger miracle was her generally intact brain function. Who else gets tossed around by the world's deadliest tornado and lives to talk about it, let alone walk after such an ordeal? So many details were beyond fuzzy—downright thick velour—but something reassured her that as long as she had her loving mother and sister supporting her, it would all eventually clear up and her memories return.

Prax spent a week binge-watching Netflix, reading books, and trying to catch any snippets of memory by exploring the house. It didn't seem to matter what each room was for; almost all of them were filled to the brim with luscious greenery and vibrant flowers, giving the place as a whole a very distinct feeling of walking through a garden. The only exceptions were the mudroom, which lived up to its name with the daunting amount of potting soil piled everywhere; and the family room, which Prax noticed contained no plants at all and very little signs of family activity.

"Nothing ever grows here," Mya piped up behind her, so unexpectedly that Prax jumped and clutched her chest with a laugh. She gave Prax a wry smile and looped their arms together, leading her away towards the atrium. "Mom's been trying, but the lack of windows and natural sunlight is making it difficult."

This explained how the domed conservatory was a veritable paradise, what with all the natural sunlight streaming through the glass to nourish the leaves canopied overhead. It was truly a place anyone could spend hours upon days relaxing in, but good grief, there was an outside world that Prax needed to reintroduce herself to.

Against her mother's wishes, which were really more like vehement protests that eventually melted into begging and pleading, Prax stepped outside the house for the first time in a week with the full intention of going for a walk. Of course, Demi had a million reasons why going for a walk was a bad idea. What if she collapsed from something the doctors missed? What if whatever happened to her before happened again? What if she met someone or saw something that jogged her memory so hard it caused a seizure?

"Fifty-four percent of all injuries happen inside the home," Mya chirped at breakfast, and Demi let out a heavy sigh of defeat. The younger daughter winked at her sister, and Prax couldn't hide the conspiratorial grin.

There was also the fact that while Mya was most certainly underage, probably closer to fourteen by Prax's guess, Prax herself was a grown woman. That much was obvious, from her stronger frame and fiercer gaze to the womanly curves she did her best to hide in a loose-fitting tee and basic jeans. Grown women made their own decisions. She understood wholeheartedly that Demi was just worried about her as any good mother should be, but there were limits. Going for a walk to grab a coffee and just stretch her legs was nothing so serious to warrant such a protest.

Bogarten possessed a unique beauty similar to the house—past and present, old and new were intertwined in the architecture of the shops and offices downtown and its charm attracted visitors from the surrounding towns. There was no Main Street so much as there was a series of parallel streets, each with its own grouping of industries. Fourth Street was where the best café—according to Mya—was nestled between a law office and hair salon. It was there that Prax decided to go, suddenly thirsty for an iced latte, and she hastened her stroll past the apartment buildings that lined the river towards the bridge. Thank heavens Mya knew how to program the map in her phone - after giving her an evening's worth tutorial on how to use the complicated smartphone Demi gifted her.

A few people cast their glances her way as she crossed the wide bridge through the covered walkway. They probably remembered her from the news, but everyone kept to themselves for the most part. Prax was relieved. Of course, she smiled in return to anyone who initiated or gave the standard Midwestern Head Nod, but she simply wasn't ready for any intense attention being "the lone survivor", as the local news erroneously referenced her. She did give an honest effort to see if any faces felt familiar, but none seemed to spark any sense of recognition. Would a long-time friend be excited to see her? Would they jump at the chance to welcome her back?

Did she *have* any friends?

"Hey, aren't you that girl from the news?"

Prax covered her sigh with a cough, cleared her throat, and forced an awkward smile to the guy standing in front of her as they both waited for the crosswalk light to change. "Yeah," she muttered.

He lifted a shoulder and had the decency to look sheepish. "Sorry, I'm sure you get asked that a lot. Just...wanted to say I'm glad you're doing well. We all are."

"Thanks." This time she didn't hide her sigh, since it was one of relief. The man was young, probably a university student taking a lunch break off-campus, and seemed polite and pleasant. She wondered if she knew him, or was supposed to know him...but he didn't look at her with the type of expectancy she'd seen on the faces in her hospital room. Instead, he turned away from her to focus on the crosswalk, and Prax appreciated his respect for her privacy. She was also, embarrassingly, relieved at the lack of familiarity. It was enough trying to deal with the guilt of not knowing her own sister; figuring out friendships was dead last on her "to do" list.

The light turned green, the walking symbol flashed, and the young man stepped into the road.

Immediately the ground gave away, pavement crumbling beneath his feet. His scream was almost louder than the thunder of collapsing cement, cut short by a sickening snap.

"Hey!"

Prax blinked.

The young man peered at her from where he stood at the crosswalk, alive and unscathed. A quick glance over his shoulder showed a perfectly intact road. "Are you okay?" he asked, noticing her wide eyes and pale face.

Prax swallowed hard, willing her heart to slide back down into her chest, her lungs to resume   operation, her fingers to stop trembling. "Yeah...yeah. Thanks," she added with a small smile.

He didn't seem entirely convinced, but he nodded and turned back to the street. The light turned green, the walking symbol flashed, and he stepped into the road.

"Wait!"

Her voice faded beneath his scream as the ground gave away, pavement crumbling beneath his feet. She heard the sickening snap, his scream instantly silenced.

Other screams around her confirmed this was now very, very real.

Passersby rushed to her side, many scrambling to the edge of the sinkhole to pull the young man out. When it became clear he would not emerge alive, those who did not stumble in shock quickly spun around to stop oncoming traffic while others frantically dialed 9-1-1.

It was by either sheer coincidence, or great fortune, that they were only a block away from the police station. First responders arrived within minutes—seconds, to be accurate, as one squad car had been driving by on return from patrol. Prax gave her statement to an officer and declined any medical assistance; the last thing she needed was another reason for Demi to keep her inside. The moment she spotted the news van, she ducked away from the growing crowd.

"Did you see that sinkhole?"

"I heard someone fell in!"

"Poor kid didn't make it...."

Prax did her best not to wince at the not-so-hushed whispers in the cafe and kept her head low as she waited in the short line to the counter. Bogarten may be a large town, a city by Midwestern standards, but news spread among the community just as fast as if it was a small, one-street township.

Plus, it was admittedly difficult to ignore a gaping hole in the middle of one of the main arterial roadways.

"What can I get ya, hon?" The woman behind the counter, a lovely older lady with shoulder-length hair carefully styled into soft curls, smiled and poised her fingers over the tablet screen.

Shoot. Wasn't paying attention to the menu. Prax glanced at the chalkboard high on the wall above the lady's head and quirked her lips. "What's in the 'Sea Turtle'?"

"You like salted caramel?"

"Yes?"

"You like mocha?"

Prax licked her lips and nodded. "Absolutely!"

The barista grinned and winked. "Then you'll love it. What size?"

"Large, please. With oat milk. Iced." While her initial plan had been to grab a coffee and return home, she realized news of the sinkhole incident most likely reached the university campus and, by default, her mother's ears. A panicked Demi was not someone Prax was ready to deal with...at least not without a considerable amount of java. Better to sit and relax in the cozy ambiance of the cafe before going back.

"That'll be $6.50." The barista tapped through the payment on the tablet, then paused. "Wait, aren't you that miracle survivor they found after the storm?"

Prax blushed. *Dammit.* "Yeah, that's me."

"Good to see you doing well, up and around. This one's on me, okay?"

"Really?" Prax fumbled with her wallet. "I can pay, really—"

"It's not every day you get to walk away from death itself. Plus, from what I heard on the news, you could probably use the wake-up." The barista immediately stopped and covered her mouth. "Oh my word, I didn't mean—"

Prax laughed. Genuinely laughed. "No! You're actually right! Here," she giggled, stuffing a five-dollar bill into the tip jar. "At least let me tip you."

"Deal."

The barista quickly went to work making a fresh pour-over, and Prax stepped aside to find an empty table. Jefferson Java was a warm, inviting atmosphere of pine wood floors and antiquated stone walls accented by matching wood panels and antique decor from buildings of Bogarten's past. On the wall next to the chalkboard menu hung a window rescued from the recently demolished St. Catherine's Church, and exposed brick by the main entrance showed pockets of erosion where little trinkets and pictures now nestled. This was the kind of cafe that somehow maintained a quiet atmosphere even when filled with its most loyal patrons, and Prax eased herself into a corner table with a small sigh of relief. She could easily hunker down here for a while until she felt ready to face the barrage of questions waiting at home.

"Here ya go, hon." The barista slid the plastic tumbler across the table and winked. "Let me know if you need anything else, okay?"

"Okay, thanks." Prax smiled back, internally marking this place as her new go-to for all things escape-related. This notion was doubly reinforced by that first sip, the swirl of salted caramel with rich mocha and dark roast exactly what she needed. Mya's obsession with this place - denoted by the way she made sure to bookmark the map in Prax's phone - was entirely understandable.

The silver bell above the door tinkled, and almost the entire frame darkened as a man stepped inside. Prax hadn't noticed the other customers coming in and out, but this guy was difficult not to notice. He looked so out of place, his height matched by his solid-wall-of-a-chest build and his demeanor nothing short of gruff. His dark hair was cropped close enough to keep the waves under control, but even so, they curved around his face all thick and unruly. His dark denim pants were flaked with dried mud and painted with patches of gravel dust, steel-toed boots making every step louder, deeper, than the cafe was used to.

Prax didn't realize she was staring until she blinked and her eyes instantly felt dry. It was rude to stare, she knew this, but still...*who is this guy?*

Whether he was tired or just bored, she couldn't tell, but his eyes barely lifted as he made his way over to the counter. Not once did he look at the menu, just rumbled something to the barista who flitted her lashes and gave him her sweetest smile. To Prax's surprise, he returned the smile and winked at her!

As the barista stepped aside to make his coffee, Prax watched him reach into his back pocket, pull out a small wad of cash, and stuff a few fifties into the tip jar. The barista didn't notice and the man didn't say a word, only nodded and grunted his thanks when she handed him his steaming mug and saucer.

"Good lord, man, did you see that sinkhole on the way in?" An older gentleman who'd been sitting at one of the high tables reading a newspaper called over to the guy.

"Yeah, what a mess." The man turned his back to Prax and sauntered over to the gentleman, sliding into one of the tall chairs that, for him, were just about the perfect height. "I heard it's something with the limestone erosion, so close to the river."

"It's a damn shame, too. I saw that ambulance drive by. Hope no one got hurt too badly."

Suddenly the mocha in Prax's mouth didn't taste so sweet. It slid down her throat more like slime as the memories of that horrible moment flashed in her mind. If what the men were saying was true, there was nothing she could have done about it.

Right?

Her thoughts were interrupted by another patron, a middle-aged woman with sandy blonde hair perfectly coiffed, who turned in her seat and loudly addressed the two men. "Hey, Ralph, how's that project of yours going?"

The older gentleman, apparently named Ralph, sighed and scratched the side of his neck. "I tell ya what, it's all I can do just to get the right family names figured out to put them in the right lots."

"No one wants your job, that's for sure." The woman offered him a sympathetic smile. "If you want, I can talk with my genealogy club and see what we can do to help with the records."

"That would be great!" Ralph took a deep swig from his coffee mug. "Send me what you got and I'll let you know what we're missing."

The woman cast a flirtatious glance towards Ralph's companion, who remained somewhat brooding but gave her the benefit of a small smile between sips of his own java. "We'd love to come by sometime and see how the progress is going, if we can help in any way." She emphasized the word "any", and Ralph rolled his eyes. She only received a nod in response, but that seemed to be enough for her to widen her smile and tuck into her breakfast with a happy little shiver.

A soft slurping sound alerted Prax to the sudden absence of Sea Turtle goodness in her cup. *Darn.* She wasn't ready to face the music, but she'd also promised Mya an iced mocha and, like the good big sister she strived to be, she was going to deliver on that promise. When she placed the order with the barista, she realized no one would know any different—and ordered another Sea Turtle, as well as an iced coffee for her mother. She kept her back to the small group of loud whisperers while she waited for the drinks, but there wasn't much to eavesdrop on. Comments about the weather, crops, river height...at times Ralph mused about the limestone problem, but his friend only hummed or grunted a response.

Finally the drinks were ready, and Prax grabbed them and quietly ducked out of the cafe. She knew it had to be a trick of her peripheral vision—there was no way the tall, brooding man was watching her as she left.

For decades, the people of Bogarten fought the elements and zoning committees to establish housing units along the Miskwa River. Within the most recent two decades, it seemed that favor was finally granted by the powers that be, whether that was the city planning and zoning commission board or the land itself. Rather than rows of houses, rows of apartment buildings were erected, with the highest rent prices allotted to the units with views of the water. Within the past decade in particular, the local historical society gained permission—and grant funds—to add a riverwalk with historical markers to tell the stories of Bogarten's people.

Prax took the longest path possible, sipping her second Sea Turtle as she read each marker word by word, memorizing the dates and names and faces of each story. At first she only did this to kill time, but soon it was a genuine interest that prompted her to take the time to learn the local history. Some small part of her, buried deep in those places she was too afraid to confront, wondered if any of these plaques would help her regain her own memories.

Or, maybe, they'd at least distract her from constantly revisiting the memory of that horrible sinkhole...or that one guy in the coffee shop.

A young woman suddenly stumbled out of one of the apartment buildings, her blonde hair tangled and her eyes wide. Before Prax could open her mouth to say anything, a man burst out from the door behind her, his face twisted in fury as he snarled at the woman. He grabbed her by the hair just to shove her forward, ignoring her shrieking sobs.

The woman cried out as she flew across the yard, her outstretched arms unable to save her from the fall—and her head landed on a decorative stone with a loud, sickening crack. Her body instantly sagged, limp and lifeless on the cool, damp grass, a dark puddle forming around her head like a halo forged in Hell.

"No!" Prax yelled and lunged forward, then froze.

The woman stood in the doorway. Alive, alone, her satin robe tucked neatly around her fragile frame. No blood stained the grass, no man spewed curses or spit on her corpse.

Instead, the woman calmly pulled a box of cigarettes from her robe and lit one, staring steadily at Prax. "Hey," she called out softly, concern touching the corners of her eyes. "Are you okay?"

No. No, no no. Not okay. But no words could escape Prax's tight throat, blocked as it was by the lump of fear that had formed when she thought—no, when she saw the woman get killed by the angry man behind her. Her heart pounded inside her chest, making it difficult to breathe, so she quickly shook her head and kept walking.

It had to be a side effect from her coma. Maybe a yet un-discovered injury to her brain, like her mother had suggested there could be. She wasn't on any painkillers or other forms of medication, since she felt fine and had no injuries to speak of, so that was ruled out.

The only thing she did know for certain was Demi could never, ever know about this.

The rest of the day was graciously uneventful, potentially due to Prax having gone directly home after that freak vision with the smoking woman. Demi stumbled through the door a few hours later, balancing her bag and a stack of books and papers while she spoke with someone on her earpiece about the tragic death of the university student. Her questioning glance towards Prax's suddenly nervous demeanor quickly melted into a grateful smile when her daughter took the books in exchange for the iced coffee. "Yes, of course," she replied to the caller, "I'll extend my office hours just in case. He wasn't one of mine, but I'm sure there will be friends of his needing the time."

Prax quickly ducked away from her mother to set the books in her office. Maybe, if she was lucky, that phone con-versation would last long enough to distract her from asking any questions.

She spent the rest of the afternoon with Mya in the atrium, basking in the warm sunlight and tracing patterns in the leaves overhead from the hammock installed between two indoor palm trees. Prax had to admit, there wasn't any specific need to leave this homebody paradise other than the feeling of not being trapped, and after today's incidents, she secretly conceded maybe some more downtime was necessary. The light through the dome gradually shifted from blue to gold, gold to fuschia, and she wondered if painting was a hobby she'd ever taken up before the storm.

They heard their mother walk by in the hallway, her smartphone broadcasting the evening news as she went into the kitchen to make dinner.

"...was found dead today in the front lawn of her home, where neighbors inside the complex say the couple had been dealing with domestic disputes for weeks "

Prax sat up, then jumped up, her heart hammering in her ears. "Mom, can you turn that up?"

Demi frowned but nodded, and slid her phone across the kitchen island so Prax could watch the video player as well. The news camera slowly panned across the crime scene, which she recognized as that block she'd walked down and seen the woman killed, but not killed. And sure enough, even though no body lay on the grass in front of the camera person scanning the scene, the unmistakable patch of dark red soaked into the lawn made Prax's stomach drop. Then lurch.

"Prax? Honey?" Demi called after her, and when the sound of retching echoed from the bathroom, both she and Mya rushed to the closed door and softly knocked. "Prax? Sweetie, what's wrong? Are you sick?"

"Maybe the coffee was too much?" Mya furrowed her brow.

Demi tried the handle, and the door opened with ease. They were both careful to be slow and soft with their movements, especially when they saw Prax hunched over the toilet bowl. Mya immediately went over and gently smoothed Prax's hair back from her face, holding it in one hand while she rubbed her sister's back with the other.

Prax took a deep, shivering breath, then sighed. "I'm okay, really." She mustered a weak, grateful smile to her sister and then her mother, who leaned over and carefully dabbed at her face with a cool washcloth. "Just some nausea. Maybe you were right, Mom. Too soon for walks in the sun."

Demi's mouth quirked in a smile. "Can I get that in writing? Maybe framed, for my office? 'You were right, Mom'."

Even Prax managed a laugh, and she hoisted herself up to her feet with their help. "I think I'm gonna go lay down, is that okay?"

"Of course!" Demi smoothed the washcloth over her daughter's forehead. "Go take a nap while I make supper. I'll make you a nice mug of soup, to help settle your stomach."

Mya insisted on walking with Prax to her room, tucking her arm around her sister's as if she was about to collapse at any moment. She wasn't, but she was grateful for the warmth and affection from the sweet girl. Mya tugged back the quilts on Prax's bed and sat down on the edge of the mattress once the elder had slid into bed. She drew a lighter sheet over her sister and lightly rubbed her arm. "Are you going to be okay?"

That was a question yet to be answered, wasn't it? But Prax didn't want to worry the girl, so she nodded. Before Mya could get up, though, she reached out and grabbed her hand. "Sit with me?"

Mya smiled and nodded, giving her hand a gentle squeeze. "Of course."

The silence that fell between them was warm and comfortable and were it not for the horrific image of that woman's head bashed against the stone, the bloody halo spread across the grass, Prax could have easily fallen asleep. More than the images was the guilt, the sickening guilt that twisted her stomach into one large knot knowing that she could have done something. She tried with the college student, didn't she? Yelled for him to stop, but mere seconds were not enough. Only an hour or so later, she'd seen the woman's impending death, and she could have done something then as well—but all she did was brush it off and walk away.

"I..." Prax swallowed hard. She didn't want to say it, but she felt like she needed to say something, if just to ease the burden. Who better to tell than her little sister? The need to bond, the craving to assuage yet another type of guilt, opened her mouth and eased her tongue just enough to get it out. "I...I saw it." Her voice was a whisper. Maybe, hopefully, Mya couldn't hear her.

"Saw what?"

Damn. "The woman...that murder, on the news." Prax closed her eyes, then quickly reopened them when the images returned.

Mya sucked in a gasp. "You saw the murder?"

"Not when it actually happened! Before...." She sighed, heavily, and wished her whole body could sink deep enough into the soft mattress to hide her from the world. "I saw him kill her, right in front of me, and then...it was like nothing happened. She was just standing there, smoking. She even asked me if I was okay." Prax felt as insane as she knew she sounded. "I didn't say or do anything because I thought...I don't know, you know? I thought maybe it was my head, or the coma, or you

45

know…that I'm crazy, even." She sighed again and flicked at a piece of lint on her pillow. "I saw the sinkhole, too. I was there."

Mya's eyes widened. "Maybe we should tell Mom—"

"No!" Prax nearly jumped up at the suggestion but laid back down when she saw how it startled her little sister. "I mean, you heard Mom earlier before I even went outside. If she knew about this, she'd strap a tracking device to my ankle and put me under house arrest!"

Mya considered this and nodded. "Point. So what now? Do you need to call the police, give them information?"

"I'm not sure how they'd react to a former coma patient claiming to predict the future."

Now they both snorted with laughter. Wry as it was, it felt good to find some humor in all of this. It was one thing to envision Demi's reaction to such a story, but a whole other hilarious thought altogether imagining the looks on the police department's faces. Prax felt better already, especially since Mya didn't even blink at the oddity of the situation. She reached out and took the moment to return the girl's favorite gesture of affection, squeezing her small fingers with her own. "Thanks, Little Sis."

Mya grinned. "It's our secret. Promise."

At first, the people of Bogarten wanted to wait until their community recovered, until all the names were restored to gravestones either repaired or replaced, until families laid to rest ancestors they'd forgotten before the tornado ripped them from the earth. But in the light of newer events, of collapsing sinkholes and a general sense of wariness settling over the Miskwa Valley, Bogarten's government decided it was time to pull the community together to strengthen camaraderie and, potentially, hasten the recovery process through the revived atmosphere of cooperation.

Potentially.

Mayor Jove Ginnar possessed a solemn charm that both eased and inspired the people under his political influence, which led to his re-election on such a consistent basis that even Demi was hard-pressed to remember a time when he wasn't the mayor. His salt and pepper beard framed a brilliant, youthful smile that appeased women of all ages and gave men the impression of distinguished wisdom, his lean build and squared shoulders draped in tailored suits every bit the image of a steadfast leader. And steadfast is exactly what Bogarten needed in the face of such destruction.

His wave was easy and carefree even as his face showed the telltale signs of strain in the corners of his eyes. His smile was tight as he stepped onto the podium. Normally, at other events, he'd throw a wink or two at a few of the elderly ladies in the front row—and for a moment it appeared as if the old habit would resurface. But he kept himself in check. He was not there to promote a new community center or cut the ribbon in front of a small business. He was there to honor the dead.

"Thank you, everyone, for coming this morning." Mayor Ginnar's voice remained smooth and composed, despite the momentary cough and clearing of his throat. "It's always so good to see all of your wonderful faces, to gather together on such a bright and beautiful morning. I just wish this was under better circumstances. I wish, so much, to see once again the smiling faces of people we'll never stand beside again."

A hush fell over the crowd, many nodding their solemn agreements.

"On a warm, humid night, the kind we're so used to having in late June, three of our towns were wiped from the earth. We're still counting, still cataloguing as fast as we can, but to date we've been able to confirm a loss of over 2,300 lives. Two thousand, three hundred friends and family members." His voice cracked. No one faulted him for the momentary pause, the fist raised to his mouth as he took a deep breath. "I wish I had answers for you. I'm standing before you today in full transparency: we still don't know why the alarms didn't work."

This broke apart the silence with a few grumbles, but none directed towards the mayor—they knew he carried this burdensome guilt and appreciated his genuine honesty. The resentment was held against engineers without faces, technological companies without names, whoever was supposed to build and supply the very systems designed to keep them safe. He knew this. He shared in their frustrations.

Ginnar's eyes scanned the crowd, wanting so much to convey his empathy for their losses. "I, too, have had to bury what's left of dear friends and cherished colleagues. I lost property, but nothing amounts to the irreplaceable souls of my loved ones. Of your loved ones."

And then he spotted a familiar face.

"Well...I'll be damned."

This lifted more than a few gazes to where his breathless whisper echoed into the microphone. The corner of his mouth twitched, then suddenly broke into a grin. "If it isn't our Miracle In the Mud!" He held out his hand and waved towards the stage with the other. "Come, come on up here!"

Prax groaned. *Fan-freakin-tastic.* She couldn't duck out now, not with the enthusiastic nudges from complete strangers around her and the mayor himself beckoning her, then pulling her up onto the platform towards the podium. Did she look as awkward as she felt? Why, oh why, did she have to attend this social gathering when she could have stayed at home with Mya?

Ah, yes. Because one of those firm nudges was her mother, who insisted on making a public appearance "to show support for the students and their families". Now Prax was wholly suspicious Demi Sadeh may have a little crush on the undeniably handsome Mayor Jove Ginnar, what with the way the professor kept beaming at him with all the glowing serenity she could muster. Prax wanted to shoot her mother a sneer but thought better of it, instead giving her best but reluctant smile to the mayor.

"Ladies and gentlemen, I do apologize for the sudden interruption." Ginnar lightly wrapped his arm around Prax's shoulders, unable to hold back the grin spread across his face. "I don't know if you all know this, but this beautiful young lady here is a living, breathing testament to the light that always exists in the darkest tragedies. Miss...."

"Prax." She grit her teeth but managed to smile. *Should have stayed home.* Thank heavens nothing *unusual* had occurred, yet, and when that thought crossed her mind she instantly muttered a prayer that it would stay that way. At least while she stood next to the mayor in front of a few hundred or so people. "Prax Sadeh."

"Doctor Sadeh's daughter! That's right!" Ginnar gave her a friendly little shake in his side-embrace, then cleared his throat again and steadied his tone. "Prax, here, is a literal walking miracle. We found her in the mud of the tornado's path, alive and uninjured. Forgive my blatant words, Miss Sadeh, but by all accounts and from what we can tell, you should be dead."

Is it too late for a redo? Prax kicked herself for the thought, but still—she'd almost rather be in one of her mother's biology classes without any pants on than gawked at by half the city. She did her best to pretend to feel somewhat gracious and nodded with a small, awkward smile. "That's what they tell me. I'm just glad to be home with my family."

"As I'm sure your mother is glad to have you home." Ginnar patted her back, his eyes serious again. "There's nothing so horrifying as the loss of a child."

Prax nodded again, her sigh calming her nerves. "Yeah. My heart goes out to everyone who's lost someone. My sister and I pray for your families every night."

For the barest, briefest of moments, Ginnar's smile faltered. Had she blinked, she would have missed it—but there it was, a flicker. He held up his free hand to shake hers, warm and firm, his gaze steady as she glanced up at him to return the gesture. "We really appreciate that, Prax. Thank you."

He seemed just as ready to help her down from the podium as she was to leave it, but instead of reprieve she was met with a small swarm of well-wishers and friendly supporters who all wanted to pat her shoulders or back or arms and murmur their blessings. Finally, Demi appeared in the crowd and helped shoulder the attention back a few feet with her signature, graciously glowing smile and silken words of appreciation for their kindness. Yes, it was such a relief to have her girls home and safe. Yes, it was every mother's nightmare sitting in that hospital room watching her baby girl sleep indefinitely. Yes, she was looking forward to the new school year. No, she wasn't sure if Prax was enrolling; they hadn't discussed that yet.

Despite being very much a grown adult, Prax felt like she was as young as Mya, if not younger, with the way she hid behind her mother's social graces. But Demi didn't seem to mind, rather she seemed to actually understand Prax's reluctance to shine in the spotlight. It was hot and uncomfortable under such scrutiny, no matter how well-meaning the public.

Ginnar's voice sounded distant as he announced the plans for a commissioned memorial, something tasteful and fiscally sound to commemorate the loss of three towns and almost as many thousands of people. Applause erupted around her, but Prax felt her head start to swim and her energy overall simply deplete.

Demi noticed this immediately and furrowed her brow. "Let's go home. You need to rest."

"Sounds perfect." Prax leaned on her mother's arm as they wove their way through the crowd, Demi pointedly maneuvering them towards the outer edge. A few people patted her arm and both Sadeh women responded with nods and smiles, their steps quickening just a bit more.

Someone started to cough, loud and harsh, to Prax's left and she stopped. There, towards the outer edge of the gathered crowd, stood a woman who must have been in her mid-fifties, hunched over as she wheezed and hacked through her lungs. With every rattled breath the next one sounded harsher, dry and wet at the same time, until her fingers clutched at her chest and she fell hard to her knees.

Prax wrenched away from her mother and rushed to the woman's side. "Someone call for help! Ma'am, are you—"

"Prax?"

She stopped. Demi's voice broke through her panic, and she blinked. The woman stared back at her, wide-eyed and nothing short of terrified, trying her best to slip out of Prax's well-intentioned grasp. No cough, no wheeze, not even a sniffle.

"Oh, honey," Demi gently chided, easing her daughter away from the thoroughly perplexed and unsuspecting woman. "I am so sorry, ma'am. It's been a long day for us."

"But it's not even noon." Prax tried to protest, yet the stern look from her mother was enough to shut her up. She felt even more depleted now, which served as a great excuse to play off that momentary insanity as heat stroke or "survivor aftermath". Whatever it was, Demi muttered to the woman who now regarded Prax with sympathy. Soft laughter was shared when one of the women mentioned Prax's eagerness to help; no harm, no foul, all good intentions.

It was all Prax could do to shut her eyes tight, even if she couldn't shut her ears, to the sounds of the woman's first rattling cough as they walked away.

You need to get out more."

Prax narrowed her eyes at her little sister. "Says the girl who's paler than moonlight."

"You know I'm antisocial." Mya grinned and winked at her. "Besides, the boys can't handle my flawless alabaster complexion. You, however, look like you're about to smash through the roof with that cabin fever."

Observant as always, the teen had a point. Despite the overwhelming, debilitating fear of "seeing" things she absolutely did not want to see, Prax possessed a deep-seated hunger to explore that was currently at starvation levels. If her soul could growl like her stomach, it would be heard the next town over. "Be as it may, I have zero interest in seeing anyone's horrible demise. I'd rather become translucent and...I don't know...vampiric."

Mya rolled her eyes. "Ugh. So stubborn."

"So eager to get rid of me, huh?"

"Maybe." She stuck her tongue out and giggled. "Or maybe I just love you and want you to be marginally less miserable than you are now."

Another point. *Damn, 0 for 2 at this rate.* Prax sighed and shrugged. "What am I gonna do? People die every day, I have no idea how to shut this thing off, and no I am absolutely not, under any circumstances, telling Mom."

Mya puckered her lips in thought. Then she snickered. "You could always go hang out at the cemetery."

"The what now?"

"The cemetery!" Mya cackled and clapped her hands together. "Oh my gosh, you totally should! What's the worst that could happen? They're already dead."

Prax really, really wished the impish joke wasn't such a great idea. But it was irrevocably the perfect plan to get out, avoid people, and duck away from those horrible visions. There was no pattern to follow, no warning when or if another "death decree" would suddenly manifest as tangible and visceral as reality. The anxiety was becoming almost more unbearable than the experience itself. She'd tried making another coffee run to Jefferson Java the morning after Mayor Ginnar's memorial speech, but an SUV swerved too soon around a corner and smashed into a lightpost.

And then it didn't.

And then moments later, it did.

That was five days ago. Prax no longer possessed the courage to leave the house, at least not without Mya's metaphorical hands braced against her back in a solid shove out the door. "How far is the walk from here?"

Mya's eyes widened. "You're seriously gonna do it? Walk into the land of the dead?" She wiggled her fingers and mimicked Vincent Price's nasal narration from her late-night horror film binges.

Prax shrugged. Casual. Calm. Absolutely not insane. "You kind of have a solid point. I don't think I can see what's already occurred. I mean, if that *does* happen, what am I going to do about it? You can't undo what's done. Like you said...they're already dead."

She was suddenly grateful for her lack of a social circle, or any social media accounts for that matter, because the idea of getting exercise in a cemetery sounded weird enough in her head, let alone attempting to explain it to anyone when asked, "So what are you up to these days?" They waited until their mother left for work, muttering under her breath about students not "getting" the difference between corn and maize, before Prax dressed for her walk and slipped on her shoes. "Wanna come with me?"

Mya scrunched her nose. "Nah, I'm good. I have another three seasons of *True Crime* to binge, and it's not gonna watch itself."

Prax rolled her eyes but gave her sister a peck on the cheek. "Be good, don't melt your brain too much, and text me if you need anything."

"I need a frap."

"Do you *need*—"

"Yes."

"Okay." Prax laughed and checked her pockets for her phone. "Text me your order and a reminder, I'll let you know when I'm on my way back."

According to Bogarten's unofficial oral history, the kind that passes down from library matron to coffee-obsessed housewife and is overheard at the local grocery store, the cemetery used to be called "Field of Dreams and Memories".

Then a certain film came out and caused quite a fuss when confused tourists flooded the tranquil gates of the community's final resting place. After a rather heated, and historic, campaign to rename the cemetery—and if the gossip was to be believed, at least one fistfight at a Planning and Zoning Council meeting—the people of Bogarten eventually settled on "Nanabozho Memorial Park", a respectful nod to the Sauk Nation who used to own the land, and who also used much of it as a burial ground before the colonizers arrived.

No one argued that name. No one dared.

Once City Council acquired permission from the Meskwaki Council to use the name, emphasizing the utmost respect for their people and the genuine wish to honor them, a "facelift" was given to the whole stretch of the grounds to make it more of an actual memorial park versus the glaring reminder of death that it was. Despite another round of grumblings from those who hate change unless it's the kind that jingles in pockets, the community actually managed to band together to revive some of the older stones. In an odd but inspiring move that made news on public broadcasting, many of the faded-by-time gravestones from the previous two centuries were replaced by elegant markers with names and dates restored. Families and ancestors were honored in several small ceremonies as the new markers were put into place. The original headstones found a new home in the university campus museum's archives for student conservationists to preserve.

Now, the Nanabozho Memorial Park was a beautifully manicured work of public art, with only a few particular plots of land where Old World pillars and obelisks remained as solemn reminders of the presence of the dead. Despite the

Midwestern weather guaranteeing heavy amounts of snow every winter, the city was very proud of its groundskeeping team who endlessly dedicated their time and energy to clearing each headstone, marker, and pathway so families could still locate their loved ones in the middle of January. Every section was marked by an elegant sculpture, with decorative hedges surrounding each designated area and marble benches installed for those wishing to spend time in memory.

Prax felt a twinge of sadness, but also sympathy, for the section of land dedicated to children who passed on "before their time". A simple little playset had been donated and installed by the family of a leukemia patient who left this world at the tender age of six, so she could play with the other little spirits who welcomed her into the afterlife. Occasionally a drunk university student swore they saw the swings move on their own, or the tiny merry-go-round spin without the aid of the wind, but such stories were met with eye-rolls and offers of more booze to calm their inebriated nerves.

As she made her way down the cobblestone paths that wound through the cemetery, she felt a strange sort of peace wash over her. Peace and quiet, both outside and within her mind, for the first time in weeks. Not a soul—no pun intended—around to scare her with their fates, no clucking mothers to shoo her back inside, and no gut-twisting worry over her lost memories. At least for now, anyway. Prax smiled, really smiled, and even tugged her braid free to let the breeze dance within her curls.

Except...that wasn't a breeze at the nape of her neck.

She froze. A warm, moist puff of air hit her skin again, tousled her curls, again. And again. Someone tall stood directly behind her, panting heavily onto her neck, and she felt her chest squeeze the air from her lungs with fear.

A warm, wet tongue lapped at her fingers where her arm hung at her side, and she nearly jumped out of her own skin. The tongue was large, flat, and eagerly licking at her fingertips with a tiny, plaintive whine.

Prax slowly, so slowly, turned around.

This had to be the world's largest dog, if one could even call it that. It looked much more like a giant pile of floof on four paws, with eyes buried somewhere within all that dark fur. It panted happily and, when it saw her turn to face it, quickly sat on its haunches as if on command.

The words "hell hound" flicked into her mind, but the more Prax studied the dog, bear, bear-dog, the more she found it unlikely to be anything more than a massive furball eager to play catch, not some soul-hunting beast. Its tongue lolled out to one side as it panted and looked at her, and it cocked its head to one side with another small whine of curiosity when Prax still didn't move. Slowly, hesitantly, she reached out her hand to the dog and stroked lightly over the fur of its neck. She was instantly rewarded with sloppy wet kisses all over her face, and Prax couldn't stop the giggles that escaped her as she was happily accosted by this loving floof.

A loud whistle pierced the air, and both Prax and her new companion whipped their gazes to the source of the sound. Lumbering towards them was a tall, dark, and very handsome man—Prax felt her cheeks flush at the thought—who looked none too pleased to see her there. His dark brows were stitched together in a glower, which only made the rest of his chiseled face even more attractive...dangerously attractive. A full, curving mouth was pressed thin into the frown plastered on his face, and a vein ticked in the side of his jaw as he stared at Prax.

It was then she realized she'd seen him before: Jefferson Java, stuffing fifties into the tip jar and discussing some sort of project with an older man.

The Giant Floof trotted over to the man and licked his bare arm, which Prax noticed was covered with various patterns tattooed in dark ink. Dressed in a simple black tank top and dark blue jeans, the man oh so casually had a way of showing off his sculpted physique and, Prax had to guess, dangerous strength. In fact, everything about this man screamed, "Stranger danger!" But she found herself drawn *towards* him, not repelled.

Add this to the list of reasons why Demi kept her daughters indoors....

"What are you doing here."

His deep voice broke her from her thoughts, and Prax blinked. His question sounded almost accusatory. She suddenly felt wholly ashamed when she realized where she was, playing cuddles with a dog as if they were in a normal park—not the final resting place for hundreds of people. Prax swept her long hair to one side and quickly plaited it back into a thick braid, her fingers twitching nervously. "I was just.... I am so sorry to disturb you." She turned on her heel to flee.

"You didn't."

Prax paused, feeling that tug inside her again. Mya was going to have an absolute heyday when she heard about where her big sister was meeting men. "Is this your dog?"

The man sighed and nodded, scratching the Giant Floof behind the ear. "This is Spot. He's *supposed* to be keeping an eye on the grounds."

Spot cocked his head and gave the man a Look, at least that's the vibe both of them felt from the eyes unseeable through the thick fur which, oddly enough, seemed to be void of any spots at all. Prax bit back a giggle. "He's beautiful, and *huge*! What kind of dog is he?"

"Tibetan mastiff. One of the largest breeds in the world, and the deadliest."

Now Prax was incapable of holding back the laugh, which came out more like an embarrassing snort. To her credit, the man's mouth twitched up in one corner, but he quickly repressed it back down. "Yeah, I know," he grumbled, rubbing Spot's back. "He's more bark than bite, and even then he doesn't always *warn me* when intruders are around." His very pointed statement was met with Spot's facial fur shifting ever so slightly, and then a torrent of loving kisses all over the man's face and neck. "Yeah, yeah, okay, okay!" What could be mistaken for a low chuckle rumbled in the man's chest, and he gently urged the dog back so he could turn his gaze to the young woman watching the exchange.

She suddenly realized what he meant by "keeping an eye" and she pursed her lips into a silent "oh". "You work here."

He nodded. "Groundskeeper." His dark eyes swept over her from toe to head, but not in the way that made her feel uncomfortable or skeevy. It was more like...wariness. "Are you here looking for someone?"

Because that would make sense. Not the real reason, a casual stroll through a cemetery for recreational purposes to avoid Seeing people's horrific ends. Prax tried to think of a name, any name, but her mind blanked. "I...no." She sighed and figured a half-truth was better than an obvious lie. "I was just going for a walk."

"A walk." His brow raised.

She nodded, her gaze sliding away to look at anything but him. "Yup."

He opened his mouth to say something, then shut it again. After a beat, he tilted his head and said, "You know, most normal people choose other kinds of parks for exercise, like... anything *not* a cemetery, for instance."

"I'm not normal." She blurted it out before she even thought it, and blushed. "I like it here better. It's quiet, it's peaceful, and no one is around to bother me."

"Except the staff."

Prax quickly flicked her gaze to his and realized what she'd just insinuated. "Oh! No, I didn't mean you're—"

He smirked. "It's okay, I get it. It's why I do what I do, anyway." He patted Spot on the back and turned to leave. "I recommend taking the fork at the left up ahead, there's a reflecting pool and garden that's pretty nice this time of year."

"What's your name?" She figured it'd be good to ask, and good to know, if he worked where she planned on visiting frequently.

The man paused and almost seemed surprised. "Aidon."

"I'm Prax."

Aidon turned back to her with a quizzical look on his face. "That's interesting."

She shrugged. "It's who I am, I guess." At his silence and steady gaze, she cleared her throat and gestured to the cobblestone path. "Fork at the left?" When he nodded, she flashed him a quick, shy smile and skipped past him, not wanting to prolong the awkward conversation any more than it already was. Besides, the man was at his work, probably had lots to do, and she was only interrupting.

When she glanced back over her shoulder, she caught him watching her. From this distance, it was impossible to tell, but her trickster eyes suggested the barest hint of a blush when he realized she'd caught him staring. He straightened his back, let out another sharp whistle, and sauntered off with Spot in tow.

Prax didn't want to seem like a creep, just standing there outside the shop staring into the window.

But she also couldn't find the guts to walk inside.

She took a deep breath and practically ripped the door open, her anxiety to get this done and over with fueling her more than the three Sea Turtle mochas she'd downed prior to walking across the street to do this. Her original plan to stay home and hide from the world lasted about as long as one season of Mya's *True Crime* and that was plenty. Time to be brave, be productive. Be employed.

Thankfully the door was made from heavy oak that did not care how wired she felt, it moved on its own time. A tiny bell jingled above her head, which alerted a beautiful woman with strawberry blonde hair to her presence - as well as the police officer the woman was talking to.

"Oh!" Prax felt her already pounding heart flip and skip a whole beat. Her face flushed with embarrassment and she took a step back across the threshold. "I am so sorry! I can come back later!"

"Wait!" The woman waved her in with a giggle. "It's okay, this is my husband, Garrett. He was just checking in on me."

The police officer smiled and gave Prax a nod. "Nice to meet you...?"

"Prax."

"Oh, that is a fun name!" With a kiss to her husband's cheek, the woman nudged him out of the shop and turned back to Prax with a warm smile. "I'm Courtney, the owner. What can I do ya for?"

Prax swallowed hard, her tongue suddenly thick in her mouth and her palms practically dripping with sweat. She glanced over at the sign in the window. "I, um, I saw the sign over there, you're looking for an assistant?"

Courtney nodded, her jovial demeanor shifting into "boss mode", as Mya would call it. "I am! Do you have experience?"

"Ah, no. Well, kind of." She let out a shaky laugh. "I don't have experience as a florist, officially, but I actually live in a greenhouse. Over at the university. My mom's a professor of biology."

"Wait." Courtney peered closer at Prax, studying her face. "The old greenhouse they gave to Dr. Sadeh? *You're* her daughter?"

Prax nodded. "One of them. I'm her eldest. Mya's my little sister." She paused. "Wait, you know my mother?"

"Know her? She nearly failed me out of her botany class." Courtney snickered and gestured Prax over to the work table where a huge tome of a design catalog lay open and stained with water droplets and pollen. "She took pity on me, though. After I bawled my eyes out and begged her to give me a passing grade so I could prove to my parents that opening a flower shop was definitely a wise career move." She giggled again and flipped through the pages to the section on bridal bouquets, skimming her finger over each design as she puckered her lips. "Here we go," she grunted, turning the book around to show Prax a cascade of champagne roses and stargazer lilies. "What do you think?"

"It's beautiful."

"Awesome. Flowers are in the fridge, tools in the cabinet to your right, there's more in these apothecary cabinets around here."

Prax whipped her gaze back up to Courtney's face. "What?"

The florist grinned. "Ya gotta audition, hon. Book smarts are one thing, but skill is something entirely different. Even if you had years of experience, I'd still need to see whatcha got in those fingers of yours. Besides," she added with a wink, "I wanna see what Prax Sadeh can do with the family green thumb." She glanced at her watch and nodded. "Perfect! Think you can be done by two?"

"Uhhhhmmm...." *As if there was a packed schedule to get back to.* "Sure? I'm not sure what I'm supposed to do, though...."

Courtney nodded and handed her a dark green work apron. "Just study the picture, see if you can recreate it. Bridal designs are always the hardest to make, and the hardest customers to please. Usually I'd run you through more paperwork and background checks, and training, but you're a Sadeh. Can't go *too* easy on ya." She gave her another cheerful wink and ducked away into the small backroom office, leaving Prax to figure out the rest. *A floral arrangement?* Prax peered at the picture in the design book. Of course there wouldn't be any instructions; she's never that lucky.

After a few minutes quietly opening and closing cabinets and drawers (lest her potential future boss hear her confusion), she slipped on the work apron and tugged heavy vases of champagne roses and stargazer lilies, and a few different variations of fillers, over to the work table. *Screw the book.* Time to make the Sadeh name proud.

Courtney's eyes bugged out of her head when she saw the finished bouquet.

And the matching floral head wreath.

And the six bridesmaid sprays, coordinating boutonnieres, and corsages.

"Oh, sorry." Prax blushed and took a step back from the flower basket she was adding finishing touches to—an enchanting, ethereal weave of delicate vines and miniature roses to match the rest of the ensemble. "I, um...I kinda got carried away."

The bridal bouquet Courtney held in her hands looked plain next to the artistic liberties Prax took with her own interpretation of the same design. The shop owner had only just emerged from the storage fridge to package the order, but stopped in her tracks when she laid her eyes on the full ensemble neatly arranged on the work table. "You did...all of this?"

Prax nodded, swallowed hard, and felt her blush deepen. "I had some leftovers from the sprigs for the bouquet, and saw some of the coordinating designs in the book, and thought.... I am so sorry, I should have asked." She didn't actually remember at what point her nervousness, her confusion, gave way to an almost zen-like state of automatic movements. Her thoughts drifted while her fingers twisted wires and wrapped tape, her eyes monitoring the arrangement of blooms with greens. She didn't even remember where she was, or what she was supposed to be doing, until she heard Courtney come back out from the office and pop open the storage cooler.

Truth be told, Prax was almost as surprised by the sight of the work table as the florist.

Before Courtney could respond, the bell above the front door tinkled and a loud gasp, followed by a squeal, pierced the air. Three women shuffled into the shop, their leader an enthusiastic blonde with perfectly manicured nails who fluttered her fingers over her mouth as she blinked back tears. "Oh. My. Gawd. It's perfect!" She reached for the bouquet in front of Prax but stopped herself, instead turning to the older woman who joined her side. "Mom, look at this! This is...I don't even have words for how perfect this is!"

"My word." The mother shook her head slowly with awe. "Miss Courtney, you have thoroughly outdone yourself!"

"How much do we owe you?" The bride snatched her wallet from her purse and rifled through a stack of hundred dollar bills. Prax did her best to not gape, reminding herself that soon-to-be-brides probably would be flush with cash.

Courtney stammered for a moment, at a loss for words as she did her best to navigate the flurry of excitement. "Well, you did only order the bouquet—"

"We'll take them all! How much?"

The florist glanced at Prax, who could only offer a small, perplexed shrug. "Six...hundred?"

"Here's a grand. Keep the change." The bride shoved a wad of hundreds in Courtney's hand and scooped up her luxurious bouquet into her arms, cradling it like a small child to her bosom. Prax quickly stepped in to help the mother and maid of honor pack up the remaining arrangements—including Courtney's, now the "tossing bouquet"—into storage boxes, tied each with a satin bow, and helped them balance each box on their way out to the car. It was a flurry of giggles and squeals and reassurances from the mother of the bride that yes, they will stash the flowers away in a cooler the moment they got to the venue, no, she hadn't heard from who Prax assumed to be the father of the groom, yes, they can absolutely stop over at Jefferson Java for some coffee.

They left as quickly as they came, with Courtney and Prax slack-jawed and leaning heavily against the work table in their wake.

"So." Courtney blinked, then thumbed through the wad of cash in her fist. She tugged out a couple bills and handed them to Prax. "I'd say you earned this!"

"Wait...really?"

Courtney snorted a laugh and nodded. "Seriously. You passed that audition with flying colors. Do you have any idea how difficult brides can be - how difficult *that* bride can be?" She tucked the money into Prax's fingers and grinned. "I just got one question for ya, hon. When can you start?"

"Behold! I come bearing gifts!" Prax called out into the house as she kicked the front door behind her. A cold splash of iced coffee spilled over her fingers and she hissed a curse, licking up the droplets before anything stained her mother's beautiful wood floors.

"We're in here!"

That always meant the atrium, the favorite room of the family. In its earliest days, this was the heart of the university's botanical center, a paradise of warmth all throughout the year regardless of rain or wind or snow. Now it was the

Sadeh's living room, with the macrame hammock strung up between two palm trees serving as Mya's "second bed" and rattan couches stuffed with exotically woven pillows framing the space.

Mya swooped in from out of nowhere and snatched one of the iced coffees from her sister's hands, a movement so smooth and practiced it reminded Prax of an eagle diving for fish. Demi retrieved her own drink a bit more delicately, thanking her eldest for the kind thought before taking a small sip. Everything the professor did was with such elegance and grace, at times Prax felt a twinge of envy that she moved like a tromping elephant in comparison.

"Okay," said Demi, "what's the news?"

She knew her mother would be instantly suspicious once she tasted the indulgent add-ins she saved for "special occasions"— like bribery. "I met one of your old students today, Courtney Johnson? Ring a bell?" Keeping her tone light and casual was part of her negotiation strategy, a trick something in her gut told her she'd learned from the elder Sadeh at some point before the storm. Prax flopped down on the couch next to Mya and swirled the ice around in her mocha.

Demi raised a brow, but played ball. "I think I know who you're talking about. Used to be Courtney Schmidt. Married a police officer, right?"

"Yeah, Garrett Johnson, I think he said his name was."

"Mhm." Another sip, and the professor's eyes narrowed. "And?"

Prax continued to play it casual, even as she could clearly see her mother was not buying it. "And she owns a floral shop now! She said you helped her convince her parents. Actually, she attributed a lot of her success to you."

"How sweet."

"Yup." Prax took a long draw through the straw. "And... she hired me."

"Prax."

"Woohoo!" Mya slapped her sister a high-five and beamed. "Get dat monaaayy!"

Demi was not so excited, or remotely pleased. She leaned into her hand and rubbed the bridge of her nose, seemingly taking a moment to breathe and choose her words carefully. "I am proud of you, Baby. I really am. Don't get the wrong idea."

"But...." Prax braced herself for the lecture sure to come.

"But we talked about this. About you moving too fast, especially so soon after your coma, your injuries, all this added stress can't be good for you." Demi swirled her ice around, unintentionally mirroring Prax, and pursed her lips in thought. "Have you talked to your doctor about this?"

Prax balked. "About getting a job? I didn't know I'd need a permission slip from the hospital to stick flowers in a vase." She heard Mya snort and quickly mask it with a cough and sniffle. "I understand your concern. I really do. But I'm fine." She felt her sister's foot suddenly, gently, press into the small of her back from where the teen reclined in her comfy corner, and she knew what that meant. *Are you really?* Mya was the only one who knew about Prax's visions; she'd kept her promise to preserve the secret. And the idea of working, of being in public where anyone at any point could suddenly keel over in front of her wasn't...*ideal*...but neither was staying cooped up in the house.

Demi thumped her straw inside the cup a few beats, then nodded with a very resigned sigh. "I guess it's better you're with Courtney. At least I know her, and she knows where and how to find me should anything happen."

"I promise I'll wear my medical bracelet at all times."

"Want me to geotag her?" Mya grinned, a little too excited.

For a very brief, rather scary second, it looked like Demi actually considered that idea. But she waved her hand and laughed. "Heavens no! I trust Prax, and I trust Courtney to still be afraid of me enough to keep things in line."

Prax let out a sigh of relief, unaware she'd been holding her breath. She expected resistance from her overprotective mother, but she figured it could have been much worse if it was over a job somewhere else, where Demi didn't have connections or couldn't keep tabs. Which, after a second thought, made Prax inwardly groan.

Did this mean she'd exchanged one gilded greenhouse cage for another?

Courtney Johnson was the kind of boss who valued the work day as much as anyone—and respected, down to the second, closing time. Every evening at five o' clock sharp, the doors were locked, curtains drawn, and whatever project still remained in Prax's hands would be quickly snatched away and stored in the cooler for tomorrow. "No use working if you don't allow yourself to live!" She'd sing as she whipped off her apron and threw it onto the nearest hook.

On this particular summer evening, Courtney's step had an extra bounce to it and she grinned from ear to ear at her new assistant. "Hubby and I got a babysitter for tonight! Are you free?"

"Free?" Prax blinked.

"Yeah! We're going to dinner, of course, but I thought it'd be fun to meet up at the pub and hang out. Get to know ya. Garrett almost never gets a night off, and it didn't take much convincing when I mentioned bottomless pitchers at Hawkeye's."

Was Prax a drinker? Of coffee and all things java, absolutely. But it suddenly occurred to her that at no point did she ever feel the urge to imbibe on anything alcoholic—not that the opportunity readily presented itself. Her mother only drank wine on occasion, and Mya was too young. "Sure, thanks! You said at Hawkeye's?"

Courtney's grin threatened to break her face. "Yay! Yup, right around the corner from here. I know, it's not *really* going out on the town, but the owner knows us and we'll get a good deal on pretzels."

Only on her way home did Prax realize her mistake: thrusting herself into a public, crowded room full of beer and bad decisions would only invite the horrors she was trying so desperately to avoid.

She waited until her mother was locked away in her bedroom for the night, and Mya was in her own room nose-deep in a book, before tiptoeing out the front door. Not that anyone would outright object to her going to meet her boss, and Demi's former student, just to hang out—there was just no telling how long the Overprotective Sadeh would keep her pinned to the foyer with questions about where she was going, who was all going to be there, does she have all eighty emergency phone numbers logged in her cell, blah blah blah.

Note to self: figure out how old I am so I can remind her.

Hawkeye's really was around the corner from the florist shop, a tidy middle ground between dive bar and classy pub. From the talk around town, they boasted one of the best corned beef sliders and a mean spinach dip—Prax made a note to order lunch from them soon, maybe for a takeout potluck dinner with Courtney.

She scanned the crowded pub but didn't see any signs of the jovial florist or her tall, straight-laced husband, and figured it may still be a bit early for them. Date night, after all, was not something to be rushed between a married couple with kids. Prax slipped over to an empty stool at the bar and ordered a ginger ale to start. She didn't feel confident adding alcohol to her drinks without a friend to keep her in line or rush to her aide; no telling what even a few sips would do to Prax's still-unfamiliar constitution.

As her eyes roamed the room once more just in case she overlooked Courtney and Garrett, she suddenly choked on a sip of her drink when her eyes met the very dark glower of the cemetery's groundskeeper. *Aidon, was it?* He sat in a corner booth nestled deep in the shadows, clad in dark denim and black leather over his fitted tee, but no amount of low lighting could hide the heat in his gaze as he stared back at her. And it wasn't the good kind of heat, the kind that made toes curl and skin tingle.

Prax was very much aware that this was a heat more like hellfire.

"Don't take it too personally. He's always had a stick up his ass about one thing or another." The guy sitting next to her at the bar, swirling a shot of whiskey in one hand, shrugged. "Not much of a people person, really."

Startled, Prax whipped her gaze to the man and took a deep swig of her own drink to prevent the gasp that threatened to escape. Turquoise eyes glittered back at her, and his sensually full mouth curved upwards into a genuine smile. That act alone served to accentuate his elegant face with high cheekbones and smooth planes, and all Prax could think at that moment was how Michaelangelo would have experienced a joy-induced aneurysm trying to carve this man into marble. "Friend of yours?" She managed to ask, surprisingly calm and steady despite the flutter in her nerves.

The man scoffed and nodded. "As much as he hates to admit it. But, to be fair, he's had a rough go of things lately.

Best to just humor him and let him pout it out."

"Ah. The storm?"

His smile wavered for a flash of a moment, and he cocked his head as he seemed to weigh his response in his mind. "You could say that."

Prax knew it was none of her business, but she also couldn't ignore the daggers Aidon was throwing via his eyeballs, especially now that he saw her talking with this guy at the bar. "So, tell me, because I gotta know," she smirked with a discreet nod towards her hater, "what's his story?"

"Hm." The man regarded her carefully, the shot glass poised at his lips which pursed for a moment as he studied her. He seemed to reach a decision, knocked the whiskey back, lightly slammed the glass down on the counter, and signaled the bartender for another. "I actually don't know the full details, you'll have to get those from him. But what I do know, the man just woke up one day and his wife was gone."

What?

The question mixed with reaction must have been on her face plain as day, because the guy nodded in response, his expression somber. "Yeah. No letter, no warning, not even an argument the night before. For all anyone knew, it was the happiest marriage on the planet until she just up and left him."

Prax shook her head, a knot forming in her gut with sympathy for the groundskeeper. No wonder he carried a chip in his shoulder. "Who would do that? I mean, I don't know him, but still. What kind of horrible person would just up and leave like that?" A sudden thought occurred, and she straightened. "Wait. Do you think maybe she was kidnapped?"

The man studied her closely, his eyes searching hers for answers to questions he didn't dare ask. His brow lifted and he sighed, a new sort of smile playing at his lips. "You know, I gotta be honest. There are more questions than answers in this case. But I see your point—maybe he jumped to conclusions."

"Says a lot more about him than her."

He coughed on his whiskey and barked out a laugh. "Oh my god, I am so telling him that."

A freckled arm swathed in perfume snaked around Prax's shoulders, and Courtney's signature grin appeared in her peripheries. "Hey you! So glad you made it! Garrett's got a table for us, let's go hang!" She shifted her slightly inebriated gaze towards the handsome gentleman sitting next to Prax and her jaw dropped for just a second. "On second thought, maybe I should leave you two here—"

"Which table?" Prax quickly slid off the barstool, ginger ale in hand, and flashed the complete stranger an apologetic smile. He smirked and winked, then slid off his own seat and sauntered over to his glowering friend in the dark and shadowy corner. Prax's ears picked up a mumbled grunt and what sounded like someone getting elbowed in the gut, but Courtney's slurred chatter about ribeye and mashed cauliflower drowned out any chance of eavesdropping.

As they approached the booth where Garrett sat with a pitcher of beer and empty mugs waiting for them, something caught Prax's attention in the corner of her eye. A biker, burly and tattooed on every inch of exposed skin save for his face, slumped over in his chair, head on his arms.

Beer and spittle dribbled from his parted lips, skin ashen with the deathly gray Prax knew all too well. Her heart stopped, her lungs tightened.

She was going to be sick.

"Hey." Courtney gave her arm a gentle shake, her own face suddenly serious and sober. "Are you okay?"

Prax blinked at her, then turned back to the biker at the table. He was sitting upright, mug fisted in one hand, the attempts to lift it to his mouth slow and clumsy. Even at this angle, she could see the glassy look in his eyes, the reddened tint in his cheeks. His head bobbed and lolled, infrequent but frequent enough.

She nodded to her boss and quickly stepped to the man's side, placing a very hesitant hand on his shoulder to give him the same kind of gentle shake. "Hey, are you okay? Can you stand?"

The man only bobbed his head to one side, his breathing labored.

Prax shot her panicked gaze to the bartender. "We need some water! And call an ambulance!"

The noise in the bar dimmed, everyone's focus shifted to the young woman hovering over the inked biker slumping in his chair. No one moved at first, only watched with curiosity as Prax waved at the bartender to hurry with the glass of water. "Somebody call 9-1-1! I think he's got poisoning!"

Murmurs and mutterings, but still no one whipped out a phone to call. Even the bartender seemed skeptical, but he still brought over the water and watched as she tilted the man's head back to try to feed it to him.

A warm hand settled on her back, and the handsome man from the bar was suddenly by her side. "Don't worry, we've got this." Behind him towered his friend, who still eyed her warily but seemed more concerned—genuinely concerned—about the thready breath wheezing from the biker's nose. "Aye,

Connor! It's not your time, buddy! We've still got a round of darts I need to beat your ass at!"

Connor lifted his bearded face, eyes still bleary and tongue lolling, but he squinted and smacked his lips with a sudden increase of alertness. "Is that right?" His words slurred almost as heavily as his posture, which leaned into the arms of both men who hoisted him to his feet. Aidon bore the bulk of Connor's weight, but he made it seem effortless as he tugged his phone from his pocket and quickly texted someone.

"For the love of all that's holy, Connor, we've talked about your drinking problem," Aidon grumbled, but his demeanor was surprisingly gentle.

"Bah." Connor grimaced and stumbled over his own two feet. "I can hold my poison."

The other man snorted. "Right."

Aidon rolled his eyes but clapped a hand on Connor's shoulder. "Let's get you home, buddy. And that clear stuff in your tumbler better be water, or so help me...." He cast one more quick glance in Prax's direction, and his expression was unreadable. At least he wasn't glaring.

Behind her, the Johnsons whispered fiercely back and forth until Prax turned back around to join them in the booth. Garrett's frown softened and he offered her a small smile. "You did good, there. Probably save that man's life."

"Are you sure there's nothing you could do?" Courtney asked him, her brow furrowed as she bit the inside of her cheek.

Garrett shrugged. "I'm off duty. And I bet that guy's got a rap sheet longer than the menu here."

"So?"

Yeah...so? Prax did her best to hide her own frown from

him, not wanting to give any cause for judgment from either her new employer or employer-by-marriage, but his flippant demeanor bothered her. A life was a life, no matter who it belonged to.

But then again, not everyone experienced the departure of life quite as intensely as she did. She stifled a sigh and buried her face in the mixologist's menu, doing her darned hardest to ignore the nagging tug in the back of her mind about the two mysterious men shuffling a bleary-eyed and bloated Connor down the street.

A particularly large order of floral arrangements had been scheduled for delivery to the local hospice, and Prax was vehemently opposed to being the one to make the delivery. It was bad enough to unwillingly see someone's untimely demise at any random moment—going to a place specifically intended for the dying was just asking for a special kind of torment. But what could she do? She needed this job to establish more responsibilities—like a phone bill under her own name—not to mention everything else she wanted to enjoy without being beholden to the good graces of her lovingly overbearing mother. It felt amazing to not need to borrow a credit card when that first paycheck arrived, at least not to feed her coffee addiction. Plus, the job was a plausible excuse to get out of the house without an inquisition.

She'd just never considered floral arrangements being sent for purposes other than weddings and funerals.

What could she tell her new boss, anyway? "Sorry, Courtney, I can't do what you hired me to do because you're sending me to my own personal hell." Yes, that conversation would go over *so well*.

As she hopped out of the florist's van, she quickly wiped the sweat from her palms on her dark jeans—and nearly forgot her cell phone on the passenger seat. She couldn't help but snort a little laugh at the absurdity of her personal issues as she grabbed her phone and slid it into her pocket.

One thing that struck her as a bit strange, and mostly a bit concerning, was Bogarten's overtly public pride in its hospice program. Signs boasted "excellent care" and "immeasurable compassion" all over the small city, and even advertised the services of Sunrise Hospice to neighboring towns over the local television channels. Just how many people did Bogarten—or Sunrise Hospice, for that matter—expect to die? Was there an inordinate amount of the terminally ill or elderly in this particular region? Or, like so many other things in the community that tugged at Prax's attention, was it yet another undercurrent of fascination with death itself?

The first couple of bouquets felt heavy and lopsided in her arms as she carried them from the van and across the white pavement to the sliding glass doors of the hospice's lobby, and Prax was grateful she didn't have to fumble for any handles. Judging by the elegant shape of the wisteria wrapped with ivy, she guessed these were decorative arrangements for the hospice itself; the personal deliveries for patients still back in the van. She tried to shift both arrangements into one arm's hold so she could sign the guestbook, but the bases were too thick for her hand to reach all the way around.

"Here, let me help you with that," said a warm, familiar deep voice from the other side of the wisteria, and Prax muttered her thanks as she scribbled her signature on the clipboard. When she turned her gaze back to more sincerely thank the person holding one of the arrangements for her, she froze.

"Ummm...thank you!" Prax covered her embarrassment

for her deer-in-the-headlights moment with a laugh. "Here, I can take that."

Those turquoise eyes glowed behind unruly chestnut curls as he peeked over the blossoms. "No worries, I've got it. Looks like your hands are full enough with the other one." The friendly man from Hawkeye's gestured with the wisteria sculpture in his hand towards hers, and she blushed with another laugh.

"Truth. Thanks! I'm looking for...." She checked the tag on the base. "Oh, the chapel. Which is...."

"This way."

Prax was grateful for his help and was painfully aware she must appear as clumsy and new to this job as she felt. He led her down the hall and around a corner, down another quiet hall of rooms that appeared to be more like offices than residential spaces until they reached a set of double doors decorated with stained glass. He tugged a door open and held it for her, and she ducked inside with yet another blush and a nod of thanks.

"I'm Donn, by the way." He set the heavy arrangement on one of the side columns by the altar, and Prax mimicked the placement on the other side. "I don't believe we exchanged actual pleasantries the other night."

"Prax."

"Interesting." Donn flicked his gaze over to her with a somewhat quizzical look, but returned it back to the floral arrangement. "These look great! I'm sure the people will love them."

"So you work here?" The question felt stupid the moment she asked it, but Prax got the sense that he didn't mind.

He shrugged and quirked another smile. "Volunteer."

At her barely concealed look of surprise, he blushed and shrugged again. "It gets lonely here, as you can imagine, for people who know...well, you know. Families don't like confronting death. They tend to feel like it's just that, a confrontation. The patients, though...." He sighed and turned his eyes back to the flowers, adjusting the leaves on one of the vines. "Families only visit when they feel comfortable enough to face the inevitable. Which isn't often. And for some of these patients, their families have already passed on, or just never come around."

"So you volunteer, to give them company." Prax felt her heart warm at this man's altruism, and knew without a doubt that anyone who had his smiling face by their side as they approached death's door would do so with a lot more courage than if they were alone. It wasn't just his blatant charm, but something more that exuded from him, even in this very brief moment of meeting him. Donn had a warmth to him that made her feel instantly comfortable, and at peace.

"And you bring beauty into their lives." He grinned and nodded at the floral arrangement.

She blushed, never having thought of it that way. And then another thought occurred to her. "How's...Connor?"

Donn's face fell and he sighed. After a moment's pause, he sniffed. "Bought him a few extra hours, but his liver and kidneys were shot. There wasn't much anyone could do, and the ER said it was a miracle he made it that long."

So that pattern was consistent: it didn't matter if she stepped in to save them, her interference only seemed to prolong the inevitable. She'd hoped maybe this time her assistance saved a man from drowning in his beer, but she hadn't considered just how long his organs might have been swimming in alcohol before that fateful night.

Still, she felt better for trying.

Donn cleared his throat and, in an instant, was back to being his cheery self. "Want help with the rest? I can give you the 'official' tour."

"Yes! Thank you!" Prax wasn't sure if it was against company policy to have complete strangers help carry deliveries into businesses, but technically Donn "worked" at the hospice so maybe that counted.

He was cheerful and immensely helpful with every trip between van and building, navigating the winding hallways for Prax so she could focus more on making sure petals and leaves didn't fall and trail behind them. Sunrise Hospice was a fairly large building, all one level save for the basement, which Donn explained was due to a combination of consideration for wheelchairs and wariness of tornadoes.

With the decorative arrangements placed in their assigned locations, the personal room deliveries were next. Donn's face lit up when Prax handed him several smaller bouquets neatly arranged inside colored glass vases, and he quickly recognized the names on each card. Every room they visited, he announced their arrival with a quick rap on the door and a bright, cheerful greeting as if each and every patient was a dear friend. And, to Prax's surprise, each and every patient greeted him back with the same happiness at seeing him, even those who were visibly weak and very much nearer to their end. Several of the elderly women blushed and giggled at his charming way of flourishing the bouquet for them as if he were about to ask them on a date. The men either chuckled or rolled their eyes in good nature, appreciative of the fresh decor for their rooms.

Occasionally "it" would occur, but not always in the horrific ways she was used to seeing. In one room, she saw the woman tucked peacefully into her bed, skin ashen and not a flicker of movement or breath shuddered. But before Prax could say, "She's dead", Donn slipped into the room and greeted the woman with his charming smile. Prax blinked, and suddenly that same woman was sitting upright in her bed, rosy-cheeked and smiling ear to ear as she breathed in the floral bouquet.

Another instance was not so...dignified. Prax was just about to call for the nurses to attend to the gentleman who absolutely just passed away in the bathroom, but stopped mid-shout at Donn's confused expression. He lifted a brow as if to silently say, "You okay there?" before he returned to his conversation about the recent Bears game with the very much alive, not-on-the-toilet-seat gentleman sitting in an overstuffed chair by the window.

It was the children's wing where Prax felt her steps falter.

Even Donn seemed a bit more solemn, his face set in firmer lines as they walked down that particular hallway. Brightly colored paintings decorated the walls, and it was heartwarming to see the hospice's efforts to make this place as cheerful for the little ones as possible. But nothing could truly mask the sorrowful truth of what this place was—a final home for those who were barely given enough time to live at all.

During these deliveries Prax was especially grateful for his help because she wasn't sure she would have been able to enter the rooms by herself. Each child lit up with joy at seeing one of their favorite volunteers, and Donn had a brilliant smile and a playful joke to give in return. It didn't matter if they were a girl or boy, all of them beamed at the beautiful flowers and hugged him with gratitude. The act made Prax pause and wonder where the flowers even came from; who ordered them all? But she shrugged it off as probably being a combination of families sending their love, and the hospice ensuring everyone was recognized.

At one particular door, Donn paused. His eyes tightened in the corners, and Prax felt her own heart tighten as well. He took a deep breath and lifted his hand to knock, then paused again. "Foster child," he muttered, and rapped on the door gently before opening it.

The room was quiet, in a way that almost felt tangible to Prax. It wasn't as if the other children's rooms were boisterous by any means, but something felt particularly solemn, thick even, about the quietness that filled this room. She noticed the countertops did not have any opened greeting cards propped up, or notes of well-wishes like so many of the other children whose families struggled to cope with their impending loss. A few stuffed toys were nestled on a chair in the corner, and the dresser was scattered with costume jewelry and a few storybooks propped up by a jewelry box.

"Hello, Beautiful." Donn smoothly pulled up a chair to the bedside and sat down, flourishing the bouquet like a besotted knight painted on one of the storybook covers. "I brought these for you."

The little girl tucked inside the bed sleepily blinked her eyes open, and she gasped. "For me? Really?"

"Really really."

She started to sit up, and Donn quickly reached out to help her by adjusting her pillows so she could recline more comfortably. Her head was completely bald and her skin deathly pale, with various tubes attached to her arms and one for oxygen threaded through her small nose. And yet, despite the shadows beneath her eyes and her delicate frame, Prax could see the beauty radiate from within this sweet little girl whose sunken eyes sparkled with joy at the sight of the flowers. "Thank you," she breathed, and Donn helped her hold the blossoms just below her nose so she could enjoy their fragrance. "I love them!"

"Want them on your dresser, by your bed?" At her nod, he turned around in his chair and handed the vase to Prax, who gave the little girl a warm smile and carefully set the bouquet by the books. "This is my new friend, Prax." Donn winked as he introduced her to the girl. "Prax, this is my best friend, Jennifer."

"You can call me Jenny." She smiled at Prax. "It's nice to meet you."

"Nice to meet you, too, Jenny." Prax returned her smile and folded her hands in front of her, unsure of what else to do or say. What does anyone say to a dying child? Especially one seemingly forgotten by those who were supposed to love her and be there for her in her final days?

Donn, however, seemed to know exactly what to say and do in the presence of this dying angel. He grinned at her and pulled out a coin from his pocket. "Should we play 'Groundhog'?"

Jenny giggled, and so did Prax, who asked, "Ground-hog?"

"Yeah, it's a game Donn and I made up." Jenny coughed briefly, and graciously accepted the cup of water Prax quickly handed to her. "It's like Heads or Tails, but kinda like

Groundhog Day, too. Donn flips a coin and if it's Heads, I get six more weeks to live."

Prax's eyes widened and her thoughts immediately wondered what it meant if it landed on Tails, but before she could ask, Jenny grinned. "It always lands on Heads," she reassured.

"Ready?" Donn waggled his brows and grinned when Jenny gave him the nod, and he flicked the coin into the air. For a very fleeting moment, the way the sunlight hit the spinning silver metal made it flicker like it was gold, and the little girl giggled again at the magical illusion. Donn caught it on his wrist, dramatically sweeping his gaze around for added suspense, then took a sly peek under his palm. His shoulders slumped, and he sighed. "I'm so sorry, Jenny.... It looks like you'll be dealing with me for another six weeks."

Prax didn't realize she'd been holding her breath until Jenny burst into another giggle, and she felt like smacking the man upside the back of his head. *What kind of morbid game was this to play with a child?!* But Jenny seemed to genuinely enjoy it, and in a way it made sense, the spark of hope that life might continue on for her at least for another month or two - plenty of time to make a miraculous recovery. Donn winked up at her and slid the coin back into his pocket. "Well, Beautiful One, I think we should let the pretty flower lady get back to work, don't you?" He grinned and gestured to Prax with a nod of his head. "And I think it's your nap time, too."

"It's always my nap time," Jenny pouted, but she did seem very tired and easily lay back down with his assistance. "Bye, Prax. Nice meeting you."

"You too, Jenny. I'll be back again soon." It was an easy decision to make, work or no work, for Prax's heart still broke for this lonely little girl. There may not be enough time in the day to fully volunteer like Donn did, but at the very least, Prax felt the urge to brighten the sweet child's room with more flowers and laughter whenever she could.

Donn waited until they rounded the corner at the end of the hall before he spoke again. "There was a car crash, a couple of years ago. Semi-truck just plowed through their van. Killed her parents instantly. Dragged her out of the back, barely alive. And that's how they found the cancer."

All the blood seemed to drain from her head and thicken in her feet as Prax absorbed the tragedy of Jenny's young life. No amount of brightly hued flowers or successful—suspiciously too successful—coin toss games could ever create enough happiness to replace the deep sorrow that must fill the child's heart. But despite this, she glowed with such radiance, such hope and strength, that Prax felt both awed and inspired. It was impossible not to.

When all the flowers had been delivered and Donn waved goodbye from the lobby doors, Prax was relieved to finally be able to drive away from that emotionally confusing place. She was doubly relieved when her boss told her the shop was closing early for the day to catch a softball game. As she walked closer and closer to her home, the weight in her chest grew heavier until, at the threshold, Prax felt like she couldn't breathe.

Her hand touched the door handle, and the pressure in her chest burst into a sob. Part of her wanted to tug herself inside to relieve the overflow of emotions deep in the shelter of her mother's conservatory, but another part just wanted a moment on the threshold. Leaning heavily against the door, Prax felt her legs weaken and she slid down to sit on the doorstep and cry.

The vines that encased their home like an emerald blanket crept forward from the old brick and gradually withered away where the gravel driveway began. And that's how she felt, everywhere she went, with or without her visions—always on the edge between life and death. Prax stared at the tapered ends of the ivy where the white and beige pebbles innocently rested on top of the leaves and felt her sobs slowly ease into shaking breaths through which tears still fell, but not as heavily. There was a certain sort of beauty to that shadowy line on the ground, the resilience and determination of the vine meeting the unmoving stillness of stone. The rocks never, and could never, pick themselves up and hurl damaging blows to the ivy; they simply remained where they were, meeting each tendril that came to them in the natural flow of growth.

Prax sighed. If she was going to keep finding meaning to life, and death, in the gravel driveway of her mother's home, she was going to need some coffee and a pillow to sit on. Wiping her eyes and checking for traces of mascara, she pulled herself back up and straightened out her clothes, dusting off the small bits of soil she'd accidentally sat in next to one of Demi's prized hydrangeas. Her mouth curved up in a smile. Demi Sadeh was loudly, unashamedly, and eternally all about life, growth, and vibrancy. It was an energy that wrapped her daughters in a warm embrace and tucked them safely inside the oasis she created for their little family, and after a day—more like weeks—of dealing with death, Prax suddenly realized just how much she appreciated her mother's sometimes overbearing exuberance.

S eriously, Mom, you don't have to do this." Prax flicked her gaze towards the flower shop, still dark and locked in the early morning, as they walked towards Jefferson Java for breakfast. "I can get my own—"

"Oh, shush." Demi grinned and nudged her. "I'm so proud of you! And I'm happy to see you recovering as well as you've been, even if your memories are still a struggle. Let a proud momma treat her baby to breakfast."

The bell overhead jingled in that pleasant, now familiar, tone Prax knew meant coffee was within reach, and she breathed in the rich aroma with a happy smile. *Such a perfect way to start a busy day.* She led the way through the small entrance to the counter, grinning at something her mother pointed out on the community bulletin board—then stopped in her tracks when she nearly bumped into the guy at the counter.

Aidon stared at her, his face unreadable. For a very brief moment his mouth opened to say something, but he flicked his gaze over her shoulder and quickly clamped shut. His face noticeably darkened and he was quick to turn back to the barista, who also noticed his sudden shift in demeanor. "Two creams," he grumbled with a nod.

"Well, well." Demi casually strolled around Prax to stand

in front of her, very much placing herself between her daughter and the groundskeeper. She kept the smile on her face, but the look in her eyes was venomous. "It's been a while, Aidon."

He scoffed and only marginally shifted away from the counter after he swiped his card, not bothering to give her even a glance. "Dr. Sadeh. Here for a coffee? Or do you brew your own in students' tears?"

Prax snickered and tried to hide it behind a sniffle, but Aidon's lips twitched momentarily towards a smile and he did steal a glance her way. Demi made a show of taking out her luxurious wallet from her equally luxurious bag and smirked. "Fresh out, I'm afraid. Summer sessions tend to run dry."

"Ah. That explains the sudden lull in burials."

"Burials?" It was obvious these two knew each other, but Prax was completely lost.

Aidon actually grinned, but just like Demi, it didn't touch his eyes. "We have a whole burial plot at Nanabozho just for the hopes and dreams of Dr. Sadeh's students. It's on my schedule to mow today, now that I think about it." He took his coffee with a genuine smile to the barista, then darkened back into that signature scowl as he regarded Demi and her continual shifts in posture as if she were hiding Prax. "You should visit sometime. Come pay your respects."

"We're good, thanks." Demi snapped her wallet shut to punctuate the last word.

He hid the grunt behind a sip of his coffee and made for the door, but not before stealing another glance at Prax and giving her a courteous nod. Prax watched him leave, thoroughly perplexed, so much that she almost completely forgot to order her breakfast. She waited until they slid into their respective chairs at one of the tables, then asked, "You know him?"

Demi quickly glanced at the door but seemed to relax when she saw it was clear. "We've met."

"He seems to know enough about you beyond 'we've met'," Prax prodded.

"We've met on several occasions. And it's true, my reputation at the university is a little...ruthless."

Somehow Prax believed it. She knew her mother to be a warm, loving woman who doted endlessly on her beloved daughters, but she'd also seen the way Demi's gaze sharpened to a point at a careless driver; heard the ice in her voice during conference calls in her home office. The graded papers sometimes scattered across the dining table "bled" with red ink and scathing comments, and at one point a sobbing sophomore student practically fell to her knees pleading for an extension right there on the front porch. The recent memory made Prax giggle to herself, and she shrugged at her mother's inquisitive look. "The thing Aidon said about the burial plot," she explained. "It was actually kinda funny."

Demi straightened in her chair, but before she could snap a response, their breakfast trays arrived and she opted for graciousness towards the server. But once he stepped away, she stared at Prax and very stiffly stabbed her fork into her bowl of fruit. "Aidon. You know him?"

"We've met." Prax meant it as a jest, but the stormy expression in her mother's eyes made her tuck into her egg and salmon sandwich just to avoid the glare.

"Where?"

Ummmmm.... Prax attempted a casual shrug and glanced around the cafe. "Obviously we come to the same place for coffee." *Yes, go with that.*

"I see." Demi shifted in her seat and in her mood as well,

suddenly cheerful and pleasant, as if the most confusing exchange didn't just occur. She hummed her delight when she bit into her own breakfast sandwich and dabbed a napkin at the corner of her mouth. "You know," she said after a sip of sparkling water, "they deliver, now! I bet you could order your coffee at home, no problem."

Prax scrunched her face and let out a little laugh. "Right, I'm sure, but I work right across the street—"

"Even better! They'll probably knock your delivery fee since it's so close."

"Mom." Something was up, and the subversive nature grated against that instinct deep inside—the same instinct that tugged every time Aidon happened to be nearby. "What is going on? What do you know about him?"

Demi carefully chewed her bite, took her time to swallow, washed it down with more sparkling water. Finally, she sighed and looked Prax in the eyes. "Just promise me you'll stay away from him, okay? Aidon Elrik is a dangerous man."

Prax wanted to laugh, but she worried it would upset her mother even further. "Mom, this isn't exactly a large city. And obviously we'll run into each other, it's bound to happen. I'm not going to start ordering delivery to avoid someone I don't even know."

That seemed to visibly relax the professor, who nodded and softened her gaze. "I just want you to stay safe. You're finally home, finally getting settled in, and I just don't want to lose you again."

She rested her hand on her mother's and gave it a gentle squeeze. "I love you, too."

Demi's phone buzzed on the table and she frowned when she checked the caller ID. "Ugh, don't tell me...yes? I *know* he said to postpone the midterms, but you can't un-grow a corpse flower!" She pursed her lips impatiently, casting an apologetic glance to Prax, who nodded with understanding. Work called, literally, and soon it would be time to open up the flower shop as well. Business as usual for the Sadehs.

Design orders were minimal for the day, so Courtney insisted Prax take an early afternoon and "enjoy the sunshine". It certainly would be a beautiful afternoon to bask in the sun, were it not for the thick humidity clinging to her skin as she walked around the sequestered sinkhole near the bridge and ducked into the covered walkway. Here the breeze provided only marginal relief, lifting cooling mist from the river bluffs beneath the bridge, but it was something.

Nanabozho was closer to the river than home, so it was an easy excuse to detour through the grounds on her way back. The gates remained open during visiting hours, and today looked like a fairly quiet day with only one or two cars parked in different sections of the cemetery. Prax sighed with relief. Between the quiet early breakfast at Jefferson Java, little to no walk-in customers at the shop, and now this quiet walk far away from the living, the day was potentially the most uneventful and non-terrifying day in public she'd experienced since leaving the hospital.

There was one individual she did want to see, and he happily trotted over to her from his nap in the shade of a willow tree, tongue lolled out to the side. Prax felt for poor Spot—his fur must feel stifling in the heat and humidity. "Hi, Spot!" She cooed, rubbing his neck as he covered hers with wet kisses. "Awwww, who's a good boy? Who's a good boy?"

Spot whined and panted and nuzzled her so happily, as if she, too, was exactly who he'd been waiting all day to see. With a laugh and then a cough, remembering where she was, Prax returned his nuzzles and nudged him to come walk with her. As they strolled down the gravel path, she couldn't help but feel like he was pressing her in certain directions, nosing her down one fork in the path then another, licking her arm whenever she started to ask him where they were going. Spot only licked and panted, nosed and nudged, distracting her with his fluffy affection and making her laugh louder than she meant to.

The sound of someone digging broke through her giggles and Prax followed Spot's sudden shift in gaze to a circular clearing surrounded by more willows. Freshly dug mounds neatly arranged in perfect rows lined the back edge of the clearing, one after the other until the pattern stopped near the middle of the open lawn. It was here where the dirt flew over the broad, bronzed shoulder and increasingly familiar tattoos of Aidon Elrik, who stomped the shovel into the ground and leveraged a fresh clump of grass with a grunt. He leaned against the shovel for a moment to wipe the sweat from his brow with the hem of his tank, giving her an clear view of the ink that continued from his arm and trailed down over his very solid pectoral and skimmed his chiseled abdomen in tendrils that led to where she could only imagine the designs met at his side.

Oh, sweet merciful heaven.

Prax swallowed hard, which stuck within her dry mouth. *When did she suddenly get so thirsty?*

Spot let out a happy little bark in greeting, and Aidon wiped his face again, slower, almost as if another once-over would make Prax disappear. Obviously it didn't work, and he chunked the shovel into the dirt with a grimace. "Isn't it a little hot out for a walk?"

Her initial attempt at a response only managed to come out as a sticky, dehydrated wheeze. *Smooth.* Prax definitely caught the smirk on his face as he dipped his head into a large cooler by one of the headstones, and suddenly the heat in her cheeks had nothing to do with sunburn. But before she could stammer or wheeze out another lame excuse for speech, Aidon held out a bottle of water dripping with melted ice, and she crossed the emerald grass to take it. She nodded her gratitude and chugged, gathering her wits while he sipped and stared at her, eyes narrowed. "Thanks," she finally said, more like gasped, smacking her lips together with relief. "It's on my way home, figured I'd get a stretch in. And...." She shifted her weight between her feet. "I wanted to apologize for this morning."

Aidon frowned. "For what?"

"Mom. I don't know. She seemed really tense and shouldn't have snapped at you like that, especially in public."

"Mhm."

Prax wished he would say something more, literally anything. "She said you're dangerous."

"I am." He didn't even flinch towards the hint of joking.

"Is that all she said?"

Not nearly as much as she probably should have. The nagging suspicion Demi was less than forthright only grew as Aidon peered at her, his jaw set in that tight grimace he seemed to reserve especially for her. "Do you two...know each other?"

Now he laughed. Not a real laugh, more like a snort and a scoff and a huff all at once, and he glanced across the grounds as if the answer was grazing out in some pasture somewhere beyond the dead. "Oh, we go way back. She didn't tell you?" When Prax shook her head, he wiped a hand over his mouth and scoffed again. "Yeah. Figures."

"What did you do?"

"What—" Aidon narrowed his eyes at her. "What did *I* do? Are you kidding me?"

Prax took a sudden step back, alarmed by the way his voice deepened into a growl. A *dangerous* growl, just like her mother said. She swallowed hard and wiped her hands on her jeans, her heart pounding in her chest for all the wrong reasons. "S-sorry," she muttered, taking another step back as she debated between running or just power walking away. "Forget it. I gotta go."

Spot whined and cocked his head at Aidon, who immediately dropped the glare and almost, *almost* looked regretful. "Prax, wait."

But she didn't feel like waiting. Not with the way he stalked towards her, the shadows practically deepening around him with every step—and that wasn't due to the slowly setting sun of the late afternoon. Something about him called to her at the exact same time that it pushed her away, like a siren song threatening to drown her in the depths. She wanted to run, she wanted to fight, she wanted to find words for the things swirling deep in her chest. Heat flared under her skin, and she took yet another few steps back towards the gravel path, her foot slipping in the thick mound of grass she forgot was there.

He caught her before she fell, his hands grabbing her arms as she stumbled backwards. For the quickest, flicker of a moment, the hard lines of his face softened…his face that was now so very, very close to hers. But when he glanced down at the ground beneath her feet, he frowned again and gently pushed her back. "You should go," was all he said before he turned around and went back to his project.

He didn't need to tell her twice. Prax spun for the path and forced herself to not run, *don't run, don't let him have the satisfaction of scaring you away.* She almost faltered, almost skipped a few steps to jog back towards the gates, but the friendly panting and comforting whine at her side kept her feet steady. She wouldn't feel any better if she ran out on the sweet floof who managed a huff over his shoulder towards his master. If she didn't know any better, Prax could almost see Spot roll his eyes.

D emi would have an absolute aneurysm if she knew, if she had any idea, of where Prax was at this exact moment.

Which, given how far removed it was from any place the professor would be caught dead or alive in, was a bit of a relief.

Prax still nonetheless felt awkward and out of her element as she walked into the semi-seedy bar, careful to step along the shadows (of which there were plenty) and avoid anyone who seemed drunk enough to fall off their bar stool. The air was thick and heady with beer, vapor, and old leather mingled with the various attempts at cologne the mate-seeking men splashed on before they arrived. One such "peacock" winked at her, and Prax reflexively ducked deeper into the shadows and flicked her gaze away. It didn't matter how cute the guy was - her alarms went off and she wasn't there to pick up a date, anyways.

Nope, there was more urgent business to attend to.

The confrontation with Aidon was only a few days ago, less than a week really, but the horrors she'd endured since then all but broke her. The fact that she even managed to get up each day and leave the safety of her bed was a miracle, fueled by her solid determination to not let this terrible curse rule her life. But by the time she returned home every late afternoon, after walking through town, sometimes through campus, the deaths she'd seen made her crawl into bed almost immediately and pull the quilts over her head. It didn't matter that it was summer, too hot and sticky for the heavy weight of the hand-stitched bedding—the thicker the layers, the safer she felt hidden away from the world.

This morning's delivery of Get Well flowers to the hospital was the proverbial straw that broke the camel's back, starting with an elderly woman slumped in her wheelchair and culminating, one death after another through nearly every hall she walked, into the most horrific of all: the ghastly sight of the young doctor's scorched body moments before the defibrillator paddles in his hands malfunctioned. The literal shock and screams of the nurses blended with her own, and Prax doubled over when her gut clenched between shrieking and retching until an aide pulled her away and led her to a quiet room to calm down. She'd called Courtney once her fingers stopped shaking, and the florist closed up shop to personally drive over and make sure Prax was okay.

Prax was definitely not okay.

It was Mya who caught her when she stumbled through the front door, Mya who stroked her hair and practically carried her to the atrium where she unceremoniously dumped her older sister into the hammock but quickly made it as comfortable for her as possible. Prax could not stop shaking, head to toe she trembled and spasmed, her eyes unfocused between slow, tear-filled blinks. The hammock rocked back and forth, back and forth, nudged by Mya's arm as she stroked Prax's hair and hummed a soft lullabye. She tucked the heavy quilt from Prax's room around her quivering sister and kissed her brow, whispering sweet nothings to soothe her to sleep.

When Prax finally woke, the sky over the glass dome was dark and glittering with stars. Mya was gone, probably sound asleep in her room, and a cursory check of her phone told Prax it was late enough for Demi to also be in bed. There were texts from Courtney, screenshots of the evening news report about the hospital incident, and a direct order to take the day off tomorrow.

Prax inwardly groaned at her own weakness. Did she really break down like that?

Oh no. Did Demi know?

She eased herself out of the hammock—after a few tries—and slid her feet into her sandals waiting by the front door. The night air felt surprisingly cool and crisp, a welcome relief from the recent bout of stifling humidity. Prax remembered walking by a convenience store several times between work and home, and Demi had mentioned a few times that it was a favorite spot for the university students seeking late-night junk food. Considering how her day went, a midnight corn dog sounded *heavenly*.

It was an older couple rifling through the potato chip aisle who caught her attention with his mumbled name. They kept glancing around, muttering about "favors" and owed debts, interspersed with Aidon's name whenever she couldn't quite hear what they were saying. They spoke of him with such reverence, such fear, and the woman croaked with her chainsmoker voice that "the godfather of Bogarten" was the one they should go to for money, since "tonight was the night for favors."

Was *this* the "dangerous" thing Demi warned her about? Prax tried to casually step closer to hear better, but they both shot her a glare, grabbed a bag of chips and scurried away.

Was it possible? Could Aidon really be this revered overlord or something?

Only one way to find out.

A new sort of tension tightened in her chest as Prax neared the booth where the moody man himself sat, a pitcher of beer in one hand and a frosty glass in the other. His face gave nothing away as he tilted his head to listen while he poured, the woman leaning over the table towards him begging with her body as much as with her voice. "I'll do anything, I swear, you name it, I'm your gal," she pleaded. Her voice cracked, but whether from emotion or smoking, Prax couldn't tell.

Aidon nodded and took a deep swig from his glass. "I know you will, and that's a big part of the problem. Isn't it?"

The woman straightened, her fingers clutched at the throat of her faux fur jacket. "I don't know what you mean!"

His voice was calm, warm even, but firm. "How many times have you said that exact same phrase to your landlord? To your ex? To literally any man other than a genuine, legal employer?"

"Are you calling me a slut?!"

Aidon's brows shot up. "What? No. If that's what you're hearing, it's your own voice in your head, not mine." He tossed back another gulp of beer and smacked his lips together.

"I want to help you, but you have to start helping yourself, Charlotte. You're a beautiful woman and incredibly intelligent to boot. Stop wasting yourself away on your back and make something out of your life!"

Charlotte sputtered but came up with nothing. Finally, she took a deep, calming breath and settled with a smile. "Okay, Aidon...fine. What do you suggest I do, then? Apply to a goddamned drugstore?"

"Better cough syrup than cocaine, don't you think?"

Someone choked on their own beer at that, and Prax stifled her giggle. Charlotte wasn't the least bit amused, but she clearly saw a losing battle and the foolishness in clawing for a hopeless victory. "Fine. Whatever. Still doesn't fix my immediate problem."

"Right." Aidon shifted in his seat and pulled out a wad of cash. He didn't even bother to count it, just slid the whole bundle across the table to her. "Get yourself a room, for the month if you need to, and figure out the grocery situation. Go clothes shopping. Whatever you need to do to stop doing... this." He waved his hand in a small circle.

Charlotte's eyes went wide, and she snatched up the cash quicker than Prax could blink. "Thank you, Aidon! Thank you! I'll pay you back, I swear!"

He only grunted his response. But before Charlotte stepped too far away, he called out after her, "Oh, and Charlotte? I'll know if a single dollar of that goes where it's not supposed to, you hear me?"

The bar fell quiet at the low growl that tipped the edge of his deep voice. Charlotte froze, and her face clearly displayed her sudden fear at probably being caught thinking that exact thing right then and there. Her shoulders slumped, but she nodded, and one of the other women patted her arm in en-couragement.

Damn. What the hell kind of underworld favor-giving was Aidon actually doing?

Prax figured out how the "line" to request his help and favors was formed and took her place in it, which worked out when the procession started at the edge of the bar, giving her time to order something fruity and sweet. He'd probably make fun of her for it, but whatever, her poison is her poison - she'd been able to figure that out when Courtney and Garrett took her out for drinks. The bartender was cute, too, and he winked at her when he slid the cosmotini across the countertop into her hand. "On the house," he insisted when she tried to pay for her drink. Prax blushed, thanked him, and quickly turned her focus back to waiting in line.

All that was left in her glass were ice cubes and a tiny umbrella by the time the procession shifted to her turn. Aidon just stared at her. Was this his way of balking?

Given the sudden drainage of color in his face, Prax was going to guess that it was.

Another familiar face grinned at her. "Prax! Fancy seeing you here!"

"Oh my gosh! Donn!" Prax beamed at her new friend and leaned into his sideways hug where he sat on the outer edge of the booth. "Wait...you know Aidon?"

"You two...have met?" Aidon interjected before Donn could answer.

"Yeah, a couple of times, but really at the hospice." Prax grabbed a nearby chair and sat down at the table, making everyone behind her groan with impatience. One look from Aidon shut them up quickly.

"Hospice."

"You know the one, where I volunteer?" Donn arched his brows and sipped on his own fruity drink.

Aidon rolled his eyes. "I will literally never understand you."

"I will literally never understand why you keep trying to." Donn flashed another cheeky grin in Prax's direction. "This handsome eejit's been my best mate for eons and he still tries to figure me out. I gave up on him ages ago."

Try as he might to hide any hint of a sense of humor, it showed in the way Aidon's eyes crinkled in the corners as he took another swig. He set the mug down a bit harder than necessary, but to her credit, Prax didn't flinch. He seemed to regard this for a moment and then shrugged a shoulder. "Alright, I'll bite. What can I do for you?"

Prax straightened in her seat and cleared her throat. "I'm asking for your permission to hang out at the cemetery whenever I want."

Donn raised a quizzical brow at her, and so did Aidon. He smirked and shook his head, reaching for a worn deck of cards she didn't notice before until he started shuffling them between his hands as he spoke. "It's open to the public until ten, and I don't see you as the kind of person to camp out overnight among the tombstones. Why do you need my permission?"

"Because it's obvious you don't want me there."

Aidon stilled, and Donn was suddenly very interested in the condensation on the side of his glass. Both men exchanged an uneasy glance, with Donn cocking his head in a silent gesture that urged Aidon to clear his throat and glance back over to Prax. "I'm just the groundskeeper. You don't need my permission."

"I don't like going where I'm not wanted."

He sighed, and his expression softened. Was that...guilt? He did seem a little sheepish, which was kind of adorable to see on the face of a man so solid and sure and in command of the room. "It's not that you're not wanted. Trust me, it's nothing like that."

Prax furrowed her brow. "Then what is it? What did I say, or do? I must have done something, you're always so angry to see me." Not to mention the other day, when he'd downright lost his temper and literally shoved her away.

"Yeah, Aidon, what did Prax do to earn your ire?" Donn hid his smirk behind his raised glass but did nothing to conceal his cocky gaze from his best friend. "It seems so unfair to treat this lovely lady like she did something to *intentionally* piss you off." His voice thickened with meaning that flew over Prax's head but landed squarely on Aidon, who did actually flinch. He shot the Irishman a fleeting snarl, but relaxed when he returned his attention to the young woman before him.

"Fine. You have my express permission to frolic among the dead all you want, any day, any hour during normal business hours - on one condition."

Prax gulped.

"Tell me why. What's so important about the cemetery to you?"

Well...frick.

She sighed and slumped in her chair. Should have planned for the possibility that he'd want to know details. It was an odd request, after all. "It's stupid and you won't believe me," she mumbled in the hopes that neither of them could hear her. But they did.

"Try me."

His piercing gaze brooked no argument or escape, and it held her pinned to where she attempted to slither casually down off the chair and slink away. When it was obvious even Donn wasn't coming to her rescue in this, she sighed. "I see death."

Donn grinned. Aidon cocked his head. "Come again?"

"I see...death." Prax leaned forward so they could hear her mumbled words through gritted teeth, not needing or wanting the rest of the bar to hear her insanity. "Like when a person is about to die. I see it, and then it happens."

The men leaned back in surprise. Neither of them snorted or smirked or scoffed.

Prax felt a little encouraged by this and relaxed. "It's everywhere I go, and it happens without warning. It's terrifying, honestly. My sister and I figured out if I spend my time where people are already dead, I won't see the visions as much or at all."

Donn gave Aidon a Knowing Look and nodded. "Makes sense." He tilted his head towards her, his gaze warm and caring—such a stark contrast to Aidon's typical glower. "But obviously you can't just pack up and live in the cemetery. How are you getting around? Work and such, especially when you're at a place like the hospice." At her sudden grimace, he pursed his lips. "Ah. That must be...nothing short of horrifying."

She nodded, and the memory was bad enough to bring her near to tears. It was all she could do to pretend she didn't see the cardiac arrests, the sudden collapses, or hear the gasps and wheezes for final breaths, just to get through the delivery with professionalism. Leaving the hospice was like surfacing from the deep, and she'd spent several minutes sobbing in the delivery van before she drove back to the shop. This morning was even worse, and she felt the tremors return to her fingertips as she fought to keep her nerves in check. *Breath, Prax. Don't lose your head in front of them.*

"Hey."

Prax slowly looked up at Aidon, whose voice was suddenly as soft as his expression. He almost looked sympathetic, but she didn't want to get her hopes up. He glanced at Donn again, who shrugged as if to say, "might as well", and sighed. "We...I...know a thing or two about having...visions." His gaze slid back to hers, and for one breathless moment, their eyes locked and Prax felt as if all the noise and lights suddenly dimmed, the world faded away until it was just them. Aidon never held her gaze before, not like this, and she didn't know what was happening to her insides. But she felt...warm.

Just as quickly as it started, Aidon blinked and returned to nursing his beer. The lights and music and hum of drunken gossip returned to their normal levels, and Prax realized she'd been holding her breath. Donn grinned like the cat who ate the canary and cleared his throat as nonchalantly as possible. "Like he said, we're fairly experienced with the odd and unusual. When did you start seeing...things?"

"It started right after I went home from the hospital." Prax picked at a flake of veneer on the table. "But I don't...I don't honestly remember anything before that. I don't know if this has always been a thing. For me." She almost retched at the sudden realization that maybe this *was* something she'd lived with "before". With a quick shake of her head, she dismissed it internally and externally. "We're pretty sure it's a side-effect of my head injury, or whatever caused my amnesia."

"We?"

"My sister. She's the only other one who knows." Now it was Prax's turn to lock eyes with Aidon, albeit with more don't-you-dare intensity. "My mother does not know about this."

Aidon nodded and tapped his cards on the table while he regarded her, more like he was lost in deep thought rather than judging her. Finally, he clicked his tongue against his teeth and leaned forward. "I might have something that can help." He rummaged behind himself for a second, then pulled out another deck of cards and set it on the table in front of her. This deck was brand new, the box barely creased, and when she opened it, she startled slightly. "It's...blank."

He smiled. "Try it out."

"What do I...?" Prax slid the deck from the box and fanned it open. The design on the backs was different, not the standard woman on a bicycle, but was still beautiful with intricate filigree all the same. When she tilted the fanned cards, the light caught on the gold foil and revealed an enchanting shimmer in the details, like veins of gold in a cave. "These are beautiful! But why are they blank?"

"It's a custom set. Figured it'd come in handy at some point. Now it has."

"And you just carry these around?" Prax shied under his raised brow, blushing as she scolded herself to just be grateful. She tapped the cards in her palm to close the deck, then fanned it open again. "Thank you, really. So...how will this help me?"

He shuffled his own deck and fanned them out. "It's going to take some practice, but it's mostly about focus." He flipped a card from the fan and turned it between his fingers. "When you're able to focus your Sight, the kind that your mind sees without your eyes, then you can start to create what we call a Veil." Aidon tucked the card back into the deck and shuffled them between his hands. "The Veil stands between you and everything you don't want to see when you're not ready. When you *are* ready, pull the Veil back." He flourished his hand, and the same card suddenly appeared in his palm.

Prax sucked in a breath and stared at the card in his hand. "And this...helps you?"

Aidon nodded. "It took me a while to build my Veil, but once I did, peace and quiet."

"You see...death?"

At this, he smirked and looked over at Donn, who chuckled. Aidon slid the card to the bottom of the deck and gave another small nod. "I see death, and a whole lot of other things I'd rather not. At least, not when I'm trying to maintain my sanity."

He understood. Aidon Elrik, the last person on Earth she'd ever guess to be on her side, actually understood her struggle. And he was offering help to ease the strain. She turned the glimmering deck in her hands and bit her lip in thought. "You really think this will work? For me?"

Aidon suddenly grinned that wolfish, dangerous, untrustworthy grin. "Let's test it out, shall we?" He nodded to the man standing next in line a few feet behind her. "Derrick, my man. Come to pay back on that loan I gave you three months ago?"

The man stepped forward and almost shoved into Prax's side, but Aidon's quick glare stopped him and he kept a respectful distance from her. His fingers shook slightly as he wiped his palms on his jeans and let out a nervous laugh. "Yeah, man, that's why I'm here. I need another extension."

"Mhm." Aidon exchanged a quick glance with Donn. "Do you remember how I originally was just going to give it to you? But you said no, you're a man of your word, you'll pay it back, make it a loan, let everyone know Derrick Bosic pays his debts." His voice mocked the man, mimicking the sounds of a cockier version.

Derrick laughed again, nervously, and nodded. "And I am! I just...ran into some unexpected expenses, is all."

"Blackjack can be very expensive, my friend," Donn chided. "Unexpected, though? Hardly."

"Listen—"

"No, *you* listen." Aidon sat back in his seat and gave the man a solid, intimidating once-over. "What exactly do you think I do with people who don't pay their debts?"

Derrick swallowed hard. He attempted to look calm, casual, at ease, but it wasn't fooling anyone. "You're a good guy...."

"If I'm so damn good, why does half the town fear me?"

"Because you never know when a good man will snap." Another voice chimed in from the bar, and Prax turned to see an older man slide off his barstool and saunter over to the booth. His presence was immediately warm and reassuring, jovial even, with the way his face lit up with a genuine smile framed by a white goatee and silver-rimmed glasses. He carried a glass mug in his hand, but Prax realized it was just soda with a wedge of lime. "Got room for one more?"

Aidon returned his grin and gestured to the empty space in the booth. "Always, Pastor."

Prax nearly choked on her spit. "Pastor? *Here?*"

"Why not?" He chuckled and held his hand out to her. "Most people just call me Davidson."

"Prax." She took his hand and shook it, instantly at ease with his magnetic warmth.

"It's lovely to meet you, Prax. Now, Aidon," Davidson addressed the man without taking his gaze off of the very nervous, and damply perspiring, Derrick, "what's this about not repaying debts?"

Aidon smirked. "Our friend here swears he's a man of his word. Witnesses say otherwise."

"You could always just cancel the debt."

Prax expected Aidon to slug the preacher for suggesting this, but to her surprise, he actually seemed to seriously consider it. "I could," he said, taking his time in mulling it over as he stared long and hard at Derrick. "But that wouldn't teach him anything. And before you get on me about mercy and shit, I've been very merciful. So," he shifted his gaze to Prax, "what's it going to be?"

She leaned back. "Huh?"

"Prax, here, has a very special gift." Aidon's voice boomed loud enough for the whole bar to hear, and the voices lowered enough for even the casual listener to catch up. He stared down the middle-aged man. "She can see a person's imminent death, just by looking at her cards."

"I...can?" Prax felt the air leave her lungs and her stomach lurch. *So much for not telling anyone.* She quickly nodded when she felt his boot suddenly nudge her foot under the table. "I can! I can. Yes." She turned in her chair to face Derrick directly, who seemed less than convinced at this charade. It helped to be surrounded by a group of men who were far more intimidating than she felt, and she let this thought steady her fingers as she fanned out the cards, face down. "Pick a card. Any card."

Derrick snorted, but a low growl behind her and his quick

snap back to seriousness let her know Aidon wasn't having it. The man reached for the middle of the deck and tugged at a random card. Prax slid it out of the deck, flipped it over, and looked up at him.

At first she began to see it like she always did, the fading of color in his skin, the shimmer over his neck where bruised ligature marks started to appear.

But then she felt her mind shift, refocus, and the vision faded from standing in front of her, to appearing on the blank space of the card. The image was somewhere between a photograph and a GIF, slight movements in the way he struggled for air, twitched as his lungs failed to fill. His eyes rolled back...and a faint smile appeared on his lips before the final sigh weighed his body down against what she could now see was a belt wrapped tightly around his throat.

Prax blinked again, and gazed into the man's eyes, her own still partly glazed over as her mind adjusted to this new sorting of Sight. She slowly looked back down at the card, her fingers visibly trembling as she held it up. "You...you should pay your debt."

He scoffed. No one moved. The longer the silence held, the more uncomfortable he became. "Wait...seriously?"

Prax's solemn face unnerved him as she slowly, oh so slowly, tucked the card back into the deck. "You should pay your debt, and quickly. Or else...."

Derrick nearly wheezed, his eyes wide and face pale as he glanced between her and then Aidon. When not even the pastor came to his defense, he shoved his hand into his back pocket and threw a thick wad of cash onto the table. "Here! It's all there, I swear! The whole twenty grand! Just leave me alone!" He stumbled backward into a chair and nearly toppled over, but caught himself and quickly scurried out the back door.

The bar was eerily quiet. All eyes were on Prax, who suddenly wished she could teleport to the safe sanctuary of her mother's atrium. Aidon grinned at her, his eyes full of amusement and curiosity. "Okay, I gotta know," he said, "what exactly did you see?"

"Auto-erotic asphyxiation."

Donn choked on his drink. Davidson closed his eyes and shook his head, mouth pressed in a firm line to hide the sigh. Aidon scoffed in disbelief. "Seriously?"

She nodded. "They'll probably find him tomorrow."

"But you told him—"

"Dead men can't pay their debts."

Donn rested his head on his hand and grinned at her. "It's official. I like you."

Aidon was still processing this turn of events. "How did you know he could, though? Even I wasn't expecting him to just have it all there."

Prax smirked. "His pants bulged in the wrong spot. Seemed like either he just won it big or had a serious medical problem." She grinned, thoroughly enjoying the reactions of the men around her. "It worked, by the way. Kind of. I saw the image on the card for a second, but then it went back to the normal type of vision."

"Keep practicing. You'll get the hang of it."

"Do you think they will help?" Donn asked. "Now that you've taken them for a spin?"

Prax nodded. "With practice, definitely. Thank you, Aidon." She offered him a shy smile.

He cleared his throat and nodded, which seemed to be the

only final word she would get from him for now. She tucked the deck into her pocket and said her farewells to her new friends, then quickly made her way past inquisitive barflies to the front door.

She couldn't wait to show Mya her new card trick.

Y ou are a blessing and a half, Prax!" Courtney beamed her gratitude at the proffered frap, quickly gulping down a deep sip. "I could give you a raise just for this!"

Prax laughed and set the carrier tray filled with coffee orders for the rest of the staff in the small fridge and grabbed her own favorite "morning wake up". It only took a few sips for the sugar and caffeine to hit, but once they did, she was ready to take on whatever—or whoever —would come through the door.

She slipped on her apron and followed Courtney out to the shop's floor where the project tables were prepared for the day's orders, somewhat discreetly veiled by purposely arranged display bouquets surrounding the workspace. This was one of the things Prax loved about working as a florist: when customers came in, she could sell products and make commissions, but when the foot traffic was slow, she could pour her creative energy into sculpting beautiful arrangements. Of course, there was always the added bonus of being the daughter of a botanical scientist who was always happy to give tips and tricks to the biggest blooms and most seemingly impossible sculptures.

Ever since Courtney gave Prax the Nanabozho delivery route, Prax felt even more attentive to the designs of the arrangements ordered by families - especially the ones specifically ordered for funerary services. It was her opinion that carnations were far too simplistic and death-related to keep as a standard, and this strongly expressed opinion paired with a prototype design using chrysanthemums convinced Courtney to let her have free reign over the designs contracted with Nanabozho. A new order for an elderly veteran's funeral had rung in while Prax was out grabbing coffee, and Courtney's notes were thorough enough to let her know poppies would be the best focus for the day's project.

Prax was carefully lifting a delicate bunch of bright red poppies from the cooler when she heard the front door open, the antique bell ringing as the heavy door swung in. She carefully set the poppies on the workbench, wiped her damp hands on her apron, and plastered on her genuine, helpful smile as she rounded the corner of the workspace to greet the customer. "Good morning! How can I help you?"

Bony, wrinkled fingers trembled as they clutched a stack of papers, and the woman's eyes were rimmed with redness and tears behind her glasses. She opened her mouth to speak, but quickly closed it again. In lieu of words, she grabbed one of the papers from the top of the stack and thrust it at Prax. "Could you please hang this in your window? Please," she begged, her voice crackling and thick with emotion. "They're missing, and...and...."

With a soft, reassuring smile, Prax took the piece of paper from the tearful woman's hand and skimmed it over. Two pictures of two little girls smiled up at her from the black-and-white, printed-at-home copy now stained with teardrops that smudged the ink. The oldest looked to be no more than ten years old, the youngest closer to seven. The bold typeface claimed they were last seen the afternoon before, riding bikes in the park near their home.

In a not quite town, not quite city like Bogarten, everyone practically knew each other, and for two little girls to suddenly vanish from sight in broad daylight without a plausible, reasonable explanation was extremely unlikely. This would not be the first time a family panicked over the sudden disappearance of their child, only to find the wayward son or daughter safely playing video games with the kid next door.

Still, Prax didn't want to discredit this grandmother's worry, especially as shaken as the woman seemed. She nodded and took another look at the flyer. "No words from their friends?"

The woman shook her head. "No, it was the first thing we checked. They were supposed to just cross through the park to their cousin's house, but—" She choked back a sudden sob, and Prax tentatively reached her hand out to comfort her. "They never made it. We don't know where they are. They never came home."

The park itself wasn't especially shady with trees, either. Sure, there were plenty of oaks and birches to provide decent enough shade, but it wasn't like these girls traipsed off into the woods. Something about it did seem...troubling.

Prax nodded again. "Here, let me take a few more. We can hang these up in all the windows, maybe put a few more in the displays."

"Oh, thank God!" The woman let out a heavy burst of tearful relief and quickly handed Prax a small stack of flyers. "Bless you, bless you!"

"Of course! And here, take our card, let us know if you hear anything or need anything more." Prax snatched a few business cards from the checkout counter and gave them to the lady, who took them and tucked them into her purse. "And I promise, on my soul, if I see either of your granddaughters walking by, I'll make sure to grab them and call you."

That did make the woman laugh just a little, and she wiped the side of her nose. "Oh my goodness, they are in so much trouble when we find them—after we hug them to death, of course!"

When the woman departed, Prax took the flyers to the worktable and grabbed the heavy tape dispenser. It probably was just a lack of communication, a well-meaning family friend who gave them a ride and forgot to call their parents.

But still, they would be home by now. Right?

Could be a relative unaware of the panic they've caused. A cell phone battery drained, sitting on the charger this very moment so they can let the Evans family know the girls were safe and sound. Maybe another neighbor near the park, a school friend whose parents invited them over for a slumber party, and contacting the Evans just slipped their mind.

Prax furrowed her brow. No matter which scenario she thought of, it still didn't explain why they weren't home by now - especially as the day ticked closer and closer to noon. She rolled pieces of tape onto the corners of each flyer and pressed them to the glass where anyone who walked by, or walked in, could easily see the information.

"What are these?" Courtney asked when she emerged from the backroom to see the papers seemingly floating around the shop.

"A couple of girls are missing." Prax realized then that she probably should have asked her boss, the shop owner, for permission before "decorating" with the flyers. But before she could apologize for the oversight, she saw Courtney's pensive frown as the florist held one of the papers still on the workbench.

"Fulton Park?" Courtney sipped her frap and squinted at the flyer. "That's so weird. They're probably just at a friend's place, right?"

"That's what I was thinking." Prax shrugged. "But their grandmother says no one's heard from them or seen any sign of them, and they checked with all the friends."

The florist shook her head, her strawberry blonde curls bouncing in the messy bun knotted on top of her head. "Uh-uh. If my kids pulled a stunt like this, you bet your ass they'd better stay missing until I've calmed down. That poor mother." She reached for the tape and gave Prax an approving nod. "Good idea, hon. Let's keep an eye out for these sweethearts, too. God knows their momma must be worried sick."

Prax suddenly had a thought that made her snort, and at Courtney's raised brow, she blushed. "Sorry, it's just...my mother practically herniated when I told her I got a job. You know, because of the accident." She smirked. "I can't imagine what she'd do if my sister or I—or both, really—went missing."

"*Your* mother?" Now it was Courtney's turn to snort out a laugh. "She'd destroy half the town, I have no doubt."

By the end of the workday, the poppy arrangements were assembled for the veteran's funeral and Prax's fingers itched to do anything other than wrap floral tape around stems and wires. She hoped the extra effort for elegance would be worth it, both in giving some semblance of serenity to the grieving family and also maybe earning herself a generous tip upon delivery. "A girl's gotta pay for coffee somehow," Courtney joked the first time Prax approached her, perplexed, with a wad of cash from a grieving widow. Prax didn't spend the gratuity until after the Thank You card arrived in the mail, singing the shop's praises, and only a day before a lavishing Google review appeared from the same family to further express their gratitude, and awe, for the "above and beyond" beauty of Prax's creations. At that point it was clear: excellent work earned excellent praise, and it would be rude of Prax to turn down the offerings.

"I'm home!" She called out to her family once she tugged the front door behind her. A distinct garlic-y aroma wafted to her nose from the kitchen, and Prax eagerly kicked off her shoes by the door to go see what supper would be.

Before she could, she was suddenly wrapped up in a somewhat desperate-feeling hug. "Oh, my god! Prax! You're home!" Demi rocked her side to side, crushing her eldest daughter to her chest. "Thank heavens! Are you alright?"

Prax gently pried herself free from her mother's surprisingly strong grip and laughed. "Um, yes? I'm totally fine! Why, what's wrong? What happened?" Her amusement faded into concern and she glanced over Demi's shoulder. "Where's Mya?"

On cue, Mya poked her head around the corner. "Yo!"

"Mom, what—"

"Mom's freaking out over the missing girls." Mya shrugged as she spooned some yogurt to her mouth from a small container. At Demi's half-glare, she shrunk back a little and widened her eyes. "What? You are!"

"I'm also just about done cooking dinner." Demi's voice was low, in that maternal way that made Mya quickly hide the yogurt container and duck out of sight. She sighed and turned her gaze back to Prax. "It's all over the news. The family is panicked and quite frankly, so am I. I just worried about you, is all."

Prax scoffed. "Mom, really, I'm fine. I'm also *way* older than those girls and perfectly capable of defending myself. You'd know if there was any trouble."

Demi's eyes softened, and in the evening glow of the lamps, looked as if they were misting over. "Would I?" She shook her head quickly, then sighed. "You're right. I know, I can be a little—"

"Overprotective?"

The sharpness returned to Demi's eyes, but the warmth remained as well. "Considering all that's happened to you, I'd say 'overprotective' is more than reasonable. What I meant to say was 'intense'."

Prax inwardly admitted maybe her mother had a fair point. In the excitement of her new job and budding social life, she'd forgotten that there was a brief moment in their lives when Prax did, in fact, go missing. Putting herself in Demi's shoes, she could see how age, size, strength, all the things she assumed to be advantages against disappearing, still didn't actually work for her when she did mysteriously vanish and eventually reappeared, naked and face-down in a cornfield.

With this realization in mind, Prax offered her mother an apologetic smile and pulled her into a warm embrace. "I'm sorry, Mom. I know you've been through a lot. I promise, though, I'm totally fine. Courtney keeps an eye out for me, and if anything were to happen, you know I'd give them hell."

Demi sighed. "Yes, I know. I worry because you're my daughter, but I shouldn't worry because, well, you're my daughter." With a wink, she caressed her daughter's cheek, then turned and walked away. "Dinner's almost ready," she called over her shoulder.

Prax breathed a sigh of relief, having caught herself before she mentioned anything about Aidon. Not that he'd come bursting in to save the day—it was a miracle of miracles he even gave her advice on managing her visions. The deck of cards suddenly felt heavy in her pocket and she slipped her hand inside just to feel the smooth edges.

That strange tug and squeeze in her chest that seemed to always happen whenever he was around now occurred at the mere thought of him. It was ridiculous, stupid, and the last thing she needed or he wanted. Just because he'd given her permission to hang out at Nanabozho, just because he'd gifted her some very expensive-looking playing cards, just because that hellfire heat in his eyes kept flickering to something else whenever she caught him looking at her…. Prax shook her head and just about slapped herself. *Nope.*

Nopity nope nope.

She joined Mya in the dining room as Demi set out platters of rice, chicken, and greens for their meal on the kitchen island. The younger Sadeh sister quickly picked up on Prax's blush and shot her an impish grin, a waggle of her brows, and Prax shot back her own perplexed look. "What?"

"Oh. Right. Like I don't know you've been sneaking off to the cemetery to go see that insanely hot groundskeeper," Mya grinned.

"What? No!" She set the plate down a bit harder than she intended and flinched, but Demi didn't seem to hear her. In fact, upon looking closer at her mother, Prax noticed she seemed almost distracted, off in some deep thought that made her brow furrow and her normally vibrant olive-green eyes fade into shadows. Prax wanted to ask if everything was okay, but something in her gut said it was best to leave it alone.

S oft whispers echoed down the corridor and signaled to Prax it was time to finish with the final touches and leave the floral arrangements around Mr. Callendoun's casket as they were before his family arrived. This was the part of the delivery job she loved most: stepping out of sight and out of mind, but still able to see the impact her work made on those who came to mourn their loved ones. She was never satisfied with "simple wreaths" and insisted on customizing each to the personality of the deceased from as much information as she could tactfully glean. Mr. Callendoun had been a naval officer in the Second World War, a trickster personality who faked his birth date so he could join the ranks at only sixteen. He met his wife while stationed in Hawaii, had five beautiful children with her, and lived a peaceful life as a farmer until he passed away in his sleep earlier that week. From the way his children spoke of their parents, and from the pictures displayed remembering his life, Prax felt a bittersweet lump in her throat form at the thought, rather the certainty, that Mr. Callendoun walked straight into the loving arms of his beautiful Eleanor who'd been waiting for him on the other side.

Despite not being an official participant of the ceremonies, it was considered customary and just plain considerate for vendors to wear black while on delivery for such solemn occasions. Prax was grateful for the overcast day, as summertime inside a mausoleum could quickly become unbearable, especially in clothing that tended to absorb heat. She let her light pashmina slip down her shoulders enough to feel the gentle breeze on her skin that drifted between the open doors, and did one more quick check to make sure all the floral arrangements remained upright and sturdy.

"Beautiful work, as always." Aidon's voice was a soft rumble behind her, and she nearly jumped out of her skin in surprise. His brow raised and he bit back a grin. "Did I scare you? Sorry."

"You don't typically expect voices to just pop up suddenly in a room full of dead people," Prax blurted, careful to keep her own voice low despite the hammering in her chest. She took a few deep breaths, hands on her hips, and finally let out a quiet laugh. "Better that than anything...*else*...popping up, I guess."

Before either of them risked ruining the solemn space with laughter, Aidon gently nudged her elbow with his hand and led them out a side door into the open air and away from Mr. Callendoun's family and friends. Prax squinted up at the sky, noticing the overcast was just thick enough to hide the sun but thin enough to brighten the world with muted rays. Weather like this always seemed to make the grass glow a bit greener, the trees etched sharper to the eye...something that made the world seem just this side of unearthly. In the memorial park, on the day a loving gentleman would be laid to rest beside his wife, it seemed perfect and fitting to illuminate the marble statues and make the water of the pond glitter like sapphires.

Prax and Aidon walked for a while in comfortable silence, down along a gravel path that wound between family sections and opened to a labyrinth-styled pathway lined with small white flowers. Well, as comfortable as it could be with the tension she felt between them. *"Beautiful as always?"* No, he'd said "beautiful *work*", which made sense since her designs now lay across the grounds and filled the mausoleum during every funerary service. Still...the Aidon Elrik who walked beside her right now seemed different from the constantly glaring centurion she'd grown accustomed to.

Was he...warming up to her?

As they strolled into the winding circle, Prax absentmindedly pulled the pack of blank cards from her dress' pocket and began shuffling them. Her brow furrowed, her gaze on the white cobblestone as her fingers strummed the cards back and forth.

"Uh-oh. I know that look," Aidon muttered. "What's on your mind?"

She shook her head. *Nothing I'm ever telling you.* "Any word on the missing girls?"

"Sarah and Rachel Evans?" At her nod, he sighed and shook his own head. "No, none that I've heard. Police have been busy, though. It's the second day they've been gone?"

"Yeah. And that's...I don't know." Prax flicked a card between her fingers, rolling it over her knuckles, and tucked it back into the deck. Not once did she bother to glance at her hands, her eyes somewhat unfocused as she let her mind drift deep in thought. "Something just doesn't feel right."

"I know what you mean."

That made Prax look up at him, curious. Aidon offered her a small smile and cocked his head to the side. "I like to take Spot out on walks in other parks, too. Get him away from the dead for a while. We've been to Fulton Park, several times.

It's open and airy and not as many trees as one would think—"

"And not so easy to disappear. Not without a trace."

"Right. And that's what has me uneasy, too." Aidon nodded his head in the direction where Spot trotted amongst the markers, long tongue lolled out and fur bouncing happily despite the summer heat. "There's no trace at all. He can't pick up a scent for either of the girls anywhere in that park. We tried, I offered his nose to the Evans and they gave him a few shirts. Still, nothing."

Prax inclined her head towards Aidon as she stared at Spot. "How likely is it that the scent vanished overnight? You know, after wind and dew and such."

The lines on Aidon's face hardened, and a muscle ticked in his cheek as his eyes darkened with something Prax couldn't quite place. "We were there that same night, just a few hours after they were supposed to be home. Went out for a walk and ran into Mrs. Evans calling for the girls, which is why I offered to help. So...how likely? Not very. Not at all."

Little girls didn't simply vanish into thin air. Much less in broad daylight, where everyone could see them and yet no one saw them. Prax wasn't sure what bothered her more: the fact that they were missing, or the fact that in the middle of a city, surrounded by people who knew and recognized them, they disappeared without a trace. Her fingers thrummed the deck of cards back and forth, and for the first time since her horrible visions began, she wished she could just flip up a card and see the fate of the girls painted on it. Sadly, that required at least one of them to be there in front of her.

She sighed. "Not much we can do, can we—"

A car door slammed, and a burly man hopped out, his calloused hand wrapped tightly around the arm of a flailing little girl.

"No! I want to go home!" She kicked out at him but the leaves under her feet were still damp from the morning dew and she slid, held up only by his grip on her arm.

The man took a deep breath, holding back his temper even as it seethed through his teeth and turned his voice into a growl. "I told you, we're getting there! We'd go a lot faster if you'd stop fighting!"

The little girl pouted but remained still, and he loosened his hold. She looked ready to bolt but remained where she stood when he yanked the back passenger door open. Another girl slid out of the car, only a few years older and a little taller, but still just as scared. She didn't fight, however, only took the hand of who looked to be her sister and kept her gaze to the ground.

"See?" The man gestured to the older girl, glaring at the younger. "She gets it. Don't make a fuss, and no one gets hurt. Everyone goes home."

Their watery eyes widened, both quickly looking up at him. "You're gonna hurt us?"

He ran a frustrated hand through his hair and sighed. "No. That's not...no. I'm not going to hurt you. I just need you two to cooperate while we get this figured out."

Small fingers tangled together and clasped tightly, trembling, but the girls nodded and meekly followed the man deeper into the woods.

Prax blinked. Once. Twice.

She was still in Nanabozho Memorial Park, no longer surrounded by trees. The only man in sight was Aidon, who suddenly stood very close to her, his brow knit with worry. Her lungs expelled a heavy, almost wheezing breath, and that's when she realized she'd been holding it for who knows how long.

"Prax...are you okay?"

The question of the century. Prax nodded and swallowed hard, her fingers shaking slightly as she held the deck of cards in front of her. She flipped the top one up and studied the card. Nothing. Again, she quickly shuffled the cards and flipped the top one over, expecting another vision or sketch, or *something*. But it was blank, just as all the other cards were.

"Here. Pick one." She fanned them out and held them up for Aidon to choose.

He raised a brow. "I don't think—"

"Just pick one. Any card. Please."

Aidon hesitated, then sighed and drew a card from the deck and handed it to her. Prax turned it over in her palm, then let out a plaintive whine. "Nothing! What the hell?" She felt half-tempted to toss the whole deck into the air with the hope that at least one of them would provide an answer, a sign, anything at all, but the breeze picked up and she quickly changed her mind. A quick glance up at Aidon's face made her suddenly very aware of just how crazy she must look and sound. The explanation, she knew, would sound crazier.

The way he looked at her, though...the same way he seemed to always look at her after the night she'd confessed her deepest, darkest torment. The hard edges in his eyes were softened, the tightness in his jaw not as frequent, and he seemed more inclined to walk with her, just like now, than the old dismissive way he used to treat her. All things considered, she couldn't ignore the fact that he stood by her through her first round of crazy.

Round two.

Ding.

"I saw them." Prax pursed her lips and debated on saying

anything more, but figured to just out with it and see what happens. "Just now, without my cards."

"The girls?" Aidon stepped back, and she felt her shoulders tense. But he seemed more surprised, genuinely surprised, than skeptical.

Prax nodded. "They were in the woods, I don't know which woods or how far from here, but they were there, with a man. They seemed...safe? So that's something."

"What did he look like?"

Shit. That would have been something to pay attention to, and her memory was already beginning to blur the images together in her mind. "I didn't see his eyes, or if I did, I don't remember. He's not too old, more middle-aged? I don't know, really. But he was wearing a t-shirt! And jeans, and work boots."

Aidon did his best to hide the sardonic grin that dangerously threatened to spread across his face. "So, basically you saw half the male population of Bogarten."

Prax shot him a glare, but it was short-lived. He had a point. "Look, I was more focused on the girls. Also, I wasn't exactly expecting a vision to just slap me in the face like that." She sucked in a breath. "But I do remember...he had facial hair, and like, a beer belly, kind of."

"That does narrow it down quite a bit." His lips twitched. "To a quarter of the male population of Bogarten."

Prax wanted to smack the sexy off his face but decided it'd be a waste of energy. And then she felt her own face heat at the realization that she'd just now, in that moment, thought of Aidon as *sexy*.

Time to schedule another MRI, double-check on those residual injuries mom keeps worrying about.

"I need to tell the police about this," she said, slipping her cards back into her dress pocket and tugging the pashmina higher around her shoulders. "Maybe it will help them narrow down their search."

"Prax."

Just as he recognized her pensive expressions, she'd grown to learn the different tones in his voice—and this one was gentle in the way that made her hackles raise. "I have to, Aidon, it's the right thing to do."

His hand lifted from his side, then lowered again. "I know, it's just.... What exactly are you going to tell them? If you leave out the 'vision' part, they're going to assume you were there and part of the abduction. If you tell them you had a vision, then...."

"They're going to assume I'm crazy."

"I wouldn't say 'crazy', but...yeah, something like that."

"One look at my recent medical history, and I'd get thrown out, anyway." Prax sighed and tugged on her braid, then yanked it in frustration. "Gaaaahh! I hate this! I hate these visions, I hate this whole situation, I hate—I hate, hate, *hate* feeling so useless!"

Now both his hands lifted and gently rested on her shoulders, and as much as Prax wanted to yank herself free and run into the pond to muffle her scream of frustration in the water, she felt a strong sense of reassurance and comfort wash over her. Aidon was built like a tank and could probably easily hammer-throw her into the pond from here, but his touch was gentle. His fingers lightly tilted her chin up until their gazes met, and he smiled. "You, my lady, are *not* useless."

If Prax's insides were about to combust like they felt right now, at least she was in the perfect place to do it. Aidon's gaze briefly flicked over her face and momentarily settled on her parted lips, but he simply smiled and gave her shoulders a reassuring squeeze. "Go home. I'm sure your boss will let you have the rest of the Saturday off, and as far as I know, there are no other services to prepare for at least until Tuesday."

Well, *now* Prax didn't want to go anywhere, so long as he kept his warm, strong hands on her body. She was pretty sure he misinterpreted the sheen on her brow as coming from the humid air, but it most certainly had nothing to do with the weather and everything to do with his very, very close proximity. And the thought of a weekend with no work or responsibilities, the freedom to do what she wanted... with whoever she wanted...made something unfamiliar and pleasantly naughty swirl in her abdomen.

Aidon's eyes sparkled with mischief but quickly blinked it away as he cleared his throat and stepped back. "You can call me if you need anything, okay? Visions, work-related stress, boredom...." That twinkle was back, and again he seemed to intentionally snuff it out.

A very breathless Prax nodded dumbly, then quickly shook her head free of the not-too-unpleasant cobwebs and smiled. "Thanks, Aidon. You, too." Before she could do or say anything else that might steal what little dignity she had left, she turned and walked across the labyrinth pathway towards the parking lot, acutely aware of his eyes watching her leave.

Spot stopped chasing the bird he'd been obsessed with moments before and padded over to Prax's side, falling in step with her pace. Despite the heat and humidity, Prax felt an urge to bury herself within the comfort of his soft fur and she did, at least partway, rubbing his neck as they walked together. The Tibetan mastiff nearly reached her height, not that she was particularly tall herself, and he used this to his advantage to lick her face with warm, gentle kisses that made her giggle - and earn a few disapproving stares from people making their way to the mausoleum.

One of those faces actually smiled at her, and on second glance, Prax recognized the cheeky grin of Donn Morrighan. He ducked away from the line of funeral attendees and sauntered over to her, the summer breeze touseling his chestnut waves and stealing for himself a few sly glances from some of the women nearby.

"Prax!" Donn immediately regretted the loudness of his voice and ducked his head sheepishly, too tall to hide behind the mastiff. "Fancy seeing you here," he greeted again, this time closer to a whisper.

Prax grinned. "I had a delivery, for Mr. Callendoun's service. I was just heading out."

Donn stole a glance over her shoulder, then smiled at the dog. "Hey there, buddy-o!" He reached out to scratch Spot's ears, and the mastiff happily slobbered the man's fingers in return. Donn crouched down to Spot's eye-level and rubbed the fur of his neck. "Who's a good boy? Yeah? Who's a good grim?" When he glanced up and saw Prax's confused stare, he flashed her another suddenly-self-aware smile. "It's an old tale, dogs in cemeteries. From 'Ye Olde Country', as it were. Church grims were dogs buried before the people so there'd be guardians over the churchyard, chasing away grave robbers and the like."

Prax tilted her head to one side as she regarded her furry friend with new respect. "Well, Spot, that certainly sounds like your job description! Is that what you are? Aidon's church grim?"

Donn's eyes flicked to hers at the mention of the groundskeeper's name, but he made no comment and instead pulled a dog biscuit from his suit coat. "Rule Number One in the land of the dead: always feed the dogs." He stood as he offered the biscuit to Spot, who very eagerly lapped it up and crunched it down in two bites. The dark, beady eyes nearly buried in thick, black fur peered up at the man with such polite request, but Donn sighed and turned out his pockets. "Sorry, my friend. I ran out."

"I'm surprised you carry dog food in your pocket," Prax chuckled. "A suit, even!"

He grinned and winked at the mastiff. "Hey, always be prepared. You never know when you'll need it." At the muted sound of organ music emanating from within the mausoleum, Donn looked over his shoulder and saw the last few guests trailing inside. "Well, that's my cue. I should go pay my respects."

"You knew Mr. Callendoun?"

He adjusted his tie and nodded. "We met at the hospice. Lovely man. Nice family, good kids. Even in his old age, he was quite the trickster, always playing little pranks on the nurses and once, even me." His grin widened. "Joe often joked that he lived this long by tricking death. I let him have that one."

Prax warmed at the thought of the sweet old farmer, loved even by those who met him briefly, like Donn, and in a strange sort of way by those who never had the opportunity, like herself. She bid her farewell to Donn, who nodded quiet greetings to the ushers and took a seat in the back, one last glance over his shoulder to her with a smile. The organ music faded, the gentle voice of the minister echoed through the chamber, and as much as Prax was tempted to stay for the service, she knew she still had a delivery van to return. Spot also took his leave, ears perked up at the faint sound of a whistle, and Prax smiled to herself as she climbed into the van. Crazy or not, it felt good to finally have a few friends.

"Where are you taking us?" The little girl whimpered, glancing back over her shoulder every other step, her hand clutched tightly in her sister's.

The man sighed and grit his teeth, but took a few moments before responding with as much calm, quiet patience as he could muster - which wasn't much, judging by the tension in his shoulders. "There's an old house up here just a ways, we can take shelter for the night. We need to get somewhere safe; they'll be looking for us."

The older girl, Sarah, bit her lip. "Um, I'm pretty sure they're already looking for us."

"I don't mean the police."

Even the woods itself stilled, the low warning in the man's voice enough to send chills through the trees. He paused and turned to look at the sisters, his face pale and cold. "Trust me when I say this, both of you: we do not want to be found. Not by them."

"Who?"

He shook his head and held out his hand. "Come, this way. It's not too far now, I know you're tired. We'll go in and get some rest."

Rachel clung to her sister's arm, and Sarah edged herself forward, keeping Rachel safely behind her. She didn't take the man's hand, which seemed well and fine to him, but he was satisfied enough that they quietly followed him further into the woods. After a few yards he ushered them ahead, even gave them a small smile probably intended as reassurance.

He waited for them to pass before looking back behind them, his smile quickly fading into a mask of fear.

Prax's knuckles whitened, her fingers practically forming dents in the steering wheel.

Again, she didn't realize she'd been holding her breath until it wheezed out of her lungs, long and strangled. This wasn't like her other visions. No one was about to die, at least not from what she could see - but she still felt that unearthly tension, like an invisible hand fisting around her ribcage and squeezing, as if she was the one to die.

She rested her forehead against the steering wheel to catch her breath, to think.

All she could do was sob.

It was a good thing Prax only needed to walk to work, because traffic was at an absolute standstill—and that was an unusual event all on its own for central Bogarten. Cars lined the streets bumper to bumper. A few people shouted from driver side windows. Most just sat and occasionally threw up their hands with impatience.

But it would be impossible for any of them to negotiate with the caravan of squad cars and a few unmarked vehicles with tinted windows sectioning off six whole blocks near the park.

Prax hurried into the flower shop, nearly knocking the doorbell off its hinge in her rush. "I am so sorry, Courtney! I got here as soon as I could!"

Her boss waved her hand and scoffed. "Are you kidding? I'm lucky I even made it in! I don't think we'll be getting too much business today, anyhow, with all that racket." She nodded out the window at the scene unfolding on one of the grassy lawns of Jefferson Park. "Did you hear the news?"

Prax shook her head.

"They found blood."

That invisible fist was back, squeezing the air from Prax's lungs. "What? But I thought they went missing from Fulton Park."

"That's what we all thought! But my husband came in late last night, said it was because someone found one of the girls' backpacks. Right over there, in Jefferson Park. With blood on it." Courtney's expression darkened, her brow furrowed against the early morning sun.

At this angle, Prax suddenly noticed the dark ring under her eye. "Oh gosh, Courtney, ow! Your eye! Are you okay?"

The older woman startled, but quickly let out a laugh and waved her hand again. "Oh my gosh, it's the dumbest thing. Playing soccer with my kids and the stupid ball caught me before I caught it." She laughed again and walked over to the design desk, quickly scanning the order binder for new requests printed overnight. Prax felt it was a rather quick and easy response, too easy, but she shook it off as paranoia from her visions.

Neither vision showed any injuries on the girls. In fact, their captor seemed keen on keeping them safe and unharmed, going so far as to check his own emotions lest he traumatize them as some sort of "bad guy" type. And he wasn't injured, at least not as far as she'd been able to see.

Whose blood was on the backpack?

"Hey, Prax, we don't have any ceremonial orders but I think the hospice could use a little refresh. You up for it?" Courtney flashed her a conspiratorial smile. "We could smuggle you out the back, duck the feds."

Prax slinked over to the table and drummed her fingers against the faded wood, her face quirked into an equally cheeky grin. "Can I get some coffee on the way?"

"Only if you bring me some!"

Deliveries to Sunrise Hospice were much easier with the deck of cards in her literal back pocket, and Prax was prone to remembering those and forgetting her phone because—priorities. Once she figured out a back alley way around the Federal Bureau of Investigation's roadshow with the local police, she drove the fresh floral bouquets to the hospice in decent time.

After finding out the flowers were a charitable donation by Courtney and the shop, Prax felt more pride in her work delivering these gifts to the people who only wanted to be remembered by someone, anyone, who cared. A "simple bouquet" was never good enough for her over-achieving tastes, which both thrilled and frustrated her boss to no end. Like this morning, when it took an additional hour of Prax's fussing over calendula arrangements before she felt satisfied enough to finally load the van.

And then another half hour when she noticed one of the petals wilting.

News of the missing "Evans girls" spread quickly throughout the hospice, which now buzzed with gossip and rumors between staff and residents alike who all felt they knew either the girls, the parents, or someone who knew someone related to either. Prax made the mistake of whispering her warning about the sectioned off streets downtown to one of the staffers she knew who lived in that area—the word "FBI" set off a whole new wildfire of gasps and comments about "the feds getting involved".

"I always told Donna that girl of hers was trouble, and now look what's gone and happened," said one of the healthier residents who sat playing cards in the open lounge area, her eyes sharp as she skimmed her hand. She folded the fanned cards with a clean snap on the tabletop and sighed. "Poor dears."

"Oh now, come on, Doris," chided another woman in the game, peeking over her own hand. "Donna may have had her issues with little Lacey, but she cleaned right up! I bet she's worried sick."

Prax knew she was eavesdropping, but this was information not shared on the news just yet. So she quietly moved closer to listen, casually setting a vase of flowers on a coffee table nearby.

Doris huffed and fanned her cards again, plucked one out and flicked it onto the pile with an elegant flourish. "Mark my words, Lacey Wilkins—I mean, *Evans*—has something to do with their disappearance. I've never liked that girl, she's always up to no good. Only ever did what's best for herself, never anyone else. Not even her own family. Not even her poor mama, sweet Donna."

The other women playing the card game tsked and shook their heads at Doris, but a few of them exchanged knowing looks with her. Prax couldn't help herself, couldn't stop from stepping closer and interrupting. "Excuse me? Hi...you said Donna? Their grandmother's name is Donna?" At their narrowed gazes, which felt very much like being silently scolded, Prax quickly added, "I met her the other day, where I work. At the flower shop."

A chorus of recognition arose from the small group and a few even reached out to playfully pinch her arm, all of their glares instantly replaced with cheerful grins. "Yes, Donna is a dear friend of ours, we all went to school together back in the day," said one of the women.

"Way back in the day," joked another.

Doris smirked at the joke and shifted her gaze to Prax. "Donna was a bit younger than us, but we still played together when we were girls. You said you met her?"

Prax nodded. "I think so. She came in with posters, the first day they were missing."

"Sounds like her." Doris gathered the cards from their finished round and began to skillfully, almost magically, shuffle them from one hand to the other, flying steadily through the air, perfectly caught. "I met them, you know. Once. They were so little, I'm sure they don't even remember." She noticed Prax's transfixed gaze on her shuffling skills and winked. "You like these tricks?"

"Yes! I've been practicing myself, with my own deck." Without a second thought, an excited Prax took her deck of cards out from her back pocket and showed them to Doris, who let out an appreciative whistle.

"Whooo-whee! Girly-girl!" She peeked at the glistening gold foil filigree and licked her lips. "Where did you get a deck like that? And can I have one?"

Prax laughed and blushed all at once. "These were a gift. I don't know where he got them, sorry."

Doris leaned back in her chair and lowered her reading glasses to thoroughly stare at the young woman. "A man gave you this deck? *This* deck? Did he ask you to marry him, too?"

All the women burst into giggles, and the one who'd scolded Doris earlier leaned in closer towards Prax. "What Doris forgot to mention was that she used to be a professional, out in Las Vegas. Once dealt a winning hand to Elvis Presley! So playing cards are a bit of an obsession—"

"Obsession! Ha!" Doris huffed. "What else am I gonna do around here besides shuffle cards and beat his ass?"

Prax quickly turned to see Donn walking over to them, his mouth twisted upwards in a lopsided grin. He winked at the ladies and gave Doris a playful pout. "One of these days, Doris Finkley, I'm going to figure out how you keep cheating."

"Oh, posh." She clicked her tongue and rolled her eyes. "Just because you've never won a single round against me doesn't mean I'm cheating. Maybe you're just that terrible at poker."

Donn gasped. "I never!"

Doris grinned. "And you never will." Wily, cheeky woman.

It was all Prax could do to stifle her own giggle, which earned her a sidelong glance from her purse-lipped friend. He sighed and folded his arms across his chest, which earned him a few appreciative smiles from the elderly women ogling them. "I came to see if you need any help with the deliveries today," he said to Prax after another narrow-eyed moment with the very smug Doris Finkley. "Jenny's been asking about you."

"Oh! Yes, thank you!" Prax also bid her thanks to the woman and tucked her cards back into her pocket, suddenly grateful none of them had asked her to play.

As gracious and sweet as she always was, Jenny didn't exude her usual cheeriness Prax was used to. Instead, her little brow was stitched together with worry as they walked in and Prax set the (biggest of the bunch) bouquet on her table. "Have they found Rachel yet?" she asked.

Donn sighed and shook his head, slipping her tiny hand in his as he sat down next to her in his usual chair. "Police are looking everywhere, I promise. We have the whole city turned upside down to find them."

"You know Rachel Evans?" Prax asked.

Jenny nodded. "We went to school together. She's my best friend. See?" She pointed to a crayon-on-construction paper card leaning against the dresser mirror. "She and her big sister used to come see me sometimes, whenever their grandma came to visit her friends."

Prax wasn't sure how she'd missed it before, but there it was—faded yellow paper with multiple crayon-drawn stick figures in skirts and long, squiggly hair, propped up to the side of the mirror. *Get well soon!* was written on the inside, the handwriting suggesting it was most likely Sarah who carefully swirled the elementary cursive letters in marker.

"Sometimes their new daddy would bring them, if Rachel asked."

"New daddy?" Both Donn and Prax looked over at Jenny, who nodded.

"Yeah, he's real nice. He only came a few times, but he brought me flowers and told us stories." Jenny shifted to sit up more in her bed, and smiled at Donn when he helped her fluff her pillows. Her face suddenly grew serious, and she beckoned both of them closer. "I'm not supposed to tell anyone," she whispered, "but he's teaching Sarah how to fight."

The adults exchanged glances but nodded for her to continue.

"Rachel told me he's been teaching Sarah how to kick and punch and stuff. And sometimes he takes them camping, to teach them how to survive in the woods. Rachel didn't learn any fighting stuff yet, she's too little." Jenny scrunched her nose. "But Sarah is bigger and stronger."

"Do you know his name?"

"No." She sighed and settled deeper into the pillows, her eyelids slowly starting to droop. "Sorry. I never asked."

Donn stroked the back of her hand with his thumb and smiled. "It's okay, Beautiful. Why don't you get some rest, have some sweet dreams." He pressed a warm kiss to her brow, which made her blush with a smile. "I'll be back later for supper, okay?"

"Okay."

He tucked her in snug and warm for her nap, and quietly slipped out of the room behind Prax. She noticed the lines on his brow, the way his eyes closed for a moment and his chest moved with a heavy sigh. "Hey," she whispered, "are you alright?"

Donn nodded and cleared his throat. "Yeah. I'm fine."

They walked down the hallway in silence, a heaviness almost tangible around his shoulders and in his mind. Prax opened her mouth to say something, but was interrupted by the very official-sounding voices of two men and a woman around the corner. Sure enough, the two men dressed in suits were accompanied by a high-ranking police officer, a woman with short blonde hair and a serious grimace on her face. They appeared to be thanking Doris Finkley for her time, snapping shut notepads and stuffing badges back into their pockets.

The officer glanced over to where Prax and Donn stood and straightened her stance. "Donn! Fancy seeing you here."

"Brigit." Donn mustered a wry smile and nudged his companion. "Prax, this is Sheriff Brigit Sulis. She's an old friend of Aidon's."

"Really." For some reason, Prax didn't even question it. It actually made a lot of things make a lot of sense, most especially how Aidon could oversee Bogarten's underbelly with impunity. Apparently it paid to have friends in high places.

"And this is Special Agent Fuller and Special Agent Madsen from the FBI." Sheriff Sulis fisted a hand on her hip as she introduced them, seeming none too pleased at their presence. "They're struggling for leads and I figured Doris here might know a thing or two, given her friendship with the girls' family."

The agents sighed and disregarded the jab with a shared look. Madsen gave Donn a once-over, then Prax. "I don't suppose either of you have any information regarding the disappearance of Sarah and Rachel Evans?"

Doris huffed from behind them and shouldered her way through with her wheelchair, head held high with the kind of look a wisened mother threw her grown children. "I told you already, do you have wax in your ears? Follow the money."

Fuller muttered something akin to, "Yes, Mrs. Finkley," with a barely concealed eye roll, which made Sheriff Sulis scoff. But Prax was curious. "What money?" She asked.

Another huff, another sidelong glare at the agents. "As I told these two, Lacey Evans has been nothing but trouble since the day she was born. Beautiful girl, but greedy as they come." Doris patted Sheriff Sulis' arm with a slight tug on her sleeve. "Mark my words, if that woman has anything to do with this, there'll be money involved. She's got all sorts of addictions and financial problems."

To her credit, Sheriff Sulis regarded the elderly woman with respect and squeezed her bony hand. "You've been a big help, Doris. Take care of yourself, you hear?"

"Alrighty then." One more cold stare at the feds, just for good measure, then a warm smile towards Prax. "It was good to meet you, dear. Always such lovely flowers." She smirked at Donn. "I have a bone marrow biopsy next week, Tuesday. Feel like a game before then?"

He scoffed and bit his cheek, but nodded. "Maybe the feds can help me figure out how you keep cheating."

Doris laughed and wheeled herself away, every bit the healthy woman for someone who was supposed to be so close to death.

The search expanded into the woods surrounding Bogarten. Expert divers were called in to dredge the lakes, and volunteer fishermen cast nets into the river in case the current would reveal any secrets. The biggest fear everyone had was the possibility that they fell, or were thrown, into the Miskwa River's powerful current. If that were the case, all hope of finding them was lost far down in the rocky depths miles and miles away.

Lab reports would take a few days to fully identify the source of the blood on the backpack, which the Evans' family confirmed belonged to Rachel. Sarah's phone was stuffed into one of the pockets, which confirmed to officials this was absolutely a kidnapping. No one found blood anywhere else, not inside the pockets or around the backpack in the grass, which also suggested the bag had been dumped in Jefferson Park as an afterthought. Agents Fuller and Madsen took a quick peek into Lacey Wilkins-Evans' current financial records, but nothing out of the ordinary flagged their attention. They chalked it up to the ramblings of a well-meaning old lady near the end of her time and felt it best to pursue other, more credible, leads.

Which is exactly why Prax decided to not tell them about her visions.

There wasn't much she could do, anyways—she was

a florist, for Pete's sake. A florist's assistant, to be more specific, and one who was still recovering from severe head trauma caused by miraculously surviving the world's deadliest tornado.

Oh yes, Prax Sadeh was the "more credible" lead the FBI needed.

As if.

Prax realized that if she couldn't go directly to the authorities with her own insights, maybe she could find another way to help the girls. People loved to spill their secrets when they thought no one was listening—and no one listened to a drunk person's incoherent babbling.

What courage she'd felt walking into the bar quickly vanished when she saw the booth Aidon usually sat in was empty. No Aidon meant no backup. No regulation over the rowdier crowd. But she'd already stepped across the threshold, in more ways than one, and turning around felt considerably cowardly. With a deep breath, Prax squared her shoulders and sauntered over to the bar counter, ordered herself a pitcher of cider, and slid onto the pleather seat of the crescent table.

At first no one paid her any attention, for which she was actually quite grateful. She poured herself a glass of cider and sipped it to calm her nerves, studying the room over the rim. A small group of college dudes bantered over the pool table. A biker and his girlfriend played a competitive game of darts. The DJ tested the sound system and flicked through karaoke screens. The bartender wiped down the countertop and polished a few glasses, greeting newcomers as they trickled in. All in all, it was a quiet night, and possibly not the best night for seeking answers to questions Prax didn't have the words for.

Her mind wandered back to the visit to Sunrise and Doris

Finkley's masterful shuffling, and she felt herself smile as she tugged out her deck and fanned the cards on the table. The gold filigree glinted in the low lighting, sending sparks of magic into the air when she flipped the bottom one over and the rest followed suit. She swiped her hand across the deck and they neatly folded back into the stack. Then, another sweep of her hand, another beautiful array of gold woven into midnight, and another flash of magical light danced before her eyes as she flipped them over. She picked the deck up and tried the hand-to-hand shuffle Doris made look so easy, but that only resulted in several cards flying across the table. Prax scrambled to pick them back up before anyone noticed and quickly resumed her more familiar shuffling tricks.

"Hey."

Prax looked up to see a middle-aged woman with a snake-skin purse and equally dry skin on her collarbone lean over the table. "Hey," she said, reminding herself how Aidon would be all cool, calm, and collected whenever total strangers approached him. "What can I do for ya?"

"You're that death dealer, right?" The woman pulled a chair over and sat down, teasing an unlit cigarette between her fingers.

Prax flinched, but quickly caught herself and straightened. "I'm not sure I'd word it like that, but—"

"You see people's deaths, right? With those fancy-ass cards of yours."

"Um...yes? Yes." She cleared her throat and took another sip of cider. At second thought, she turned that sip into a chug. "Yes I do."

The woman grinned and shimmied her hips with a giggle. "Do me!"

Okay, crazy lady. Prax shrugged and gave the deck a quick shuffle, then fanned the cards out for the woman to admire. "Pick one." She bit the inside of her cheek when the woman used her cigarette to tap on a card at the end of the deck, reminding herself to "do as Aidon would do" and pretend nothing drove her nerves up the wall. With a slow, dramatic pause, she lifted the card and peered at the blank side. "Hm. Interesting."

"What?" The woman's eyes widened, her smile quickly faded. "What is it?"

In reality, there was nothing to tell. The card remained blank, and no visions appeared before Prax's eyes, bidden or otherwise. This meant that death wasn't right around the corner, but there was no telling just how far away it truly was—it could be a few days, a few weeks, a few decades. But the insistent tapping of the unlit cigarette against the table gave her an idea, and she let out an exaggerated sigh. "I've got good news and bad news."

The few moments of silence irritated the woman, who quickly gestured for Prax to continue. "Yeah? What's the bad news?"

Prax took another quick look at the blank card and slowly met the woman's impatient gaze. "If you don't quit smoking, and I mean immediately, you're looking at a few months. Tops."

The woman paled. Then quickly shook her head and threw up a hand. "Wait, wait, wait. You said, 'if'."

"Yeah, I did. That's the good news. Every now and then someone's death is potential, rather than imminent, and that's what yours is." At the silence and blank stare, Prax swallowed back her eye roll and offered a small smile. "The good news is, you can control when and how you die, starting with the smoking."

This seemed to sink in at least a little bit. The woman regarded the cigarette in her fingers, her nose slowly curled into a sneer. "So, what, I'm supposed to just quit cold turkey and it magically fixes everything? Are you kidding me?"

Prax channeled her best Aidon impression and poured herself another glass, held it to her lips, and shrugged. "Quit, don't quit, it's your life. And death." She cocked a brow as she tossed back a hearty gulp and smacked her lips. "Anything else?" When the woman shook her head and walked away, it was all she could do to not slump in her seat with a sigh of relief. Maybe she was in over her head, trying to act like someone she wasn't.

"Hey, I told you it was her!" The group of college students playing pool nudged each other excitedly and pointed over to where Prax sat, and when they saw her looking at them, they all simultaneously grinned and shuffled over to her table. "Hey, yo, you're that death dealer we've heard about!"

She nodded and hid her sudden spike of anxiety behind another sip. *Was this why he's always drinking? To hide his nerves?* The thought made her smile, made her appreciate him just a little more, and she set the glass down with renewed confidence. "Yeah? What's up?"

The two on either side looked to the guy in the middle, who smirked and shrugged a beefy shoulder. "So...can you do it? Can really see how I'm gonna die?"

"Let's find out." Prax flit her lashes at him with a flirty little pout, which made his two friends chuckle and playfully nudge him. Instead of letting him pick his card, she fanned the deck out with both her hands and gazed up at him over the edges like a lady over a delicate silk fan. She plucked a random card from the middle, flipped it back and forth between her fingers, then focused on the blank side.

Just as all her visions before, the images didn't appear on the card like an illustration—they were still very tangible as if she was there at the scene of the accident. His head hung over the edge of the steering wheel wedged into his chest, the horn blaring endlessly under his literal dead weight. In the passenger seat slumped one of his companions, head smashed halfway out the side window at an angle a seatbelt would have prevented. In the backseat—well, would have been in the backseat—the third friend lay twisted between the front two seats, his ribcage nearly crushed by the sudden and instant thrust into the tight space.

Prax slid the card back into the deck and tapped the stack neatly on the tabletop to settle the edges. "Well, boys, it's a three-for-one deal." They all leaned in closer, and she twitched her lips into a small smile. "Any chance I could talk ya'll into just ordering an Uber?"

They chuckled, glancing at each other with no small amount of worry. "Um...what?"

She sighed. "Whether it's in an hour or at closing time, I have no idea. What I *can* tell you is, Mr. Huskers Fan here is way too drunk to be behind the wheel. Better take his keys now if you want to wake up tomorrow."

Suddenly the guy in the middle was not so sure of himself, his fingers self-consciously tugging at the hem of his Nebraska Cornhuskers jersey as his friends eyed him suspiciously. The one on the left furrowed his brow. "So what if one of us," he gestured to the friend at the other end of their group, "drives instead? We've barely had anything to drink."

Fair question. Prax took a look at another random card and pursed her lips. "Ooo, sorry, no go. None of you make it."

This did not sit well with any of them, and for good reason. "All because of a few drinks?"

She shrugged. "Good question. It might be, it might not be. Could be a deer, could be a sinkhole, could be the wrong turn on a gravel road in the middle of a dark night. All I know is, no matter who is behind the wheel, all three of you die in a horrible crash." She didn't even realize her hands were attempting the fancy mid-air shuffle until it happened, successfully, and her eyes widened for an instant before she corrected herself with a cough. "Anyways, it seems like the best way to avoid this fate is to just not drive. Get someone else to do it, or get a hotel room. Whatever you need to do."

The guy in the middle winked at her and smirked. "You offering a place, sweetheart?"

Before she could respond, a familiar hand slapped heavily onto the dude's shoulder and gave him a firm, "friendly" little shake. "Seems like your cards are off," Aidon grumbled, brow raised. "This boy's gonna die long before he gets to the car if he keeps it up." He winked at Prax and slid onto the seat next to her, stretching his arm across the back of the booth—not unlike wrapping a protective arm around her. He stared at the students with his signature glower, cocking a brow when none of them came up with a response. "As I overheard it, you got what you came for. Anything else?" At their quick head shakes and even hastier departure, he chuckled. "Amateurs." He glanced at Prax, his expression softening. "Sorry I'm late. Didn't know you'd be here tonight, or I would have come sooner."

A whirlwind of emotions swirled in her chest and in her stomach, a flutter of excitement, nervousness, and uncertainty. He was here for her? No, she must have misheard. She kept her gaze on her cards as she felt his gaze remain steadily on her.

"Why are you here, anyways?" Aidon asked. "I never figured you for a barfly."

How to tell him without telling him...was that even possible? Yet again she'd been caught encroaching on his territory, inserting herself into his world. Prax bit the corner of her lip and tapped the deck nervously against the tabletop a few times before she sighed and gave in. "It was a stupid idea. I just figured...." She stole a quick glance up at his face and almost jumped in surprise at how close he actually was to her. And it felt...really, really nice. "I've been hearing some things around town about the disappearances, the little girls. I thought maybe someone here would know something, something useful anyways." She let out a small laugh. "You know, because they're drunk."

Aidon leaned back against the booth, deep in thought. Then he chuckled. "That's actually all sorts of brilliant." He gave her a rare, genuine smile and nodded. "You're pretty good at this, you know."

"At what?"

He didn't answer her. Instead, he raised a hand to get the bartender's attention, then announced loud enough for the whole bar to hear, "Drinks are on me tonight! Anyone with information about the missing girls gets double on the house - my house!"

The entire bar erupted in cheers, whoops and hollers, half the patrons immediately beelining for the bartender. Prax chuckled and shook her head. "And how will you know they're telling the truth? Free booze in exchange for information may lead to some wild stories."

Aidon grinned. "I always know. And they know I always know." He watched the chaos unfold with no attempts to conceal his amusement as he drank his favorite beer and drummed his fingers on the back of the booth. It felt so distinctly like he was putting a protective arm around her, without even touching her, and she was not opposed to the feeling of safety the motion gave her.

He's married. He's married, he's married, he's married....

Was he, though? She quickly glanced at his hand which now rested close to her head, and saw the glimmer of gold wrapped around his ring finger. Ah. He never spoke of his wife, or her departure, and it looked like some part of him was still dedicated to at least the idea of being married to her. Whoever she was. Wherever she was.

Something tugged at the deepest recess of her mind... and her heart. It bothered her to no end that whenever he was around, and even more whenever he did things like this, he kept sending her mixed messages: pulling her close and shoving her away at the exact same time; protecting her, showing off his nonexistent claim as if warning others away from her, while showing a gold band of loyalty on his hand to a completely different woman.

From the other end of the bar came a woman still dressed in what looked like a service uniform, the polo shirt tied on one side to show off her belly piercing, her long, dark hair tugged out of the ponytail it must have been bound up in during her shift. She looked every bit the overworked employee just wanting to unwind over a few drinks and flirt with a few cuties...and right now, she looked like she had something juicy to share with Aidon Elrik and his Death Dealer.

"*Hola, su majestad,*" she purred, kicking out a chair and sliding into it with a wink.

Aidon leaned back, his eyes keen but his smile just as flirtatious. "*Hola, mujer hermosa,*" he murmured in response. He must have felt Prax stiffen beside him, with the way his smile broadened just a fraction more and his foot nudged hers under the table and stayed there. "What have you got for me? I know those beautiful eyes see everything."

Prax puckered her lips and focused her gaze on her deck of cards, deciding now was as good a time as any to practice a new shuffling trick. Anything to not have to watch him make goo-goo eyes with this woman who looked ready to devour him as slowly as humanly possible. Married or not, he was eating it up and feeding her more.

"*Si,* and boy did I see some shit today." The woman smirked and drummed her long, artistically manicured nails against the tabletop. "You know those missing girls, the ones you were just asking about?"

"Yeah?"

She leaned closer. "Guess who decided today, of all days, was perfect to hit the tables? I swear to you on *mi madre y hermana*, I know it was her because I made up some excuse to card the bitch just to make sure I wasn't suddenly seeing things." She quickly glanced at Prax. "No offense."

Aidon leaned closer as well, propping his other arm on the table. "You're not serious."

"If I'm lying, I'm dying! Plain as day, with fifty grand! Can you believe it?" She scoffed and waved a hand next to her face like the thought offended her. "Her two little *hijas* are missing and that...that *perra* has the balls to show up at the casino like she doesn't even have children. Took every ounce in my body not to smack her from here to Xibalba, I tell you what."

This made Prax whip her gaze up and she frowned. "Lacey Evans was at the casino? Today?"

The woman nodded, her eyes wide in disbelief. "Ay, and flush with cash! I saw this same woman at the tables not two weeks ago begging for a twenty just to buy herself a drink, and suddenly she's back and making it rain? Nuh-uh." She shook her head and leaned way back in her chair as if it would distance herself from the memory. "I got someone else to cover me so I could take a break. No way am I touching that money. It's cursed, I don't need that on my fingers."

Aidon nodded and considered her words, the wheels in his mind turning as his finger traced the rim of his beer mug. He shifted in his seat, closer to Prax, and tilted his face towards hers. "What do you think?"

Things I have no business thinking.... Prax straightened her deck between her fingers and gave a little nod of her own. "I heard someone earlier today tell the FBI to follow the money. They did mention Lacey, said she was trouble."

"Hm." He watched her fingers for a moment, then cocked his head towards the bartender. "Ay, Bennie! Get this beautiful lady whatever she wants for the night, on my tab." He winked at the woman and gestured for her to go enjoy her open bar. It didn't take much convincing for her to giggle and scamper over to Bennie. "She definitely delivered," he mumbled.

"I didn't know you spoke Spanish." Prax didn't mean for it to sound as...*territorial*...as it did, but she couldn't chip through the frosty feeling that kept her tense.

"I speak a lot of languages." Aidon quirked an impish little smile and nudged her with his thigh, leaning just a fraction of an inch closer. "Are you...jealous?"

"What?" Prax whipped her head around to look at him, and froze when she realized just how close he was to her. Good lord, she could smell his cologne, that heady spice blended with dark leather and even darker thoughts. The man wasn't even wearing leather tonight; it was far too warm and humid for that. "Warm" didn't begin to describe the strange and not unwelcome feeling seeping through her skin, into her blood, heating up all sorts of places just by sitting next to him. Pressed to him. His eyes on no one but her, lidded with unspoken promises darker than his denim. "Jealous of what? You're married."

And then, of course, her mouth had to go and ruin it.

Whatever glowed in his eyes for that brief moment quickly shuttered behind the all too familiar wall he'd carefully constructed ages ago. He cleared his throat and turned back to his beer, lowered his arm from the booth back, straightened his posture. "Ah. That." He took a deep pull from his beer and smacked his lips, looking everywhere but at her. "I suppose Donn told you all about it."

Prax shrugged a shoulder as nonchalantly as possible. "That, but your ring does most of the talking."

He bit down hard on the inside of his lip and hissed something she couldn't quite hear over the din of the music, and she watched his left hand absentmindedly toy with the golden band. Then he just scoffed and shook his head. "Look, it's way more complicated than you may think."

"I gathered." That feeling again, that icy freeze, crept into her voice. "Good thing you're over her, huh?"

Aidon whipped his gaze to hers, and she almost gasped at

the fierceness in his eyes. "I'll never be 'over' her," he growled. He seemed to register her sudden surprise because he hissed another curse and buried his face in the mug as if he might have the opportunity to drown in it.

This was not at all awkward. Not at all. Prax tapped each side of the deck on the tabletop until every edge was so perfectly flush the whole thing looked like a solid block of black and gold. She had a nagging suspicion she was going to have a much easier time finding the missing girls than figuring out the complicated mystery that was Aidon Elrik.

On the sixth day since the girls' disappearance, the Evans family announced a candlelight vigil to be held at their church later that evening. In some ways, no news was good news, and the community wanted to gather together in a house of God to pray for the sisters' safe return.

It was always a thing of wonder how tragedy and pain could bring together even the most skeptical disbelievers in a time of prayer—as if something deeply embedded in the coldest heart still beat with the hope that someone high in the heavens would hear them. This dark time was no exception, the fear which gripped the hearts of parents who held their children just a little bit closer, a little bit tighter, compounded with the loss of neighbors and friends only a few weeks before.

Suffice to say, there was much to pray about.

Courtney insisted on donating a few simple arrangements to the vigil, wanting to "brighten up the place" with reminders that "where flowers bloom, so does hope". Demi didn't think twice about recruiting her graduate students to comb through the campus' greenhouse for particularly lovely blossoms, including a few of her prized orchids from home to give to the family in honor of their sweet angels. Mya helped box the orchids and scribbled notes of encouragement in the cards she attached with ribbon, and insisted on staying home in case anyone called or came by asking questions. By now the

FBI and local police were canvassing the area, and it would be only a matter of time before someone in a blue uniform or black suit showed up at their doorstep wishing to speak with Professor Sadeh.

Prax wasn't sure what she wanted to do. What she *could* do. Despite all the information gathered from the inebriated whispers at the bar and the rumors circulating over coffee and news feeds, it seemed like the authorities were turning a blind eye—or rather, ear—to anyone who suggested the girls had been sold.

"Nothing like that ever happens here," she heard one of the officers mutter to his partner as they grabbed their coffees at Jefferson Java. "Are you kidding me? Bringing in those psychics, come on."

That made her quickly shut her mouth, even as she'd slowly approached the pair to broach the subject. The last thing she wanted was for people to think she was crazy, or worse...*wrong*. It was easy enough to be the social underbelly's "death dealer"; everyone who entertained the notion treated it just like that - entertainment, the kind that mimicked watching a horror film or reading a thriller novel. People loved the adrenaline rush of knowing their time could be up at any moment, it inspired them to either make better choices or utilize what they had left.

But no one ever actually wanted the truth.

She hissed and sucked on her finger when one of the thorns pricked her skin. *That's what I get for pondering the depths of the bar scene.* Prax pressed the corner of her apron to the small cut and hissed again, frustrated with herself for being so careless. Fortunately, Courtney kept the First Aid kit stashed close to the work table, and Prax easily tugged it out and opened it with her pain-free hand to fish for a Band-aid.

Her fingers paused.

Her chest felt tight, too tight. It was like someone took a vacuum and sucked all the oxygen from her lungs, and now her organs scrambled to retrieve precious air. Her heart hammered in her chest, and it was all she could do to grip the edge of the table and brace herself from collapsing.

"NO! I wanna go home!" Rachel shrieked and wrenched her arm free from Sarah's grasp. Tears streaked her face, smearing the dust of their long trek in muddy tracks down to her chin. Her lips trembled as she sobbed and stomped her foot. "I want! To! Go! Home!"

Sarah hugged her sister close and choked back her own sob. "So do I, but we gotta stay here. We gotta listen to him, to stay safe." She tried to stroke Rachel's mouse-brown hair, but the little girl shoved herself back with a frustrated cry.

Prax felt wetness drip from her chin, and she lifted a shaking hand to touch her damp skin. Her tears mirrored Rachel's, and from the way the girl's chest rose and fell, she wondered if their racing heartbeats matched as well.

The man quickly and quietly moved into the room, a pair of rucksacks in his hands. He nodded to the girls at first, his eyes distracted as he kept glancing out the dirty windows of the old, seemingly abandoned, farmhouse. "Here," he handed one to each girl. "We'll stay the night here and leave before dawn. But you need to keep your voices down, okay?"

"NO!" With another stomp and another shriek, Rachel threw her bag to the floor. "Take me home! I want to go home!"

He clamped his hand over her mouth and yanked her back against

his chest, frantically looking out the windows and at the flimsily bolted door. "Keep your voice down!"

"Greg—"

Sarah was cut off by his sudden yelp of pain. Rachel's teeth sliced into his fingers hard enough to draw blood, and she used that moment of surprise and his reflexive jump to launch herself out of his grasp and run towards another door in the far wall. "Sarah, come on! Quick!"

The older sister stood frozen in place, just for the barest of moments, her face twisted with uncertainty as she glanced between their keeper and her little sister, who frantically waved for her to follow. Sarah grimaced and took one step towards the man, "Greg", she'd called him, then stopped. "Sorry," she mumbled, and she darted off after her sister.

The stairs to the basement creaked and groaned under their footfalls, splinters on the old railing threatening to pierce their hands as they all but slid down into the musky cellar. Rotting crates and broken glass littered the floor, but nothing could stop Rachel from wriggling her way to the one window where the afternoon sun shone through. It was just wide enough for her to crawl through, but she was too short to reach it. "Sarah, help me up!"

"Here, let me go first." Sarah grabbed an old broom propped against the crumbling brick foundation and used the handle to knock away bits of broken glass from the windowsill. The pane itself opened easily, if loudly, and she used a crate to give her foot added leverage to climb out.

Prax's hand instinctively reached for her cards. "No," she felt her lips mutter, her eyes glazed over. Her fingers brushed along the edge of the deck, but she didn't need to pull a card out to know. "No. No, no no...."

She willed so hard, prayed so deeply, for the girls to somehow hear her. "Don't go through there. Go back! Go back!"

Sarah hesitated. She was halfway through the window, halfway to freedom, but something tugged at her to go back. "Rachel, I don't think we should—"

"He's coming!" Rachel pushed at her sister's feet, her whispered scream enough to make the elder finish the writhing crawl out onto the dry grass. She scrambled onto the crate and shrieked when it collapsed beneath her, the wood too old and brittle to withstand both their efforts. Thankfully, Sarah was quick to grab her arms and pull, and she kicked at the wall to try and push herself up. The sounds of heavier footsteps coming down the stairs made her scurry faster, and Sarah struggled to pull her up through the window.

She was almost through when Greg grabbed her ankles and pulled. "Get back in here!" He hissed, more panic than anger in his voice. "It's not safe!"

Rachel screamed, which only made him pull harder. She clung to Sarah's arms, fear pouring from her eyes as she begged him to let her go, begged her sister to pull her free.

Sarah's fingers slipped. The air was too humid, her own fear added to the slick sweat coating her palms. She scrambled to keep ahold of Rachel's small hands but that tiny fraction of give made it easier for Greg to pull back, and she watched as her little sister slid back through the basement window.

Greg's foot landed wrong on the broken crate, and he stumbled back, losing his grip on Rachel.

She sobbed. She fell.

And then she was so very, very still.

"No." Prax's lungs heaved, her stomach twisted. "No...."

"No, no, no!" Greg kicked the splintered crate aside and dropped to his knees beside Rachel, reaching and hesitating to touch her. "Rachel?

No...no, no, no, no....." He muttered over and over as he nudged her gently, then rolled her onto her side.

A shard of glass buried deep into her stomach, angled up into her lungs.

Sarah screamed.

Prax slumped to the floor.

It was just her imagination. It had to be. None of her other visions were so drawn out as these were, so it stood to reason that maybe her mind filled in blanks that weren't actually there.

But the sick feeling in her stomach, almost like a broken windowpane had speared through her as well, was unavoidable. Too tangible. Too real.

Every blink of her eyelids brought that final moment back into her sight, and it was all she could do to hold back her own scream. She thumped her head back against the table's leg, hoping maybe it would knock some sanity back into her brain. Sarah's screams still echoed in her ears, mingled with the man's groans. Shadows of him cradling Rachel in his arms flickered in and out of her vision.

Her phone buzzed in her pocket, and she checked the message—then the time. *Shit.* She was due at the church in less than half an hour, and there were still two more votives to arrange. With a heavy sigh, Prax dragged herself back up and gave herself a little slap. *Pull it together, woman.* Once she delivered the flowers to the service, she'd be able to sneak away and go home. Hide under the covers. Read a book until she passed out.

It didn't take long to finish the votives and soon she was pulling into the parking lot of the small church the Evans family attended, the chapel near Aidon's house which also skirted the edge of Nanabozho. Cars filled the parking lot and people quietly milled into the open doors, where Prax could see candles already lit. The setting sun cast an otherworldly glow through the stained glass windows, adding to the light which filled the chapel as people held hands and prayed.

Prax silently wove her way through the crowd, grateful that this particular delivery only consisted of smaller arrangements. She set each votive on the altar, on the sides of prayer benches set up front, and reached for the book of matches in her pocket.

She wasn't quite sure what made her pause. No vision filled her eyesight, no sounds echoed unnaturally in her ears or mind. But as she struck a match and leaned to light the first candle on the altar, she hesitated.

A feeling, something buried deep within, welled to the surface of her being. While her lungs gasped for air earlier, now they felt like they contained too much oxygen, her heart too full, her limbs too heavy. Her fingers trembled and nearly dropped the lit match, but she caught herself and set flame to wick.

A prayer moved between her lips. She didn't know the words, couldn't place mind to meaning, but that *something* uttered secrets to Heaven as she lit the candle on the altar. Tears kissed her lashes as she gazed into the flame.

There it was. The *something* became a presence, a warmth around her shoulders, a gentle nudge to her back. It turned her feet around, made her shift her focus to the small group huddled in the center of the room.

Davidson stood amongst the group, one comforting hand on the shoulder of a weeping, praying Donna Wilkins, his other arm cradling a Bible to his chest. Even in the midst of prayer he looked up, his gaze met Prax's, and he nodded. He didn't need to say the words, the expression in his eyes enough to confirm what she felt she needed to do.

Could her feet grow any heavier? Prax felt as if each shuffled step towards the Evans family sank into the floorboards more and more, compelled by that unseen presence to keep going. Nothing could turn her back now, not even her own doubt gnawing at her mind and tugging at her skin. And when Donna looked up, her eyes swollen with tears as they peered at the approaching woman, whatever chance existed to turn away vanished.

Prax opened her mouth. Closed it. What was it she meant to say?

"Thank you for coming." One of the men with Donna offered no smile, but his voice was kind. Prax recognized him from television, from the news. The meteorologist, if she remembered correctly, but it was clear in this moment that he was not here in an official capacity. His own hand braced on the back of Donna's chair, his stance protective. He regarded Prax with soft curiosity but didn't press her for anything. At least one of his questions must have been answered when he noticed the bits of pollen and leaves stuck to her shirt. "We really appreciate your donation. Please give our regards to Mrs. Johnson."

Again, Prax opened her mouth to say, "I will," but the words just wouldn't come out.

Donna dabbed her nose with a tissue proffered by Davidson and sniffled. "Wait...I remember you."

Prax shifted her stare from the man back to Donna. Their eyes met. And in that instant, Prax's mouth finally opened to say the words she didn't want to utter.

"It was an accident."

She felt the room still. Voices fell into a hush as heads turned towards her. Not the first time for this to happen, but the circumstances were different. So very, very different.

Donna frowned. Hiccuped. "Excuse me?"

It overflowed from within, that overwhelming feeling that had only been growing with every step from the altar to here, here where she stood and faced a family she didn't know—and yet knew more about their daughters than anyone could fathom. She choked on her sobs as the words spilled out. "It was an accident. I'm so sorry. I'm so, so sorry...."

The floor hit her knees but she barely noticed, doubled over as she was, unintentionally clasping at the elderly woman's visibly trembling hands. One of the other members of the Evans family started to protest, to ask what the hell this girl was doing, but Davidson stopped him. Donna's eyes glazed over as the shock set in, until a wail rattled from her chest and echoed through the rafters. The man beside her looked away, reddened eyes blinking furiously, his jaw clenched as he fought to control his breath.

The other relative shook his head quickly and huffed. "How do you know this? Who the hell are you?"

Davidson placed a protective hand on Prax's arm. "Prax is one of my own. And she does not say such things lightly."

The man swallowed hard, still shaking his head. He didn't want to know. He didn't want to ask, but his mouth moved for him. "But how does she *know*?"

"You prayed for a miracle." Davidson's voice was gentle but firm, and he moved to warmly grasp the man's arms. "You prayed for a sign, for answers. God heard you, and He sent a message to you."

The man went limp, held by the pastor as the grief washed over him. "Not like this," he sputtered, his face a sudden, reddened mess of tears and spittle. "Not like this."

Davidson pulled him into his strong embrace, the only thing that kept the man from collapsing to the floor as he surrendered to the weight of the pastor's words. Others in the chapel covered their mouths to hush their gasps and whispers, a few bursting into sobs as they realized the kind of news that must have just been given to the Evans family.

Prax realized she hadn't shared the other half of information she knew—and the look Davidson gave her when she glanced up to tell them made her pause. Something deep in her mind agreed with him. Something in her instincts silenced the words she so desperately wanted to say, the reassurances she wanted to give. Was it wrong to withhold this information from the family?

Her gaze shifted to the man who stood as a quiet sentinel of support for Donna, and something in his eyes made her bite her tongue even harder. He stared back, conveying something unspoken to her that translated into the silence which now held her mouth shut but quickened her heart.

If she didn't know any better, he almost looked more afraid than Greg.

Despite her earlier urge to just go home and bury herself under the thickest blankets she could find (which she still might do), Prax felt as though a walk through Nanabozho before the final rays of light faded would do her some good and help clear her mind. After a few whispered words of prayer and sympathy to Donna Wilkins and her family—which, she confirmed, included Channel 9's award-winning meteorologist Lonnie Achachak. Donna briefly introduced him as her son-in-law but quickly corrected herself, throwing him a deeply apologetic glance to which he swiftly responded with a tight smile and reassuring pat on her hand. The whispers close by informed Prax of the rest: a broken engagement, an even more heartbroken man, an absentee mother.

That last bit was all too painfully accurate: Lacey Wilkins-Evans never showed up to her own daughters' vigil.

It wasn't too far down the gravel path before the familiar sound of heavy panting, followed by a series of wet licks to her face, accompanied Prax on her walk. Spot sensed her mind was troubled despite her soft giggle and loving neck rub, and he pressed close to her side as if to say, *lean on me*. So she did, one arm draped around his burly neck, fingers absentmindedly digging into his soft fur.

"Do you ever see things?" Prax mumbled, then sighed. "Donn says you're a grim; I suppose if he's right, you've probably seen your fair share of scary secrets."

Spot cocked his head and gave her the tiniest of whines. His paws padded so quietly on the gravel, his fur so dark it blended into the encroaching night…it was no wonder he made such a good guard dog for the grounds. Maybe Aidon could be persuaded to let her kidnap the sweet floof every now and then, help her chase away the nightmares that were bound to come from this whole ordeal. As if he could read her mind, Spot panted happily and licked her face again, readily agreeing to be kidnapped for the sake of protecting his beloved friend.

A sharp whistle sang across the grounds, and both Spot and Prax whipped their heads towards the source. Aidon's steady gait faltered when he saw her, and he slowly approached with one eye on the woman, one brow arched at the dog. "It's kind of late for your walk, don't you think?"

"I was just at the vigil." Prax nodded back towards the chapel, biting down the urge to remind him she didn't need to explain herself. Well, it was getting pretty dark out in the land of the dead. "Spot's been keeping me company."

"I can see that." Aidon scratched the giant pupper's ears and cast a quick glance over Prax's face. "What's wrong?"

Damn his keen senses. She shook her head and tried to hide behind an unassuming smile, but she felt very aware that it did not reach her eyes. "Nothing. Nothing important, anyway. Just tired."

"Mhm." He gave her another once-over as if checking for injuries she might be trying to hide. "Well, Donn's over at my place with a six-pack and he's determined to beat me at Texas Hold 'Em." He hesitated. "You're welcome to join us, if you want."

Was that a legitimate invitation? Or a half-hearted social pleasantry? "Oh, thanks, but I don't want to impose."

Aidon scrunched his nose and shook his head. "Nah, don't

worry about it. I've got more beer in the fridge and Donn's about to wipe my accounts clean if someone doesn't step in and beat his ass. You'd be doing me a favor."

Prax was grateful for the settling night that hid the blush she felt creep over her cheeks—heaven forbid he'd see her reaction and suddenly have second thoughts. "If you're sure."

He smirked and patted Spot on the side of his neck. "Hey, if you'd rather walk out here all alone in the dark surrounded by dead people, be my guest." With a shrug of his broad shoulder, he turned and started towards his house at the other end of the cemetery. Spot let out another little whine, reluctant to leave Prax behind, but he followed his master down the gravel path.

Only a few seconds alone in the dark surrounded by shadowed gravestones was all it took for Prax to scurry after the pair. "You said Texas Hold 'Em? I might need a refresher."

It might have been a trick of her mind—Lord knows *that* was a constant thing happening these days—but for a moment Prax swore she saw Aidon's stony face break into a grin.

H ave you been talking to Doris Finkley?" Donn grumbled as he frowned at his cards.

Prax scoffed. "As if! You're just mad because I'm lucky."

"Uh-huh." He narrowed his eyes at her, chewing the inside of his cheek. "That's a very Doris Finkley thing to say."

Aidon smirked and tossed his cards facedown on the table. "Well, I fold. Between Lady Luck over here and Señor Sore Loser, I don't stand a chance at regaining my savings account anytime soon." He slid his chair back and stood. "Anyone else need another cold one?"

Prax blushed but nodded. The man drank the good stuff, and she was suspicious that ordering the same brew at the bar would cost her half a paycheck. "Thanks."

Donn scoffed and gaped at his friend, who smirked and sauntered off towards the kitchen. "I am *not* a sore loser! I'm just surrounded by cheaters!"

"Hey!" Prax feigned her insulted pride, unable to hold back her laughter. "I didn't cheat! Not once! You're just mad because I've never played this before and I can't help it if you keep dealing me the best hands."

"Right." Donn's narrowed gaze landed on a bookshelf by the fireplace and his eyes lit up. "Oh! We can play another game! How about chess?"

"*NO*." Aidon's voice bellowed from the kitchen, and Prax could hear the humor laced in that one word. He sauntered back over to the dining table, balancing three glass bottles of beer in one hand with a bottle opener in the other, which he pointed at Donn. "Do *not* start that again. You've lost your chess privileges for the next...millennia. No chess. No."

He might as well have been scolding Spot, whose ears perked at that familiar tone. Donn pouted and nursed his bruised excitement with the proffered bottle. "Ugh. *Fine*. Have it your way."

As Aidon settled back into his chair, he realized Prax was staring at him with questions written all over her face. He sighed. "Someone," he glanced pointedly at Donn, "takes the game a little too seriously and starts dancing every time he wins. It's embarrassing."

"For you."

Aidon rolled his eyes and tried to hide his own laugh behind a swig of beer, but was unsuccessful. His face split into a bright grin that made the corners of his eyes crinkle with genuine mirth, and Prax felt her heart skip a beat as she watched the usually guarded man let down his walls enough for the light to shine through. He was already a very handsome man, but when he allowed himself to be happy, he was stunning.

And married. Prax gave herself a little shake, a little mental slap across the face, and did her best to nonchalantly look away. But then she caught a glimpse of one of the tattoos partially hidden by the curve of his bicep, a symbol she'd seen before but kept forgetting to ask about. "So, I've been curious about something," she began.

"Uh-oh." Donn winked at her, and now it was her turn to roll her eyes at him. "The pretty lass wants to know your secrets."

Prax nearly choked on her sip and quickly waved her hand in denial. "Oh my gosh, no! I was just curious about the tattoo on your arm. You're a veteran?"

Aidon and Donn exchanged yet another Knowing Look, shadowed by some unspoken conversation that quickly passed between them, and suddenly Donn was very, very interested in the cards in his hand. Aidon squinted at the visible retreat of his friend's assistance, but nodded and took another swig. "Something like that."

"Where did you serve?"

The questions may have grated at him, but his slanted gaze softened when he saw her genuine curiosity. He sighed and shrugged. "It was a long time ago. No big deal."

Prax frowned and ignored Donn's sudden cough. "It couldn't be *that* long ago—"

"I try not to think about it."

She deflated, suddenly realizing how pushy she was being over something that's none of her business. Something that clearly made him uncomfortable. "Oh. Sorry."

Now it was Aidon's turn to chew the inside of his cheek, and he seemed to be weighing something in his mind as he stared at the bottle on his clenched fist. Again, that hardened expression he was so used to wearing softened, a flicker of regret flashed in his eyes when he looked over at her. "I... didn't really have the best relationship with my father. I did what I could to get out."

Donn cocked a brow, still keeping his gaze transfixed on those cards. "Calling that hellscape 'not the best relationship'

195

is like calling Spot 'somewhat large'."

Prax didn't know what to say. She felt like saying nothing was the best course of action to take, and inwardly kicked herself for being so nosy about the life of a man who, until recently, basically hated her. Still.... "I'm sorry."

"Nah, don't be." Aidon did that adorable nose scrunching thing again and brushed it off with a flicker of a smile. The motion sent another little skip of a heartbeat through her, and she inwardly sighed in defeat. If Mya found out about this, she'd salivate over all the little details Prax was trying very, very hard not to read into.

"Speaking of Doris Finkley." Donn made a face when his friends groaned and shushed them both with a stubborn but playful glare. "I overheard you talking with that card shark about her shuffling tricks. Got any new ones yourself?"

It took a moment for Prax to realize which cards he meant, but when it clicked, she pulled the gilded deck from her back pocket. The weight of them on her person always gave her an extra sense of reassurance, a reminder that she was in control of her visions now.

Well, most of them.

She fanned them out in a row on the table, then flicked one end over and grinned as the light danced on the gold fili-gree just as it had in the bar. Only this time, the lighting inside Aidon's house was a warm golden glow all on its own, which added an extra spark of magic to the movements. Her fingers deftly swept the upturned row back into a stacked deck, then shot them from one hand to the other with an expert flourish that she, admittedly, learned from Youtube after inadvertently playing "52 Pick Up" with Mya one too many times.

"Whoo!" Donn whooped and whistled as he watched her

showcase her newly acquired card tricks. "Give Doris a run for her money!"

Prax giggled and did the card spring flourish again, mesmerized by the glittering gold flashing in the soft light as each card flew across the space between her hands. After another shuffle, she fanned them out and cocked a playful brow at her friend. "Wanna see your fate?"

Donn grinned, a mischievous glint in his eye. He leaned back in his chair, balancing it on the back two legs. "You can flip as many cards as you want, *colleen*, but they'll all be the same boring blank nothing." He winked. "It's not my time."

"You're so sure about that?"

"It's never my time." He cocked his head at their host. "But I'd be super curious to know about this guy's fate."

Aidon narrowed his eyes again, but his indulgent smirk gave Prax the go-ahead. She flipped one card, then another, brow stitched together as she focused her Sight with all the concentration she could muster. Nothing. "Well, good news here. Nothing threatening your life any time soon."

He clicked his tongue against his teeth. "Like Donn said, it's never my time."

She started to say something in response, but the sudden loud buzzing on the table startled everyone. Donn grabbed his phone and checked the screen. "I gotta go."

There was no missing the instant change in his countenance, the way his face paled and his jaw set as he pushed his chair back and reached for his keys. Aidon quickly snatched them away when he saw Donn teeter in his step. "Where do you need to go?" He asked, reaching for his own set.

"Sunrise." Donn sniffed, cleared his throat. Stood there, reluctant to move. "It's Jenny."

197

Prax swallowed hard, that knot in her stomach returning. "Is she...?"

He started to shake his head, but stopped. Faltered. The next breath within his chest sounded strained, and when he looked at his best friend, the light caught on his lashes. "Aidon, I can't."

Aidon slowly closed his eyes, braced a comforting hand on his friend's arm. "It's time. It's *been* time." His fist closed around his keys. "Let's go."

The hall felt so much longer than before, than any other time they walked the flecked stone tiles. The low light of the nighttime shift only added to that seeming endlessness, and Prax felt her steps slow the closer they got to the door.

Donn hesitated, his hand reluctant to turn the handle. He cast one more glance towards Aidon, who only nodded his reassurance and stood beside Prax. Her fingers twitched over her deck of cards, but Aidon gently captured them before she fell into the reflexive temptation. "We'll be right here," he murmured.

She looked so much smaller in that bed. How long had she been this feeble, this gaunt? Donn swallowed hard and willed himself forward. Her eyes were closed, her breath thready, the rattle in her chest a sound he never wanted to hear coming from this sweet girl.

"Donn...." It took so much visible effort for Jenny to open her eyes, to say his name, and he quickly slid into the chair next to her bed and clasped her tiny hand in his. "You came."

"I'm here." He did his best to clear his throat, to swallow back the lump that kept reforming in it. "I'm always here."

She managed a weak, but genuine, smile. "I know." Her eyes closed again, ringed with deeper hues than he remembered seeing before. Were they always there? Did he simply choose not to see the true depths of her suffering? "I...I have a secret," she whispered. "I needed to tell you, before...."

He leaned in closer, blinking back the tears that kept stinging his sight. "What's your secret, Beautiful?"

Jenny rasped, then sighed. Her eyes opened again, this time with more clarity. "I remember you."

"I'm glad of that, Sweet One. We've been friends for quite a while."

"No." She tried to shake her head, but he caressed her cheek to calm her. "I remember you. From the crash."

Donn stilled.

She smiled. "I remember you. I was so scared. I thought I was going to die. Everyone else was dead. But then you came. And you carried me out."

The tears burned as they spilled down his cheeks. He didn't have the right words, even though there were so many things he wanted to tell her. How she was the bravest person he'd ever met, and he'd met a lot of people who thought themselves brave. How she truly was beautiful, no matter what illness sought to take that away from her.

How he couldn't have children, but if he could, he liked to think his daughter would be just like her.

Jenny sighed again, a sound full of weariness and pain. "I'm so tired." Her voice crackled, tears forming on lids that just barely had any lashes left. "I'm so tired, but I'm so scared."

"What are you scared of, Love?"

Her tiny body shook with weak sobs, and before he realized what he was doing, Donn scooped her up in his arms and cradled her to his chest. He sat on her bed and held her, rocked her, wiped away her tears. "Shhh, it's all right. There's nothing to be scared of, I promise."

"I don't want it to hurt." Every word was punctuated with a hiccup that tore at his soul, one plaintive sound after another. "I don't want to be alone."

Donn wrapped her in his arms, his thumb ever so lightly stroking her brow and catching her tears as they fell. He cleared his throat again, that damned lump threatening to break his voice. "Do you want to hear a story?" When she nodded, or what he interpreted as a nod in her weakened state, he kissed the top of her head. "A long, long time ago, when God sang the world into being, death did not exist. It was never supposed to exist, not for anyone. But eventually, it came, breathed into being through broken promises and desperate lies. It created a chasm between this world and the next, between the gardens of the earth and the paradise of Heaven.

"So God spoke to His angels and asked who would walk with His people so no one would ever need to make the journey alone? Back and forth, back and forth, who among them would walk this path? Many angels stepped forward, and they agreed to hold the hands of each person when it was their time to leave this world behind and enter the gates of Heaven. But there was one angel He gave a special task—the one job no one else wanted. The Angel of Death knew how important it was to keep the balance. And he agreed to carry that burden for all eternity, until the end of time."

Jenny's body stopped shaking, her tears slowed. "Does he ever get to walk with people?"

His heart wrenched at the innocence in her voice laced with so much concern for the same being millions of people tried to avoid. He nodded, his soft laugh broken with what threatened to be a sob. "Sometimes. When he meets someone special. Someone he doesn't want to share with anyone else. He can be very selfish."

Silence.

Donn leaned her back in his arms, just enough to check her face, her breath. It was so weak he could barely see her chest move, save for the rattles that came every now and then. She looked so tired. So worn. Now his tears flowed freely, dripping onto her pale skin. "I'm so sorry," he whispered. "I'm so sorry. I've been so selfish."

Jenny opened her eyes as much as she could, and what she saw made them widen in wonder. "Donn?"

"Yes, my beautiful girl. It's me."

A soft smile played on her lips. "I think I'm ready." She curled up in his arms, used the last of her strength to nestle in the warmth of his chest. "I don't know if I can walk, though."

He kissed her brow, held her close. "It's okay. I'll carry you."

Jenny Melrose was finally free to run and never grow tired, laugh with the music of angels, play with her brother and sister and best friend again. Where the softest breeze filled with the fragrance of flowers she'd never smelled before danced through her silken hair.

The chapel filled with people who'd been blessed to meet this sweet girl, her nurses and doctors and a few patients, like Doris Finkley, who insisted on honoring her despite their own thin threads of life. No one had been able to locate any external family members from either of her parents' side; both sets of grandparents were long passed and no clear record of aunts or uncles existed in either legal or medical documents. Aidon pulled as many strings and records as he could, but to all extent, Jenny Melrose was the last of her line.

It took most of the service before Donn was able to blink back the tears long enough to see his way to the front of the chapel. The coin felt heavy in his palm, and for a moment he doubted he would be able to part with the double-headed reminder of his stolen time with the little girl who captured his heart. He wanted to say something, anything, a final parting word before they closed her casket forever - but nothing felt right except the truth.

"I'll see you again, Beautiful."

In the old days he would have laid the coin over her eyes—two coins, in fact, but he'd been able to strike a bargain with Ralph. So instead, he pressed the coin to his lips, then tucked it between her fingers with the small bouquet of calendulas Prax personally arranged especially for Jenny.

He felt his friend's hand gently rest on his shoulder. Aidon didn't press him or rush him, simply stood by his side and let him have a few more moments. "Whenever you're ready," was all the groundskeeper said.

Donn coughed back the rest of his tears and nodded. "I think I'm ready."

If only Jenny Melrose, the little girl who once dreamed of being a princess, of riding on the shoulders of dragons and giants, could know how lovingly she was carried on the shoulders of the men who now guarded her eternal sleep. Donn was the one who insisted she was too good to be carried so low to the ground, and Aidon didn't hesitate to hoist the casket onto his shoulder, with Davidson and Ralph following suit behind them.

The Sadeh women ensured the earthly path between God's house and Jenny's final resting place was lined with the brightest and sweetest-smelling flowers, the biggest and most beautiful being the soft calendulas the little girl loved to draw. Both Prax and Demi agreed that the traditional wreaths were too solemn for such a sparkling life they now honored—instead of dreary carnations and monogrammed sashes, the procession was lined with rose petals and silk pastel ribbons. Were it not for the marble place markers and weathered gravestones, or the four men carrying a small white casket, one could have mistaken this for a celebration.

They carefully lowered her into the earth, each attendee taking a fistful of soil as Davidson stood over the group. "For I am convinced that neither death nor life," he read aloud from his Bible, "neither angels nor demons, neither the present nor the future, nor any powers, neither height nor depth, nor anything else in all creation, will be able to separate us from the love of God that is in Christ Jesus our Lord."

Most of the service blurred around Prax as she felt her mind wander—something that, she'd wonder later, might be a coping mechanism in the face of such bittersweet sorrow. She'd seen Jenny so often during her deliveries, yet never saw her death impending like everyone else who passed around her. Was this because Aidon stopped her from looking? Her fingers still felt the warm and gentle grasp of his, the way he'd silently encouraged her to let this one be.

The way he'd pulled her close when she cried, when she felt, rather than saw, the passing of Jenny Melrose from this world into the next.

Soil slipped from her fingers to join the fistfuls of the others, a soft rain of fertile earth blanketing the ivory casket. She felt her mother stroke her arm and heard her whisper something about leading everyone back to their home for refreshments; Mya had texted to let them know the drinks and snacks were ready. "With at least three variations of potato salad," the teen promised.

"I'll be right there." Prax tucked a stray curl behind her ear and hoped her mother would understand. "I just need a little bit."

Demi nodded and wrapped her arms around her. "Take your time, darling. We'll save you a plate. Can't promise on the punch, though. You know how your sister gets." She kissed Prax's brow and lightly rubbed her back, then turned to make her way towards the parking lot and guide the funeral guests to the reception.

It didn't feel right to stay by the open grave, not when Donn slumped down beneath the willow tree and tugged his tie loose, his gaze transfixed on a distant horizon as his fist clenched tightly around the soil he couldn't yet surrender. Prax kicked off her heels and stepped into the soft grass still cool with the morning dew, no destination or path in mind other than a casual tour of the names carved in marble and stone all around her.

As if on cue, Spot trotted over and nosed himself under her hand until she rubbed his ears and draped her arm around his neck. Aidon was not far behind, and the two keepers of Nanobozho flanked Prax like silent, dark guardians to her contemplative self. She glanced behind them, back towards Donn beneath the willow tree, and chewed her lip. "How long was...?"

"Six months." Aidon followed her gaze with a sigh. "The accident where he met her was three years ago, but her cancer took a turn for the worst about a year ago. She should have died six months ago."

"What kept her alive?"

Aidon's smile didn't quite reach his eyes, and he nudged them onward to give their friend some distance. "For all his teasing about being cheated, he's probably the biggest cheater I know." He shoved his hands in his pockets and kicked at a stray gravel stone. "They never caught the guy who killed her family. I think that's been bothering him more than he lets on."

Prax squinted in the light of the late morning sun. "I thought it was a car accident."

"Accident or not, the driver fled the scene. Donn watched the whole thing happen, the way the semi just plowed through the red light without even trying to hit the brakes or honk. Dragged the whole family for half a mile before he finally stopped. By the time people got there, the driver was gone." His nose curled in a small snarl. "Things stop being accidents when cowards run."

She nodded her agreement and hugged Spot just a little bit closer. "Now Jenny's gone."

S cattered showers are expected to arrive early this afternoon, with a thirty percent chance of thunderstorms following late into the evening." Lonnie Achachuk's hand swept over the green screen in practiced movements, computer-generated clouds following his fingers as the screen zoomed in closer to Bogarten's layout. "Conditions may become right for another tornado advisory, but so far these past few days have been too dry."

The camera switched to the news anchors as one of them posed a question most viewers were most likely thinking. "Yes, it has made the search for Sarah and Rachel Evans easier, despite the lack of any new evidence or leads. Do you think the rains will wash away any chance authorities may have in finding them?"

Lonnie nodded, his somber expression giving away nothing more than the general concern shared with the community. "That is a very serious risk with any sort of precipitation. We can only hope and pray authorities catch a break before the showers set in."

"Isn't he their stepdad?" Mya blurted through a mouthful of muesli and oat milk. "He's so calm, like none of this is bothering him at all."

Demi rolled her eyes and nudged her youngest to show some manners. "He's also on television being watched by a few thousand people. I'm sure the man can't afford to lose his composure any time the mood strikes." She poured herself a travel mug of coffee and refilled Prax's mug. Another mug nudged across the table, and she lifted a skeptical brow, but Mya's sweet smile and *please, Mommy* eyes made her give in. "My office hours are extended today and my charter flight leaves tonight for the conference. Will you girls be okay?"

"We'll be fine, Mom," Prax reassured her between her own mouthfuls of cereal. "I'm a big girl, I can make sure Mya doesn't burn the house down."

Mya stuck her tongue out and giggled. "Ugh, fine. I'll reschedule the bonfire party."

Prax's eyes flicked over to the small flatscreen on the kitchen countertop as images from the investigation appeared on the screen. Yellow tape wrapped around the outer edges of Fulton Park, and the subtitles suggested that all possible leads were now exhausted, prompting officials to shift away from the park and towards the family's residence. "I heard they never actually got married. Lonnie, I mean. Lacey Evans left him or something." Her brows furrowed as another piece of gossip came to mind. "And she's been seen with a *lot* of money right after they disappeared."

"'A gossip betrays a confidence; so avoid anyone who talks too much'," quoted Demi as she quickly packed her briefcase. Even without directly looking at her daughters, the raised brow and firm tone felt like the scolding it was.

"Yeah, but in this town?" Mya scoffed. "Gossip is currency and secrets come at a very high price."

Demi shot her a Look, but the young teen possessed a pair of cojones Prax envied and she barely flinched, just shrugged and busied herself with the now-soggy muesli. As for Prax, she felt her conscience play tug-of-war between the two concepts: gossip really was a dangerous flame to play with, but the people of Bogarten were pyromaniacs in that regard—especially those who dwelled in the underworld of society where Aidon ruled through influence and his own version of investigation.

A sudden image came to mind of his dark curls and sensual mouth, especially the way his lips curved and his eyes lit with something she both recognized and couldn't name every time he looked at her. Prax felt her cheeks heat and she quickly grabbed her coffee mug, hoping no one noticed. Her mother was too busy rustling through an overnight bag, muttering about deodorant and toothpaste, but her sister was now grinning at her like she knew *exactly* what had appeared unbidden in her mind. Mya wiggled her brows and blew a kiss, making the elder Sadeh sister narrow her eyes.

It was too bad Mya wasn't old enough to join them at Hawkeye's. Her sharp perception would be an incredible resource as they weeded through drunken testimonies.

The teasing did not stop once Prax left the house for work. Courtney immediately noticed the subtle enhancements in her outfit: a lace-edged tunic and dark denim which hugged her lower half in a rather flattering way. Perhaps the biggest tell was the gold jewelry that she never wore, from delicate hoops dangling from her ears to equally delicate bangles, midi rings, and a floral pendant that rested only slightly below her collar bone. She'd pinned her hair up in a somewhat messy bun, curly tendrils framing her face, held together with a gold pin Demi said was from one of her trips to Ethiopia.

The florist's eyes practically bulged from her skull. "What... who...hold up!" She laughed in shock and disbelief. "I mean you're always a stunner, but *what* is going *on*, girl? You look so fancy!"

Prax blushed deeply and immediately regretted everything, her hands reaching for her hair. "Is it too much? I got asked to dinner after work and won't have enough time to change—"

"Don't you dare touch anything." Courtney all but smacked her hand away from the hairpin and grinned. "You look breathtaking and I hate you so much for how effortless you make it. We are going to have to go shopping sometime so you can teach me your secrets." She went back to the cooler and the clipboard with the opening checklist, biting her cheek as she considered how nosy she wanted to be. "So...who's the guy?"

Prax quickly slipped her work apron on and rolled up her tunic sleeves, her phone in her pocket a solid reminder of the text she'd received that morning during breakfast.

> *Aidon: Hawkeye's tonight?*
> *Prax: Sure! What time?*
> *Aidon: 5:30?*
> *Prax: That's really early for drunk confessions :P*
> *Aidon: Early enough for dinner, if you want*

After scrambling for the phone under the bed (having dropped and subsequently kicked it there), Prax confirmed the date before her brain could catch up with her fingers. And then chanted to herself *not a date...not a date...not a date...* as she dressed and readied herself for work.

And the not-date.

"So...?" Courtney gave up on hiding her curiosity and opted for downright nosiness. "Oh come on, I gotta know. As your boss, I have a vested concern in your well-being, especially when guys are involved."

Prax coughed up a laugh and busied herself with sorting the day's projects at the register. "Fine. Just promise you won't breathe a word to my mother."

"Oh my gawd, now I *have* to know. Scout's honor, I won't say a word."

"Aidon Elrik."

Prax spun around at the loud crash of a dropped vase. Courtney barely registered the ice-cold water seeping over her shoes, tulips scattered with ceramic shards. "You're shittin' me."

"Courtney!" Prax playfully gasped and quickly glanced towards the door, grateful no one was around to hear such language coming from the shop's owner. She knelt to pick up the biggest pieces and salvage the tulips while Courtney gave herself a moment to register what she'd just heard.

"I'm sorry, I thought I heard you say 'Aidon Elrik'."

"You did, because I did." Prax peered up at her boss. "Wait, you know him?"

"Know him? Oh honey, if I wasn't married...." Courtney slapped a hand over her own mouth and glanced behind her, then laughed. "Yeah, I know him. Well, I know of him and I've seen him around. He's kinda...hard to miss."

Prax knew exactly what she meant.

"Anyways, Garrett's worked with him a few times when things go down, you know, like a drug bust or skipped bail. Aidon Elrik has a reputation with the police force and they consult with him sometimes." She scoffed. "You just won't see him at any barbeques or balls, not his scene."

"Wait." Prax carefully filled a new vase with the tulips and added water while the wheels in her head started spinning on mega-speed. "Aidon's been working with the police?"

Courtney giggled. "Don't let him hear you say it like that. It's more like, when they're facing something pretty dark and scary in his neck of the woods, he's the one they go to for help. He's friends with the sheriff or something, I don't know the details." She helped sweep and mop up her mess and cocked a playful grin at her assistant. "But speaking of details...."

"It's not a date. He's married, kinda. We're just grabbing dinner over at Hawkeye's. He knows I work close by, and I haven't had a chance to try their dinner menu yet." She felt like she was ticking off a laundry list of reasons why this was absolutely not a date. No matter how giddy or excited she felt about it.

"Um, how is someone 'kind of' married?"

Prax smiled wryly to herself. "When their wife leaves them and they still wear their ring and say things like 'I'll never be over her'," she mimicked his deep voice, very aware of the tinge of bitterness that touched her impression of the moment he snapped at her.

"Ah. That sucks. For both of you."

"Yup." *Bitch*, Prax really wanted to mumble towards the mystery woman who broke her friend's heart. Because mixed signals or not, with or without his constant tug of war, it felt safe to at least regard him as a friend now. Lord knows he's been by her side through some pretty turbulent times since they first met.

And at least he no longer glared at her as if she'd personally insulted his ancestors.

That feeling of distinct self-conscious doubt churned in her gut the closer her steps took her to the entrance of Hawkeye's. Was she too dressed up for this? Would it look like she expected anything more than casual conversation? She caught glimpses of herself and fought the urge to rip every piece of jewelry off, to go home and change into something less...*revealing*. Not that her clothes were actually revealing, by definition. She just wasn't used to her curves being hugged in ways that made them impossible to ignore.

"You're not a princess," Courtney teased her as they closed up the shop for the day. "You're a freaking *queen*. Bring 'em to their knees."

"Who?"

"Everyone."

Her boss' words echoed in her mind and bolstered her courage, and she watched her glassy reflection straighten her posture and square her shoulders.

I'm a queen.

I'm a queen.

I'm a freaking queen.

She threw open the door to Hawkeye's and was immediately, and simultaneously, frustrated and grateful the door had one of those weighted features that made her dramatic entrance no different than if she'd snuck in. No matter; she still kept her head held high and her mantra playing on repeat as she scanned the room for his familiar face.

Aidon stood by the bar, chatting with the bartender about something that had the guy—Bennie?—chuckling and nodding his agreement. Aidon casually glanced towards the door, and Prax swore she saw his jaw drop at least an inch before he snapped it shut and muttered something to the bartender. He strolled over to where she stood by the door, her unease melting from self-consciousness to lack of consciousness at the way his dark shirt hugged him like a second skin and that cologne she'd smelled the other night filled her senses like a drug.

Not a date. Not a date.

He sure cleaned up nicely for a casual dinner with a friend he had zero romantic interest in.

You're a queen. You're a queen.

You're his queen.

She almost visibly balked at that last thought and masked her internal reaction with a slight cough. "Sorry, lots of pollen at the shop today." *Compared to what? Every other non-pollen day surrounded by flowers? Idiot.*

Aidon smiled and gestured to a booth in the corner. "Shall we?"

The waitress set drinks on the table for them immediately after they sat, which answered the question of what he might have told the bartender: he ordered her favorite cocktail and a gin and tonic for himself. Prax couldn't remember when she'd ordered this around him before, but she must have because he nailed it. He also made a point to not return the waitress' flirty advances, his gaze steady on Prax's face while he ordered an appetizer for them to share. "So," he said after the waitress left, "how was work? Besides the pollen issue."

Prax hoped he didn't see the blush she most certainly felt creeping up her neck. "Busy, pretty usual this time of year. Mostly weddings, a few funerals. But you know about those."

He nodded. "You guys do fantastic work. Definitely stepped up the game since you started there. We get a lot of great feedback from the families after services."

"Thank you." She really meant it. The praise made her sit up a little straighter, his words stroking her professional ego.

"Jenny's flowers were stunning. You really went all out, and it meant a lot." His voice softened, and she could tell he didn't want to dampen the mood. "I know he's been pretty distant lately, so I'm saying it for him; thank you."

"How is he doing?" Prax hadn't seen Donn since the funeral, not even on her last delivery run to Sunrise Hospice. The staff there said he was taking a few personal days and would be back soon, but "soon" was a very subjective term.

Aidon sighed and rubbed a hand over his jaw. "Donn's always been...mercurial, you could say. I'm not too worried about him, he always bounces back full force once he's had time to get a grip on the circumstances. This one just hit a personal nerve."

"They were really close."

He nodded. "It's something he's always struggled with." Aidon flipped open the menu and skimmed the selections, and he offered her a reassuring smile. "He'll be fine, I promise."

Prax skimmed her own menu and did her best to focus on the words, even as thoughts swirled in a spiraling vortex through her mind. Aidon Elrik held this reputation of being the big, tough, don't-even-go-there kingpin of Bogarten's darkest reaches of society, but the more time she spent with him, the more she saw this continual conflict between his reputation and his personality. He genuinely cared, deeply cared, for everyone around him - friend, acquaintance, random stranger on the street. At first, Prax assumed his iron fist on the seedier enterprises was because they feared him, and maybe they did, just not in the way that someone feared a madman. If she were to take all the interactions she witnessed, it seemed more like a fear that if they crossed him, they'd lose his favor.

And losing favor in eyes as magnetic as his would be a very, very painful experience.

Dinner was delicious, and casual, and every bit as wonderful and stress-free as she could wish it to be. Aidon asked about her work, her upcoming projects, if she planned on going to the university where her mother taught. That drew a laugh from both of them, as Prax had not actually considered that option until he mentioned it. She turned the questions on him, asking about his own career as a groundskeeper, what drew him to the life, what does he love most about it?

Aidon chewed on a bite of his steak and gave her question thorough thought. "I don't know, I honestly can't remember what drew me to it. I sort of fell into it. Didn't have so many options presented to me at the time." He smiled. "I liked the quiet. Still do."

Prax blushed again and bit into her patty melt. "Sorry," she mumbled. "Quiet" was not so much of a feature at Nanabozho after she'd made it her literal stomping grounds.

He grinned. "You get a free pass."

They ate in comfortable silence for a while, exchanging bites of each other's food for the sake of trying new flavors from each plate. The waitress checked on them only often enough to refill their waters, her demure expression communicating that she got the earlier hint to cool her jets. Aidon did flash her an appreciative smile and thanked her, which added a perk in her step. Prax couldn't fault either of them; he was being a gentleman and even Prax would've simpered under his smile.

Would have? You mean "constantly does".

She gave herself a little shake and sipped her lemon water. "So, I'm curious. 'Cause I know there's just *so much* excitement at your job," she teased. The indulgent grin he gave her made her pause as if she'd made a sudden and wholly inaccurate assessment of his work. "What's probably the best thing you've ever seen happen? Or the most unusual?'

Aidon's brow quirked. "Despite what you may think, 'unusual' doesn't even begin to cover what I actually do." His grin widened at her sheepish smile and he winked. "It's okay, I prefer people just assume I dig holes and count names. Lord knows that's what I've been doing since that goddamned tornado," he added with a grumble. He saw her quizzical frown. "The damage done to the smaller cemeteries means we've been up to our elbows, literally, going through genealogy records and medical, legal, blah blah blah, just to sort out who belongs to who so we can re-bury them. So yes, to be fair and accurate, I really have been digging holes and counting names."

"The project," Prax breathed. Now it was her turn to answer his questioning gaze. "I overheard you talking with that one guy, Ralph, at the coffee shop. The day of the sinkhole."

He leaned back in the booth, memories returning. "That's right. I remember seeing you there." He watched her studiously swirl a steak fry in bleu cheese. "I do, actually, remember the answer to your question," he said in a casual attempt to ease the conversation. When Prax looked back up at him, he smiled. "It was forever ago, so forgive me if I'm fuzzy on the details."

She sipped on her cocktail and nodded for him to continue, eyes bright with curiosity.

"There was a...oh, how would you put it." He rubbed his jaw. "I've always been a keeper, over the dead, over the grounds, but even before that. I don't know, maybe it's just how I was wired from the beginning. Anyways, this one place I was in charge of had this whole section of people who didn't really belong anywhere else on the grounds, but there was nowhere else to put them. Basically homeless and kinda depressing. Frustrated the heck outta me, but what could I do? Anyways. One day my boss came in, grabbed the keys, and next thing I knew everyone sectioned off in No Man's Land followed him out. They finally had a place to go. A home."

"Wait...you mean they were alive?" She swallowed her fry. "Was this during the war?"

Aidon met her surprised gaze with his own, surprisingly wistful. "Yeah. And let me tell you, watching all those happy people finally go somewhere they could call home...that was probably the greatest day of my life. Well, topping only one other."

"Which was...?"

He stilled. And honestly, for a solid minute, it looked like he really wanted to tell her. But Aidon thought better of it and polished off his steak. "Cubs winning the World Series."

Prax pouted, but no amount of silent pleading would cajole him into telling her the true answer. Aidon simply smiled and finished his drink, watching her enjoy the last few bites of her own meal—which was, by all accounts, pretty fantastic. She knew it was far more ladylike to order a salad; that's what Demi would have insisted upon. But Prax never considered herself a "lady" and so she gave herself a free pass, as Aidon called it, to order the dang burger with fries and enjoy every ounce of it.

Aidon checked his phone for the time and clicked his tongue against his teeth—a subconscious habit Prax noticed he did whenever he was thinking a minor decision over. "It's still kind of early, but we can head over to the lounge if you want. It's Favor Night, so there's no telling who's gonna show up first."

This made her quirk a brow. "Oh, this'll be interesting."

They slid out of the booth, Aidon leaving a hefty tip for the waitress and Bennie, who nodded his gratitude and called after them that he'd see them in the lounge later. Aidon offered Prax his arm and murmured, "my lady," a gesture that surprised her and made her blush even brighter than before. She slipped her hand in the crook of his arm and together they made their way down into the lounge room of Hawkeye's.

Prax honestly never actually realized the dive bar where she'd first made her own request was attached to the pub-restaurant Courtney had introduced her to. Apparently, they were one and the same business, with the "lounge" (a generous word for it) downstairs from the nicer, more family-friendly dining area. It should have been obvious, now that he led her through to the back door and down the indoor stairs, but to be fair she'd only ever used the separate front entrances. It did feel very apropos for Bogarten - two different atmospheres, two different worlds, amicably occupying the same space.

He led them over to his usual booth, the dark crescent of leather and wood on a small platform that always gave Prax the slight impression of a casual throne. It might as well be, the way he sat there with one arm draped across the back, his hooded gaze studying every person in the room. She did her best to ignore the fact that his arm was behind her again, just like the other night...when she'd challenged his personal morals and ethics.

Maybe it was coincidental. Maybe it was his way of protecting her from skeevy barflies who might make a pass if she were alone—there were certainly plenty of those, even at this early hour of the evening. They, too, scanned the room, more like predators seeking vulnerable prey. One glance at the dark king reclining in his comfy throne, though, tended to stave off the worst of them. Even if they weren't seeking his favor, they definitely weren't seeking the thorough ass-beating Aidon Elrik's reputation promised to those who crossed the line.

One such barfly was already hunched over the counter, slumped precariously on the stool as he nursed whatever swirled in the shotglass loosely teetering in his fingers. He lifted his head and through the mess of straggled curls, Prax recognized his bleary face as none other than Donn Morrighan. He threw back the shot and smacked his lips, slid heavily off the stool, braced himself against the counter as the room spun around him, and gradually made his way over to their booth. "Hallooo! My friends! Fancy seeing you here!" His accent was as thick as the alcohol on his breath, and Prax would have laughed if she didn't feel so immensely worried for him.

"Effin' fates, man, when were you last sober?" Aidon scrunched his nose, eyes wide as he regarded his friend.

Donn snorted. "I dunno. When was the last Crusade?"

He cackled and signaled the bartender for another drink, who quickly glanced at Aidon, who gave a subtle signal to bring something else.

"Are you all right?" Prax touched Donn's arm and noticed how hot his skin felt. Was he feverish? "You look terrible."

"And you look sexy." Donn grinned at her, his Flirt Mode on full power. He let out another snort when Aidon glared at him. "Oh, come off it. Look me dead in the eyes and tell me you haven't been mentally worshipping every inch of this goddess from Day One."

Both Aidon and Prax immediately sat up in their respective seats, his arm lowering while hers reached for her deck of cards in her pocket so she could focus on something other than Donn's cheeky grin and Aidon's uncomfortable attempt to look anywhere else. The bartender came and slid a glass of clear liquid to Donn, who lit up and muttered something about vodka.

Then promptly made a face and sputtered. "What the hell?!"

"It's Favor Night," Aidon calmly replied, still steadfastly gazing out over the bar. "I need you sober. At least alert enough to pass as sober."

"I hate you. So much."

"You love me."

Prax nervously shuffled her cards, nothing fancy, just a continual tap-tap-tap between her fingers while the two men bickered around her. She didn't want Donn to collapse from alcohol poisoning, not like Connor, but she also didn't want to flip a card and see Donn's ashen body slumped in the booth. As if he could read her mind, he gently nudged her side and winked, taking an obligatory sip of his water. "Hey," he reassured, "I'm not going anywhere. And it will take a lot more than a few choice beverages to take me down. I'm invincible. I'm inevitable."

"You're insufferable," grumbled Aidon, a smile threatening to break his stern façade.

The first request for a favor came in the shape of a haggard old man trying to afford his rent after a price hike by his landlord. Aidon asked if he needed money, to which the man quickly shook his head and insisted it wasn't a financial issue as much as it was a landlord issue. "I'm not the only one facing eviction," the man confessed. "We all met together and I promised I'd at least see what you advise we do."

Aidon nodded and nudged Prax to discreetly peek at her cards. When she shook her head no, nothing seen, he visibly relaxed and offered the man a reassuring smile. "I'll have a little chat with your landlord and see what we can negotiate. Have you eaten?" When the man shook his head, Aidon pulled out a few large bills and handed them to him. "Go tell Bennie I sent you up; if this doesn't cover the tab, he'll put it on mine. Get some takeout, too, okay?"

The man looked close to tears with relief and nodded, shook Aidon's hand, nodded again, and scurried away to the stairs that led to the restaurant level. Aidon tapped a quick text on his phone and let out a low grumble Prax almost didn't hear. "Goddamned slum lords."

"Language," Davidson playfully scolded him as he joined their little group in the booth, settling next to Donn.

Aidon didn't bother to look up from his phone, only raised a brow in acknowledgment towards the minister. "You and I both know I'm no choir boy."

"You're a man with standards, and no excuse not to keep

them." Davidson nodded his greeting to Prax, who furrowed her brow in curiosity. He chuckled and shrugged his shoulders. "It's Favor Night. Someone's gotta be around to make sure Aidon's favors stay on the straight and narrow. And legal."

"I hate you. So much." Aidon grumbled his impression of Donn.

"You love me."

Donn grinned at their friend and nudged his glass of ice water in his direction. "Hey, preacher man, if you could turn this water into wine, I'd be much obliged," he implored.

Davidson let out another chuckle and nudged the water back. "You're about to witness the miracle of every alcoholic beverage turning into water before it hits your tongue, my friend."

"Ugh. You're so boring."

"And you're three sheets to the wind. We need you sober."

Donn made a face and imitated his two parental friends, but acquiesced and sipped on his water anyways. To his credit, he did manage to look far more alert and sober when the next request approached, a young woman needing money for food to feed her children, help to find a job, anything to alleviate the poverty she suddenly found herself in after her fiance was arrested and broke off ties with her. Davidson took the lead on this one, giving her contact information for the church's food pantry and the names of people who specialized in her type of situation.

Prax watched as more requests like this trickled in, one after the other. Rental assistance, food assistance, security concerns in certain neighborhoods, many of them from the university or sudden misfortune. "I don't get it," she whispered to Aidon during a gap in the line. "Why do they come here? To you?"

"Why do they have to?" He drummed his fingers on the table as he shared a sidelong look with Davidson. "You'd think social services would, you know, serve society. But half the time the restrictions are so tight and the funds bled dry, only a fraction of the people who need help actually get it."

Davidson nodded in agreement and sipped his ginger ale. "It's why so many turn to drugs, prostitution, other forms of illegal activity that either earns them money or numbs the pain. If we can step between one problem and the next to steer them in a better direction, we'll do it."

"Hence Favor Night."

As the night deepened, so did the line of people waiting their turn to ask Aidon Elrik for help—and the requests grew more and more...interesting. One person wanted seventy grand for a Tesla so he could impress his ex-girlfriend. Another demanded Aidon and his "cronies" beat the ever-living daylights out of a store manager who refused a twenty-dollar refund. That one earned the name and number of a good therapist who specialized in "entitlement disabilities", to which the petitioner indignantly gasped and huffed away. All four in the booth chuckled and rolled their eyes.

But then there was one petitioner in particular who drew the hushed attention of the entire bar.

Her hair was tangled, tied back in a sloppy attempt at a low bun, mascara smeared under her eyes only enhancing the heavy bags beneath them. She mumbled and stumbled her way to the front of the line and braced her hands on the table. "I need fifty grand," Lacey Evans blurted, the syllables slurred together as her eyes darted around, never focusing on anything longer than a second.

Prax sat up, as did the rest of her entourage. Aidon kept his calm demeanor at the forefront, even as she felt him tense beside her. His arm returned to the backrest, and she didn't miss the direct implication of protection over her as she stared at the hot mess before them. "For what?" He asked.

"I owe some people some money." Lacey shrugged. "Gotta pay it back. Don't have it."

"What happened to the other fifty grand?" Prax blurted out the question before her brain could stop her, and there was zero chance at hiding the distaste in her voice.

Lacey narrowed her eyes and snarled. "What's it to you?"

"Careful." The word was a low, rumbled warning, his expression darkened just a fraction as he tapped away on his phone and set it down to focus his stony gaze on her. "Answer the question."

The woman huffed but didn't retreat. "Fine. Things didn't go down like they were supposed to, and now I gotta pay back money I don't have."

"What didn't go down?"

She snarled at Prax. "Nosy bitch, I don't gotta explain myself to you—"

Before Aidon could fire back in her defense, Prax leaned forward and gave the woman a very insincere smile, her fingers deftly shuffling the gilded deck with the mesmerizing flourish she'd finally learned to master. It did the trick, literally, because Lacey's eyes actually focused on their shimmering light and made her stop mid-tirade. The voice that emitted from Prax's mouth sounded eerily like her mother's, but given the circumstances, she embraced it and went with it. "Allow me to explain something to *you*," she purred. Another shuffle, another flourish. "I don't have to look at these cards, heck, I don't have to see *anything* to know that your days are numbered. You're desperate for money you wasted only a day ago? Looking over your shoulder even now? Where is the desperation to find your daughters? To look for them?" She felt a growl roll in her throat. The betrayal of family, the desecration of the sacred bond between mother and daughter, sickened her on a level which now simmered into fury. "If you want anyone to help you, and I mean *anyone*, then yes you better explain yourself. *Now*."

Even Donn's eyes widened at the sudden shift in Prax. Lacey hesitated, the slightest hint of fear in her eyes, but she snorted. "Bitch, who do you think you are?"

The last word cut off with a solid thump, her head pinned down on the table by Prax's vice-like grip on her tangled bun. The move was so quick, so unexpected, several of the bar's patrons took large steps back from the booth and waited for Aidon to do something. He, however, simply watched Prax take the woman in hand with a very impressed smile playing at his lips.

"I'm someone who doesn't like that word," Prax responded, that same dangerous purr coating her tongue. "Let me rephrase the question, make it easy for you. And this time, if you decide to not answer me, whatever or whoever you're running from will be the least of your worries. Are we agreed?"

Lacey whimpered and did her best to nod.

"Good. Now." Prax slowly released her hold on the woman's hair and leaned back, eyes narrowed into dangerous slits as she watched her straighten. "Where are your children?"

For the first time since the day they disappeared, Lacey Evans choked back a sob. "I don't...I don't know. I don't know!" She suddenly shrieked, her fingers clawed against the table as whatever pressure she'd been containing suddenly burst. "It wasn't supposed to go down like this!"

The shadows in the room deepened, curling around the pair who sat and watched the woman fall apart under her own foolishness. "What, exactly?"

Lacey shuddered and tugged at a jacket that wasn't there, her twitching fingers curling against her bare arms and leaving faint pink lines. "I swear to you, I didn't think anything bad would happen. I was going to get her back just as soon as I paid off my dealer and made good on my loan."

Prax felt like she was going to vomit. "You sold your daughters?"

"No! Just Sarah!" As if that made it any better. "No one was supposed to take Rachel, no one was supposed to touch my baby girl." Tears fell from her eyes, but genuine as they might be, no one felt an ounce of sympathy for her. "Something went wrong. I thought they had her, I got my money, everything was fine! But then I start getting calls and texts for the money back, saying they never got Sarah, the girls were already gone...." She broke down into sobs, her body shaking from head to toe as she rocked on her feet. "I swear, I swear, I don't know where they are!"

Aidon was the first to speak, once the chill had time to set in. "Who did you broker the sale with?"

"Some guy was supposed to pick her up—"

"That's not what I asked." He leaned forward, dangerous warning etched on his face. "I said, who did you broker the sale with?"

All the color drained from Lacey's flesh. She took a step back, shook her head. "No. No. I'm not saying another word."

"Lacey."

The laugh that bubbled from her lips was anything but sane. "Do whatever you want to me, I don't care! Arrest me, torture me, hell, kill me if it'll make you feel better. But you want a name I can't, I won't give you. Not for all the money in the world."

"Not for your immortal soul?" Davidson quietly asked.

She slid her gaze to him and slowly shook her head. "Not even that," she whispered. Before anyone could ask her another question, she turned on her heels and stumbled through the crowd to the door. No one made an effort to stop her.

Aidon tapped his phone's screen and sighed. Donn tilted his head towards the door and asked, "Thinking I should keep an eye on her, make sure she doesn't go and do something stupid?"

"More stupid than the mountain of stupid she's already gone and done?" Aidon sighed again, replied to a text that pinged in, and set the phone down. "Already on it. But maybe pay her a visit once she's settled in, hm?"

Donn nodded.

Aidon turned to peer at Prax, who returned his gaze with an uncertain smile. "Remind me to never, ever use the 'b' word around you."

She blushed and shyly ducked a bit. "Sorry."

"For what?" He laughed. "You just got more information out of that woman in ten minutes than Sheriff Sulis and the FBI have in a week. Don't apologize, be proud. I know I am."

Prax didn't know what to do with that information, or with the way he kept staring at her as if she'd just wrestled the moon to the earth with one hand. She could only bask in the warmth of his gaze, nestle into the literal warmth of his arm not-around her, and forget, just for a little while, that this was not a date.

Authorities finally caught a break in the Evans case after an anonymous tip provided police evidence of their mother's complicity in the disappearance. Twenty-six-year-old Lacey Wilkins-Evans of Bogarten was arrested in the early hours of this morning after the FBI and local officials were able to confirm the validity of the tip, and Evans now remains in custody for questioning."

"That's right, Mark. Initial reports say that the mother of two openly confessed to *selling* her children to pay off a large debt, but she refuses to give names of others involved in the supposed transaction. Authorities are hesitant to pursue this line of investigation without further evidence, given the intensity of her substance withdrawal casting doubt on the validity of her claims, but there is no doubt she is directly involved and will face charges once the investigation is complete."

"And just in time, it seems. As you can see on the dashcam video here, officials arrived at her house right after emergency calls came in reporting a whirlwind that touched down in the Fulton Park neighborhood and, as you can see here, knocked a tree into the Evans' home. Police found Lacey Wilkins-Evans hiding in her bathtub, screaming and babbling what they described as 'incoherent nonsense'. Now, Lonnie, what has us puzzled and I'm sure the rest of Bogarten, given recent events—how common are sudden windstorms like these?

Especially since nothing showed up on the radar and the revamped alarm system should have picked up on the weather conditions, right?"

The camera shifted to Channel 9's award-winning meteorologist, who sat behind his desk and solemnly nodded. "It's a common misconception that all windstorms come with ample warning, and of course, we are continuously enhancing weather-tracking technology to catch the most minute details that may indicate sudden shifts in air pressure, wind currents, temperature, and other factors that commonly play into the formation of tornadoes and similar vortexes. Without sufficient data, it's difficult to say what exactly happened in Fulton Park in terms of barometric pressure, but we have seen this before in cases like the whirlwinds that formed in a Target parking lot last summer. Do you guys remember that?" He chuckled.

Mark and Yvonne's carefully powdered faces broke into humorous smiles and they both nodded. "That's right!" Yvonne exclaimed. "That was a strange one, too, as I recall. Do we have footage from last summer showing this?"

The screen flickered to grainy footage from a security camera overlooking the megastore's parking lot. Five medium-sized patches of dust and litter individually swirled through the parking lot, shaking vehicles as people ran for cover. Lonnie's voice narrated over the reel, "As you can see here, this is a very unusual wind pattern that obviously has people running, and I don't blame them! But you can also see there's not a whole lot of damage occurring where these winds seem to hit the sides of cars, and if you look real close at the sliver of sky above the rooftop," the screen paused and a bright green oval circled around the patch of blue at the top, "there's nothing happening overheard to give any sort of warning. It's a strange and unsettling occurrence, indeed, but these things do happen."

Mark's voice chuckled good-naturedly as the camera returned to his face. "These things do happen."

The way the rain pattered on the glass dome of the atrium sounded like an ethereal sort of music to Prax's ears, and it quickly became a habit for her to sit with Mya on one of the couches with a cup of tea just to listen. Lately, her sister also got into the habit of asking about "the tall, dark, and handsome" groundskeeper, wanting all sorts of details like the way his voice sounded, the way his eyes seemed to light up when he saw Prax walking down the gravel pathways, or how his gruff demeanor always melted with a single lick of Spot's slobbery tongue.

"I think he likes you," Mya said during one of their Late Night Rainy Teas, sipping her chamomile with a wiggle of her brow.

Prax snorted. "Right, okay. First of all, he is *way* out of my league, and *married*. Second of all, did I mention he's kind of an overlord or kingpin or whatever you call it? I feel like I mentioned that a few times."

"I love how you led with how unattainable he is. Been thinking about it, hmmm?"

Her face immediately pinkened and she tried to cover it up with a hearty sip—alright, chug—of her vanilla rooibos. "What? No!"

Mya giggled. "You totally have! I don't blame you, though. He sounds like a total babe."

"Again, I'm going to mention the criminal element."

"You said he watches over the underbelly, not that he commits crimes."

Prax took a moment to consider that. The girl had a point—while Aidon dealt out favors to every sort of person who darkened the door and seemed to know every dealer and slumlord on a first-name basis, not once did she see or hear him involve himself within the acts themselves. In fact, didn't he scold someone for selling herself and threaten her *away* from prostitution? And every interaction Prax witnessed between him and a shady dealer involved plenty of not-so-veiled threats should they continue pushing their product. Not to mention the fact that one of his closest friends was a *minister*.

She sighed and set her cup down on the coffee table. "I don't know. Maybe I just don't want to get my hopes up." As she leaned back on the couch, she felt the deck of cards in her back pocket and shifted in her seat to tug them out. They never ceased to fascinate her, from the way the gold foil shimmered to the near-dependence she felt towards them to keep her sane.

Mya leaned back and eyed the deck as her sister fanned the cards out and folded the deck over and over again. "And yet here you have it, evidence that he totally wants you. I mean, look at those! Tell me the man didn't give you some hella bougie playing cards 'just because'." She snorted. "How much you wanna bet that's real gold?"

Okay, maybe that question had been tugging at the back of Prax's mind for a while, so much that she was still considering taking the deck to a jeweler just to find out. But every time she felt the courage to go do it, she talked herself out of it by remembering how rude it would be to look a gift horse in the mouth. Plus, a part of her didn't want to know either way. She loved the mystique of possibility with every shuffle of the stiff cards.

"These definitely help." Prax flipped a card between her fingers, a trick she'd been practicing almost daily just to look cool. Mya watched with a skeptical look on her face. "I mean, the visions are still horrible, but at least I can contain them to the surface of the cards like a picture. And I've been able to stretch through time a bit, now that I'm not stressing out over the shocks and surprises. My current record is like, three days, I think? It was really faded, though, so I probably won't count it."

Mya let out a small laugh and shook her head. "You know, there's gotta be a rule somewhere that it's rude to foresee someone's death without their permission. Like it's spying or something."

"Like I'd willingly just casually peep on someone's death?" Prax snorted. "People keep asking me. They keep wanting to pay, too, but that just feels weird."

"This whole thing is weird."

Her words visibly stung Prax, and Mya immediately regretted saying them. She reached out to hug her older sister but quickly recoiled at the sight of the cards still in her hands. "I'm sorry, I didn't mean...." She sighed. "I just feel bad. For you. For all of us, really. Our family is weird enough as it is, and now you're telling people how they're going to die from a deck of playing cards like you're...I don't know...dealing death."

Prax nodded and slumped in her corner of the couch. The teen was right; their family was weird as all heck and these post-coma abilities definitely didn't help any. She didn't have the courage, or willpower, to tell Mya about her waking visions of the missing girls. The police didn't believe her; why should they? Why should anyone? It's not as if the information was useful, since she didn't recognize any distinctive features in the surrounding woods they seemed to be traveling through.

She flipped another card between her fingers, admiring the way the gold caught the faint sunlight peeking through the rain clouds. There was a small part of her that began to worry, even fear, that she was beginning to enjoy this a little too much—that being, more than the "tolerate" level she'd originally resigned to. She felt a little rush of power every time a random stranger asked to "have their cards read", and felt a little thrill of showmanship every time their eyes lit with excitement as she shuffled in increasingly complicated patterns (most of them learned on YouTube). It was even more so whenever she hung out at the bar with Aidon, who kept a close eye on her as barfly after barfly asked for their death to be seen—or not seen. Sometimes she caught him smiling with amusement at her shuffling tricks, which he quickly hid behind his mug.

Sometimes she tried reading her own fate. Was that possible? Even if it was, there existed the strong probability that she wouldn't be able to see it if it was far enough into the future. She'd tried again with Aidon, who sat very still with a thoroughly indulgent smile on his face while her shaking fingers tugged out a card. Nothing. At least that meant he didn't plan on kicking the bucket any time soon. Donn insisted on having his cards read again as well, and the same round of nothing occurred after she fanned them out and let him pick his card. His grin was wide and infectious, and that was when Prax decided to try it on herself.

Still nothing, but no complaints about it.

"Hey Mya," she said, breaking the silence of their day-dreaming as she flicked another card back into the deck. "Wanna have your cards read?"

If it was possible to be any paler than she was, it happened at that exact moment. Mya shifted uneasily on the plush cushions and slowly shook her head. "No, it's okay. I'd rather that all be left to mystery."

"Aw, come on. Worst thing that could happen is I get a heads up on tomorrow's forecast." Prax cringed. "Ugh, bad joke. Sorry. Too soon."

Mya gave her a half-hearted laugh, her fingers plucking at the lint of her hoodie. "It's okay, really. I'd rather you didn't." She lifted her gaze to meet Prax's, her face suddenly serious. "Please."

"Are you okay?"

The teen tried to summon a smile and failed, but she nodded. "Just...let's just forget it, huh? We can play a board game or something. You up for Monopoly?" She sprung to her feet and skipped over to the cabinet where Demi stored all the family board games, her sudden perkiness an obvious attempt to shove the subject aside.

Prax frowned. No one ever said "no" to having their cards read. Not that she willingly offered it to everyone in town, but still. Her little sister was acting weird about it, and as much as she didn't want to press her further...

...*what would a little peek hurt?*

She waited until Mya's back was completely turned to-wards her, then quietly shuffled the deck. There was really no need to, every card was blank, but the familiar motion calmed her nerves and gave her a few seconds to decide if she should just respect the very clear boundaries or sneak a quick look at her sister's potential fate. She wanted to know if the sweet girl was in danger, right? And if she wasn't, the card would be blank.

No harm, no foul.

Mya tugged the Monopoly box out from the bottom stack of games and turned on her heels with a proud little grin. "Got it! Which one do you want—"

Prax lifted the card.

"Prax! *NOOOOOOOO!*"

Her arm outstretched, her face twisted in surprise and horror, Mya leaped at Prax—and stopped in midair.

The fingers reaching for the cards curled into claw-tipped wisps. Her jaw slackened, more and more, the last word from her mouth melting into an unearthly howl that shook the glass overhead and reverberated through Prax's bones. Mya's eyes rolled back until they became milky whites that sank into her head, and her once lustrous amber hair whipped around her ghastly face in silvery streaks and faded away, strand by strand, until it stripped down to her bare skull. And then even that vanished, until all that was left was the echo of her screams through the hallways of the house.

It took several minutes for Prax to realize those lingering screams were her own.

The silence that followed was almost worse.

She wasn't sure when she was finally able to stop screaming, and start breathing, but eventually, the switch was made and Prax white-knuckled the couch cushions until heaving air into her lungs felt more like therapy than a necessity. Her ribcage felt like it could splinter under the constant slamming of her heart against it.

Mya was gone.

Prax blinked. Maybe it was a nightmare—maybe she'd fallen asleep on the couch and Mya was just in the other room, getting more tea or using the bathroom.

But silence hung heavy in the house. No flowing water, no soft little hums or tinkling of porcelain from the kitchen. The corner of the couch where Mya was sitting still showed an indent in the cushions where she'd been nestled all snug and warm just moments before...

...and the Monopoly game lay scattered on the floor.

The next sound that followed was the slam of the front door behind her, then the crunch of gravel beneath her feet as she ran—no, *sprinted*—down the driveway.

The stars were gone from the sky, the air thick with the heavy darkness that clings to early dawn. Adrenaline coursed through her veins as she raced down the misty sidewalk, across open lawns of the neighboring campus and its dormitory houses, cutting through private yards until she reached the singular road that led to the one place she knew she'd be safe.

She'd ask for his forgiveness later.

Something heavy landed on her back. Prax screamed and scrambled over sharp gravel rocks littering the damp grass, caring less about the scraping pain on her palms and far more about the other set of hands that suddenly grabbed her face from behind.

Prax....

Her throat burned and thickened with her panicked sobs, icy fingers she couldn't see but felt clawing over her face smeared her tears through the kicked-up dirt streaking across her cheeks. She tried to roll around, to knock her assailant off, but every time she landed on her back it was suddenly as if no one was there. The moment she crawled back up on hands and knees, the weight returned, as did the horrible hands.

Prax...help me....

She couldn't hear the voice as much as she could feel it, somewhere deep in her mind, in her soul, in the thunder of her heart slamming against her ribs.

Prax...I'm sorry....

...help me....

She took a moment. Fingers digging into the cool, dark soil, knees quickly staining with dew-kissed grass, the mists of dawn clinging to her skin and curling the tips of her hair all grounded her into that very moment. Enough to slow her heart, enough to fill her lungs.

Enough to focus.

The fingers were still there, the weight still firm on her back, but not as aggressive as before. In fact, the hands that gripped her eased and slid down until she felt a pair of arms wrap around her shoulders in a freezing embrace.

Hurry...the sun....

Nothing explained how she knew, but she did. She knew the arms around her, knew the voice pleading in her mind. And she knew she had to hurry before the first rays of sunlight pierced the sky.

"Hang on tight," Prax muttered, and she shoved herself back onto her feet. This time, however, she was prepared for the weight and braced on her heels to lift up, reaching back with her own hands to grab for what she hoped would be there. Sure enough, she felt the cold firmness of thighs and then the shift in weight as those same legs did their best to wrap around her waist. She hooked her grip behind the knees, hunched low to balance both their weights, and took a deep breath. "I've got you."

The gates to the cemetery now felt miles away compared to the few blocks they actually were. Every hurried step took more effort than the last, and Prax realized it was the phantom weight dragging her down more and more and more. The closer she got to the gates of Nanabozho, the heavier the presence became, until she was practically doubled over under the impossible burden.

Hurry!

Dawn threatened to shatter across the sky, and something deep within warned with horrific ferocity against finding out what failure meant.

Mud sucked at her shoes, clung to her ankles. It was as if the earth itself didn't want her to reach those gates, cross that threshold. The arms around her neck tightened, cutting off her windpipe. Fingers tangled and curled in her hair, nails scraped against her scalp, frantic and terrified as she began to lose hope she'd make it in time. Or at all.

A different type of cold brushed under her outstretched hand.

The gates.

A long howl echoed in the distance, but Prax could barely hear it as her vision blurred, her lungs burned, her throat closed around her thickened tongue. The weight was too much, far too much for anyone to bear, and the first ray of sunlight threaded through the clouds.

Her foot caught against a stone.

She fell.

Another howl.

Then a bark, this time closer, followed by a mournful whine.

A warm, slobbery tongue lapped the dirt and tears from her cheeks.

Prax groaned, which was immediately met with an excited huff and short yip of the giant bear-dog hovering over her. She felt the warmth of shaggy fur wrap around her, and then a whole different sort of weight made her grunt as Spot eased himself down by her side and halfway on top of her.

Morning painted the wispy clouds in brilliant hues of violet and peach, gold and turquoise. She squinted in the sudden light, her head disoriented at this odd angle, but the comfort of Spot's hulking mass wrapped around her in his version of a hug was the most blessed reminder that she was okay.

And she had, in fact, made it in time.

"Spot?" Aidon's voice called out over the gravestones. Prax blushed at the way her heart instantly skipped a beat the good way, and she did her best to bury her face against her canine friend's fur. "Spot? What do you have over here, buddy?" His voice drew nearer. "What...Prax? Prax!"

Spot reluctantly rolled onto his feet when Aidon rushed over, not without a rather jealous-sounding huff. "Prax! Are you okay? What happened? What the hell are you doing here?" Aidon's hands were warm, so warm and gentle as he eased her onto her back, then cupped the nape of her neck and firmly gripped her hands to help her upright. The world spun a lot less this way, and for that she was deeply grateful.

The first thing she noticed was the weightlessness of her back. Her limbs ached where they once burned, and as she glanced up she discovered she was only a couple feet just inside the memorial park. Deep tracks in the dirt and a somewhat lopsided gate suggested she'd collapsed against it and the momentum helped her swing on the iron bars like a giant hinge, a move that probably saved her life.

She didn't know how she knew, but she did.

"Prax?"

Aidon's voice dragged her attention back to him, and it was only then did she realize just how close he was. Under any other circumstance she would have jumped away and blushed and stammered, but not this time. This time, she needed him right where he was, and she needed him to do exactly what he immediately began to do, pulling her into his arms and cradling her to his broad chest.

Warm. Safe. Protected.

Tears stung her eyes. Prax took a deep, shuddering breath to hold them in, but she failed. That breath was all it took to burst open the gates deep within, and she collapsed against him as the sobs shook her limbs that now felt so heavy from exhaustion.

From grief.

"It's okay." Aidon murmured into her hair, stroked her curls, tucked her closer into his embrace. "It's okay, Sweetheart. I've got you." He gave Spot a quick little nod, and the dark mass of fur dipped his head in response and quietly nosed the gate shut behind them. Metal lightly clicked against metal, and the realization that the gate could have been locked, should have been locked, made Prax sob harder and her fingers clung to his shirt. "You're safe now. I promise," he whispered.

"M-Mya...." It was the only word that dared escape her lips.

"I know, Darling, I know. I'm so sorry."

She didn't know how he knew, but he did.

And for some reason that stood just outside of the reaches of her mind, of her memory, Prax felt all the better for it.

The blackout curtains in Aidon's bedroom lived up to their name, blocking out all traces of sunlight that would have alerted Prax to the lateness of the day when she finally woke up from her much-needed nap.

When she did awaken, she was thoroughly confused. This wasn't her bed—hers was just big enough to sleep comfortably in, but it was modest and tucked against a corner. *This* bed was huge, a prominent centerpiece in what appeared to be a very masculine room—all dark wood and deep leather, but clean. Tidy. Aidon's leather jacket hung on a hook on the back of the closet door, and a familiar pair of boots sat neatly in the corner by the other door which most likely led to the living area.

Prax let out a soft groan as she sat up, immediately regretting the movement. Every muscle in her body, including some she never knew existed until now, ached with a deep soreness she was positive she'd be feeling into next week. But heavens above, was the bed comfortable. It was easy, too easy, to sink back down into the overstuffed pillows and bury herself deep under the impossibly fluffy comforter.

"Knock knock." Aidon very gently opened the bedroom door and poked his head in. "I heard you stirring. Are you *up* up?"

"Do I have to be?" Prax groaned, her voice muffled by

his bedding. She heard him chuckle and didn't know if she wanted to peek at his beautiful face or continue to hide her own so he couldn't see her blush.

"After what you went through? I wouldn't blame you one bit if you decided to sleep for a month. However," he nudged the door open and stepped into the room, "I happened to hear you stirring while I was stirring...up some coffee."

The nutty fragrance that wafted to her nose promised he spoke the truth, and she flipped the duvet down to squint up at him. In each hand was a steaming mug of the blessed bean water. When he saw her eyes light up he chuckled again and handed her one before carefully sitting down on the edge of the bed. "If I remember correctly, you like yours with caramel and chocolate, right?"

Prax furrowed her brow only briefly, trying to remember when they had coffee together, but her brain was a fog and she was in no mood to push through it. "You nailed it," she said with a grateful smile. After the initial sip, she moaned and took another, deeper sip. "Oh my gawd, you *nailed* it."

Aidon cleared his throat and became very, very focused on sipping his own mug. They sat in silence for a few warm minutes, and Prax realized he hadn't once pressed her for details about how he found her that morning...or why. Instead he sat there, quiet and contemplative, stealing a few glances her way before he paused and quirked a shy little smile. "What?"

She blushed and hid behind her mug. "Nothing. Just... thank you."

He nodded. Was *that* a blush? She blinked and it was gone, replaced by a more serious look of concern crinkled in the corners of his eyes. "Do you want to talk about it?"

"I don't know." Her face dropped and she stared at the

foamy liquid tickling her nose with its aromatic steam. She opened her mouth to say something, but no words formed on her tongue, so she closed it again. Finally, something. "I don't even know what happened. Not...really."

Aidon nodded again. "I understand. Really."

Something tugged in the back of her mind, and she squinted up at him. "Yeah. You seem to understand. A lot, actually."

"Do you want to know?"

No. "Yes."

Another nod, another sip of coffee. "I'd wondered for a while. Suspected, anyways." He cleared his throat, stared at the bottom of the wall. "Just wasn't sure until this morning."

Prax swallowed hard. She didn't want to know, not really. But she *needed* to make sense of everything, she needed answers, and it felt better coming from him. She gave him a nod to continue, and he sighed.

"There are several versions of the *myling* story, but the basis is the same. The ghost of a murdered child who was never properly buried has a habit of piggybacking on unsuspecting people out for a walk in the middle of the night." He leaned over and gently eased the mug from her limp fingers before the coffee spilled onto the blankets, setting it down on the nightstand. Aidon Elrik was not known for beating around the bush on any given topic, but he winced slightly hearing his own words. Perhaps easing into it would have been better. "You lived through the second half of the story."

One shaky breath, then two. "How did you...?"

"There were lots of little signs, but I never...I don't know. Maybe I didn't want to know. But finding you like that, this morning." He paused, his jaw set tight. "The ground was still muddy from the rain. Your tracks were deeper, the

251

deepest, at the gates."

Impossibly heavy. Horrific as it was, something deep within her warred against the notion that Mya had ever, would ever, mean her harm. The madness felt like desperation, like panic, as if Prax was the only one who could carry such a burden beyond the gates and onto consecrated ground. Her little sister was always so sweet, so loving, so vibrant.

But how?

"My best guess? Your mother." Aidon cocked his brow and shrugged, not meaning to respond so quickly to the hushed whisper of a question Prax obviously thought was silent.

"My mother?" She gasped. "Oh god, my mother!" Panic immediately set in and she felt her chest tighten, her throat close up, her skin grow cold. But before she could leap off the bed, strong hands grabbed her arms and eased her back down. "What am I going to tell my mother?!"

"Hey, hey. It's okay." Aidon tucked a stray curl behind her ear, leaning close enough for her to feel his solid warmth, his steady breath. Even without realizing it, she followed his lead, drawing in deep breaths to calm her nerves. "She's at a conference, right? So you've got time to figure things out."

Prax nodded, then groaned. "She comes back today."

"Ah."

They sat together in silence, Prax feeling the weariness return while Aidon felt something dark tug at the corners of his composure. She broke the silence first with a heavy, tired sigh. "I don't want to go back there." Her words choked on fresh tears on the last syllable. *There.* "I can't."

"You don't have to go anywhere." Aidon eased her back onto the pillows and tucked the fluffy duvet around her shoulders.

For the briefest of moments, it seemed as if he wanted to kiss her brow. "Stay here and rest. Get some more sleep. No one dares come by here and if they do, Spot will take care of 'em." His wink made her giggle, and she couldn't deny the welcome pull the soft pillows and blankets had on her weary body.

He waited for her to drift to sleep, his hand resting on top of hers with the comforter between their fingers. He wanted to stay with her, to watch for her nightmares and be the face she saw when her beautiful lashes fluttered open. But he had things to do.

Spot rose from the couch with a yawn and a stretch when he heard the bedroom door open, then lazily padded over to his master and nuzzled his hand. The moment he spotted a familiar head of silken curls, however, he forgot Aidon existed and immediately hopped up onto the bed. It was both comical and sweet the way this hulking mass of muscle and fur so gingerly nestled next to Prax's sleeping form, laying his head on her lap.

Aidon was almost jealous. Almost. At least she'd still have a familiar face to wake up to, albeit one that would undoubtedly smother her with drooling kisses and hot dog breath.

He tiptoed through the living room and scanned the dining table until he spotted what he needed: her house keys. The corner of his mouth twitched at the thought of Prax, most likely and understandably terrified out of her mind, still having the presence of that same mind to remember her keys as she fled the scene. They jingled softly when he lifted them and he quickly wrapped his fist around them, casting a quick glance back towards the bedroom door. Not a peep.

He let out a breath he didn't know he'd been holding and quietly ducked out the front door.

It didn't take long to retrace the events of last night, from the scattered Monopoly game on the floor of the atrium living room to the kicked up corner of a rug and a toppled chair Prax undoubtedly tripped over on her way out. Demi wasn't home from her conference yet, no suitcases in the foyer or keys on the hanger in the kitchen.

The silence in the house was deafening; the air thick with unanswered questions.

A different type of retracing was what Aidon came here to do, and he wasted no time in scanning each room for glimpses of what might have happened to bring them all to this point.

"Aidon always knows" was practically a bumper sticker in this town, a phrase often giggled by flirtatious women who vied for his affection and whispered by those who preferred that he didn't always know what they were up to. But no one in Bogarten could ever figure out how, exactly, he always knew what they were up to. How he always knew when a greedy dealer lied or a desperate man sobbed the truth.

He took a deep breath, then lowered the Veil he'd so carefully crafted within his mind as he made his way through the house.

Demi's voice danced from the kitchen, a laugh mingled with the murmurs of a young man whose lips pressed to the curve of her neck. She stepped away from her lover and around the corner, her rounded baby bump the first thing Aidon saw. She faded down the hall, the voices melted away.

A little girl's laughter tinkled from one of the bedrooms, a flash of amber glistened as she danced away from her mother's outstretched arms. Aidon wasn't surprised to see the bedroom filled with Mya's things, pictures of her with Demi clipped to fairy lights strung across the bed's headboard. More laughter, now mixed with Demi's huskier tones, came from the atrium, the sounds of a loving mother and her sweet daughter most likely playing a game together in the shade of Demi's trees.

A new voice—no, the man's voice—from further down the hall. Aidon turned and followed the hushed tones, the harsh edge to the whispered end of a phone conversation. The man, Demi's lover, hunched over the mantel of the fireplace in the family room, phone to his ear. His shoulders were tense, the muscles in his back hardened. His voice wavered in and out, words promising to find replacements. Negotiate new terms. Ask for a different option, another way to appease the one in charge. Defeat dripped into his voice, quickly replaced by something harder, darker.

The vision faded, but the sickening feeling in the pit of Aidon's stomach only grew, seeping into his veins.

This was the room.

Maybe it was the Veil doing its job, maybe he genuinely did not want to see the details of what transpired here. He did not see as much as heard the shouts, the screams, Mya's voice sobbing and begging her father to stop, please stop....

The screams.

Aidon shut his eyes tight, wishing he could as easily shut his ears to the horrible, horrible screams. At the first sound of a sickly wet thud, he threw the Veil back up completely.

His gaze landed on the fireplace.

"Mother of...." He couldn't bring himself to finish that

sentence, nor could he bring himself to rush over to the mantel as quickly as he should have. Each step was a step towards an answer he truly did not want confirmed. Sometimes not knowing was better.

"That's where I saw her."

Aidon spun around. Demi stood in the archway that led to the hall, an overnight bag slung over one shoulder. Her back was straight and her head held high, but tears glistened on her lashes. "I came home one day, and they were gone." Her voice cracked. "I looked everywhere, filed a police report, thought maybe they'd just gone for a drive and had a terrible accident. But then one day she was there, standing by the fireplace. And that's when I knew she was gone." Demi slid the bag from her shoulder and let it fall to the floor with a dull thump, her gaze suddenly sharp and narrowed at him. "What are you doing here?" She glanced around the room, down the hallway, her breath quickening. "Where is Prax?"

"She's safe." Try as he might, Aidon could not bite back the grumbled, "No thanks to you."

Leaves rustled in the atrium, the foyer, the hallways as Demi took another step into the family room, fists clenched at her sides. "What the hell is that supposed to mean? Where is my daughter?"

"Where, indeed? Did you not bother to bury your own child?" What sympathy he felt for the grieving mother was shoved aside by an all-too-familiar rage building within his chest against this stubborn, foolhardy woman.

He more heard the slap than felt it. The sting set in a few seconds later.

Demi's eyes flashed a dangerous ivy green, her nostrils

flared as she fought to keep her temper in check. "How. Dare. You."

Maybe he deserved that one. Maybe. Aidon felt the muscle in his cheek tick as he battled his own urge to lash out, instead reminding himself that no matter how much she infuriated him, she was still Prax's mother. He steadied his own breath and ran a tense hand through his hair. "Dammit, Demi, I'm just trying to figure out what's going on."

"By breaking into my house?!"

Showing her Prax's keys dangling from his fingers didn't necessarily help the situation, but at least Demi didn't lunge for the phone to call the police. That was the very last thing either of them needed right now. "Tell me more about this room." He glanced around, not daring to turn his back to her just yet, but despite the Veil settled back into place he could still feel something was off.

Demi sighed. She folded her arms across her chest, every bit the formidable woman who made unsuspecting biology students cry...but still very much a loving, grieving mother, the pain etched in her eyes. "Nothing grows here," she mumbled, looking away as if ashamed by that simple fact.

That must be it, the thing nagging at his senses. Every inch of this house was covered in ferns, vines, roses, succulents, potted varieties of lush green things with fancy names—except in this one particular room. The room filled with Mya's screams.

He swallowed hard, slowly turning to the fireplace. That pit in his stomach turned, dread coiled low and deep with every shuffled step towards the brick and stone. No one had used it for ages, he could tell, but there were distinct marks in the ash that hinted at recent movement in the hearth. Aidon braced a hand on the mantel and crouched, using his other hand to reach up inside the pitch-black flue and feel around for something, anything—

"Oh god." Demi doubled over, hand clamped over her mouth, eyes wide and brimming with tears as she watched as Aidon carefully eased out what remained of a human arm, Mya's charm bracelet clasped around the wrist. The sight was too much, far too much, and by pure luck one of her empty planter pots sat close enough for her to retch into.

A whole new type of anger filled Aidon as he gently laid Mya's arm on the cleanest part of the hearth. It had been wedged up there, and the jagged marks on the end of the humerus told him what that sickly wet thudding sound in his vision was. Part of him wanted to keep digging around up inside the chimney to pull out any other pieces that may still be shoved in the ash and stone, but most of him recognized there was only so much Demi could take. And, truth be told, there was only so much he was willing to stomach. "This explains the plant issues," he finally said. Demi furrowed her brow, and he pinched his own as he nodded at the bones. "From what I can tell, this is where Mya died. This room, where nothing grows, is where she was murdered."

"And it's where her spirit returned," Demi added, her voice barely a whisper. "How did I not know? How did I...did I miss this?" She flicked her fingers towards the bones on the hearth and quickly pressed them over her mouth again, shuddering with another sob. "I knew something happened, I knew she was dead, but *this*...?"

Aidon sighed and rolled back onto his feet. He left the bones, and the bracelet, exactly as they lay, and pulled out his phone to snap a few pictures of the scene. The police would have to be called now, reports filed and questions answered, so he wanted to be sure that his role in this discovery would be crystal clear. It also busied himself enough to keep his gaze away from Demi. "Is it possible you just didn't want to know?" He braced himself for a second slap, but it never came. Demi just sat on the couch, defeated and pale, her lips moving against her trembling fingers as she stared at her youngest daughter's remains. "Demi?"

She blinked, then looked up at him. At this angle, in this moment, she seemed so small. So vulnerable. A shadow of the queen who ruled over such vibrant paradise. "I just wanted my baby back, any way I could have her. And here she was!" Her mouth curled in one corner, a sardonic smile in the face of such cruel circumstances. "I never told her anything, never acted like something was wrong, and I just.... I couldn't bring myself to come into this room. At first I thought it was because my plants kept dying, but I couldn't ignore that feeling...." She sighed. Such a deep, heavy sigh that almost looked like she would crumble at any moment. "I poured all my heart and soul, all my energy, into making Mya as real and alive and healthy as she'd once been. And it worked!"

"Explains why Prax never noticed until now."

Demi's eyes filled with horror. "Oh, no, no no no no." She jumped to her feet and grabbed for her keys, but was stopped by Aidon's firm hand on her shoulder. "I need to see Prax! I need to see my daughter!"

"Prax is fine." Again, not in any particular thanks to Demi, but at least now Aidon could clearly see the tragedy that unfolded rather than any cruel intent which led to Prax's near-demise in the early dawn. "She's really shaken by all this, but she's safe. Let her rest."

"Don't tell me how to parent," snapped Demi.

"Fine. I'll just remind you that Prax is a grown woman who stopped needing your parenting a very, very long time ago." He couldn't hold back the low growl of warning in his voice, and he wasn't sure he wanted to. "What she needs right now is a solid night's sleep and time to process what she's just been through. I swear to you, Demi, your daughter is safe. No one is laying a finger on her." *Not even me.*

Demi frowned, but acquiesced with the barest hint of a nod. Her gaze sharpened when she caught onto his words. "What she went through?"

He pursed his lips, words failing him as his mind tried to figure out how to navigate this turn in the conversation—how to tell the mother of a murdered child what happens when they aren't properly buried. When they're not allowed to rest. So, instead, he opted for misdirection towards something they both needed to know.

"Where is your husband?"

Eight Months Earlier

What do you mean, 'they're gone'?"

Jared McCready clenched his jaw, the icy tones of the voice on the other end of the call setting his nerves on edge. Only one man could make him sweat under the collar this profusely, and that man was pissed. "I doubled back and tracked them through the woods, but there's no sign of them."

A moment of silence.

That was almost worse than the verbal lashing.

"You assured me everything was secure."

"It was—"

"You gave me your word, your personal oath, that the shipment was secure and every head accounted for."

"It. Was." Jared couldn't keep his own anger from his voice, the pulse in his forehead ticking faster with every passing second. "They. Were. We can't figure out how they vanished—"

"Oh, no, Mr. McCready. There is no 'we' in this mess. Only you." Another pause, this time laced with a sigh. "How many?"

Jared swallowed hard.

"How many, Mr. McCready?"

"Eighty." He spat the word like the very syllables poisoned his tongue, which might as well be a true event—his stomach roiled. "Only eighty. The other trucks made it through."

"Only. Eighty." A chair creaked in the background, and the rustling hinted at the shifting of his stance, probably standing up to pace back and forth while he meted out his judgement. "You owe me a significant debt, Mr. McCready. A steep, steep debt."

He figured as much. "I'll pay you back, whatever it is."

"Oh you will, make no mistake about that. All six million dollars, not a penny less."

Jared damn near dropped the phone. *Six million?* "Y-you've got to be kidding me."

"Funny, that's exactly what I said when my men informed me of your mishap." The tone was light, too light. Too casual. This was never, ever a good thing. "You're lucky I don't tack on fees for damages to my truck, which I'm assuming there are considering the broken lock and slashed tires you described so vividly in your initial report."

He wheezed. "But that's seventy-five thousand dollars per head!"

"Per head, yes. *Virgin! Head!*"

Now Jared did drop the phone, the sudden scream in his ear physically painful as much as it was terrifying. *Shit.* As he scrambled to pick the device back up from the mossy gravel, he couldn't hold back the string of curses under his breath, each uttered in time with his pounding heart. The loss of eighty women was bad enough—he was hard-pressed to explain how such a large shipment of sedated slaves just suddenly vanished from the back of his truck before he crossed the Minnesota state line. How he'd never heard the lock break, or felt the truck shift, didn't notice a damned thing until he pulled into a rest stop to relieve himself and saw the back door wide open.

That was bad enough.

But no one told him they were virgins—the most expensive, most valuable products in the market.

Jared McCready was a dead man walking if he didn't think of something quick.

"I-I d-don't have six million dollars." His fingers shook, and he turned to go back inside the house. Maybe surrounding himself with the warm glow of home would somehow calm his nerves, at least enough to think straight. "But I'll give you whatever you want, to make up for it."

Mya beamed at him as she passed him in the hallway. "Hi, Daddy!" She quickly closed her mouth, eyes wide with embarrassment, when she saw he was on the phone. But then she noticed the clammy glisten of his brow, stitched together in very obvious worry, and her own smile faded into concern. "You okay?" She mouthed.

He nodded and offered her the best smile he could muster, which wasn't much, but he gave her a reassuring pat on her arm just for good measure before ducking away into the family room.

"You know what? That will work." Again with the beguiling tone that sent a chill through Jared's veins. "Give me your daughter, and we'll mark your debt settled."

That chill instantly turned into a downright freeze. His fingers gripped the phone as if smashing it to bits would somehow do the same to this asshole's face. "Hell. No."

"What's the matter, Mr. McCready?" A laugh, no true humor threaded within it. Just pure, cold calculation. "You've never had a problem with trading daughters before. What's one more?"

This motherf- "Not my daughter."

Another laugh. "Ah, I see. Suddenly it's different when it's your own flesh and blood, eh? Which is why this makes for fair and equal payment, Mr. McCready. I'm sure sweet little Mya is worth far more than six million dollars to you—"

"You're damned right she's little. She's barely fourteen." Jared kept his voice low, but did nothing to keep the growl out of it. "Listen here, you sick son of a bitch—"

"Careful, Mr. McCready." That warning spoke volumes in just three words. "I have more than enough over your head to ensure you never see the light of day again, let alone survive the first few nights in that iron hell. I've made my decision. Either you bring your daughter to me, or I will send my men to collect her."

Tears stung his eyes, but damned if he let anyone see or hear the fracture in his soul. "I'll bring you down with me, you depraved bastard."

"People in glass houses shouldn't throw stones. Especially in your house, with that beautiful glass atrium your wife so carefully keeps."

The click of the other end hanging up might as well have been the booming sound of a mausoleum's doors closing on his grave. Jared wiped a trembling hand over his sweaty face, his gaze unfocused as he stared at the fireplace he suddenly found himself leaning against. Maybe if he lit a fire and threw himself into it, all his problems would go away.

He scoffed. His employer was not the kind of man to simply forget debts—he'd sooner flesh them from the entire family than let a simple little thing as death clear the ledger.

"Daddy?" Mya's voice softly called to him from the archway that opened the family room towards the hall. She stepped into the room, her face pinched with worry at his pale expression. "What's wrong?"

Jared straightened. Better him than...them. He cleared his throat and nodded, more to himself than her. "I need you to go pack a bag, quickly. Grab your things, enough for a few days."

"What?" Mya's frown deepened. He hated seeing her sweet face so twisted. "Why? Where are we going?"

Still, they didn't have time to waste. "Just do as I say, Mya. Now."

She shook her head and took a step back. "But Mom is still at her conference, she's supposed to be back this weekend! Did you call her?"

Jared felt the frustration build, added to the stress already boiling in his mind and twisting his gut. "Mya! Do what I fucking tell you!" He instantly regretted yelling at her so harshly, but it was too late. Her eyes filled with tears, her bottom lip trembled, and she ran from the room. He'd never sworn at her before. He'd never even sworn around her before.

He still wasn't sure where they were going, so long as they got the hell out of there as soon as humanly possible. Would he take her...? No, hell no, despite his own sick and twisted occupation, he'd been so careful to separate the worlds. His business stayed far away from his home, his employer from his family.

Until now.

He glanced into Mya's room as he passed it to go grab his own things, and froze in his tracks. She was on her phone, frantically texting someone. No - *calling* someone.

Goddammit!

She screamed in surprise and frustration when he ripped the phone from her hands, ducking out from under his arm as she tried to wrestle it back and he tried to pin her arms down. "Get away from me! I'm calling Mom!"

"Don't you dare!"

Mya screamed again and ran from the room, but this time he chased after her. That pounding in his head matched the slamming against his ribcage, the world around him spiraling out of control. Everything was out of control - his job, his boss, his daughter. His life hung in the balance and that scale was quickly tipping against him. "Mya! Get back here!"

"No!" She ran back into the family room and grabbed a poker from the fireplace, wielding it in front of her like a sword. "You're scaring me!" She sobbed. Her whole body shook with her sobs, and it was almost enough to make him stop. "Get away from me!"

Almost.

"Give me that." He grabbed the end of the poker easily, her limbs still too young and weak to hold up any resistance against his corded strength. Still, she fought, her fists refusing to unfurl from around the handle. "Let go! We are leaving and that's final!"

"No!"

He wrenched it hard, twisting with all his might to yank it from her grasp.

Her head slammed against the stone mantelpiece.

Mya dropped to the floor.

"Mya?" Jared felt the bile rise from the twisting in his stomach as he fell to his knees, tossing the poker aside and quickly scooping her into his arms. "Mya?"

She didn't respond.

She didn't breathe.

Something warm and wet coated his fingers where he

cradled her head. He didn't need to see it to know what it was, as it dripped through her silken curls and pooled heavily onto the hardwood floor. Her skin paled into a sickly gray just as quickly as the floor stained with the darkest red, the same red that veiled his eyes in a grief, a fury that ripped through his pounding skull.

He didn't know how long he sat there with his only daughter cradled in his arms, his tears splashing on her mottled skin and dampening the curls which framed her sweet face. His throat was raw from his screams, his furious grief, his panic.

Oh, god, his panic.

Demi was due back in only two days. What was he going to tell her? How could he tell her anything? She'd call the police, open an investigation, and the more digging they'd do the more trouble he'd be in—and not just by the police.

He needed to get rid of the evidence.

Fast.

He grabbed one of Demi's gardening tarps from the shed and rolled Mya's body up in the plastic, setting her aside while he tried to figure out how to get the blood out of the hardwood floor and off the stone mantel. But as he kept glancing over at the dark bundle propped against the wall, his mind raced to figure out what he was going to do with her.

Can't call the police. Can't call the morgue—they'd call the police.

For the rest of his natural life, Jared McCready would be haunted by the memories of what transpired next—of what possessed him, in that darkest of moments, to walk back out into the shed and grab the hacksaw.

For the rest of his natural life, Jared McCready would wake in the dead of night to the vivid nightmares, the tangible, corporeal nightmares of his own hands ripping apart what remained of his sanity. His sweet, sweet sanity he once named, "Mya".

For the rest of his natural life, Jared McCready would never be able to look at a fireplace again, nor be in the same room as one. He'd be too terrified to look, too scared to see if her arm would suddenly fall from the flu.

For the rest of his natural life, Jared McCready would never be human again.

It didn't take long for his debt to be called.

"I understand you've experienced quite a loss." His boss flicked the ledger on the large oak desk shut without so much as a second glance. "Such a shame. I could have done wonders with your beautiful daughter."

His words no longer grated at Jared; there was nothing to grate against. The man who stood in the office, calm and ready for the next assignment, was merely a husk.

And somehow, in some sick way, his boss knew it.

"Given the circumstances, it seems only fitting to count at least a fourth of your debt repaid. As I understand it, you haven't been home since her 'disappearance', have you? Your wife must be worried sick."

Jared's voice was monotone. Cold. "I have no wife. No family. Sir."

"Very well. And it's just as well, considering the new job I have for you. There's no pay, of course, save for the basic expenses to ensure you actually fulfill this assignment to the best of your abilities." He slid a folder across the desk and flipped it open. "Another one of my wayward sheep also owes me a considerable debt. But she didn't put up a fight like you, didn't even argue with me when I told her how she could settle up." He tapped a finger on the school photo of a young girl, younger than most of the chattel they smuggled across state lines. "In exchange for a clean slate, she's given me her daughter."

"Sir." He felt no pity, no remorse, but he was curious.

"I know, I know. I usually wait for them to bleed, but this is a rare exception. Get 'em young enough and they can be trained to be excellent products, when they're ready. Plus, this one...this one is something special."

Jared nodded. "As you wish."

"Perfect. We'll arrange for your transport and security detail to escort you as far as Minnesota. No mistakes this time. We especially can't afford with this one. Make too much noise and the whole operation will be upended."

Again Jared nodded. "Consider it done."

The porch lights were on by the time Prax returned home, and she felt a pang of guilt over forgetting to leave her mother a note—and for leaving her phone behind. In her defense, the vision which drove her out of the house so quickly was enough to make anyone forget their phone, let alone their sanity, and Prax took a deep breath to brace herself for the onslaught of worry Demi was sure to pour over her.

No one rushed to the foyer as she expected, and Prax noticed the lights were off inside the entryway as well as the atrium room. Voices carried from down the hall, and Prax let out a small sigh of relief. Of course, they were probably hanging out in the family room.

As the voices grew louder the further she walked through the hall, she realized one of them was a man's voice. A familiar voice.

"Damn it, Demi, enough is enough—"

"No one asked you to come here! It's bad enough the way you've been treating her but, ha, why am I not surprised?"

"Careful, Demi." Aidon's voice dropped dangerously low. "Don't say something you'll regret."

Demi opened her mouth to spit something back at him, but stopped herself when she saw Prax standing in the archway. "Prax, honey...." She tried to smile, tried to look as if she wasn't just about to shred Aidon to pieces, but it was more effort than she had the willpower to give. "You're home."

Prax glanced between the two, then around the room, and frowned. "What's going on?"

Both of them fell silent.

"Mom." A knot formed deep within her gut and she forced herself to remain calm, remain rational. To not remember the nightmare. "What's going on?"

This time when Demi tried to speak, her words cut off with a choked sob. She quickly covered her mouth and looked away, leaning heavily against the mahogany wine table behind her. Aidon waited for her to answer, and when she didn't, his hands clenched into fists until he finally folded his arms across his broad chest and glared at the woman. "Demi."

Prax barely registered the warning in his voice, her gaze fixed on the bones carefully laid on the hearth. She stumbled back, feeling as if the air suddenly vacuumed out of her lungs. "Mom, is that...?"

Demi fought back tears that kept streaming down her face despite her best efforts. She sat on top of the wine table, her gaze unfocused. "You weren't supposed to look. You weren't supposed to look."

If she felt suffocated before, it was nothing compared to the complete absence of function Prax suddenly felt in her chest, her limbs, even her mind.

"Please, Prax, I don't want you to look."

She was faintly aware of someone catching her before she fell, her legs suddenly useless as her blood ran cold. The dark ink on the arms that held her reminded her Aidon was there, watching this unfold, and she would have felt mortified if she could feel anything within that moment. He gently pressed the side of her face to his chest until his heartbeat was the only thing she could hear. For the first time in what seemed like an eternity, the tension in her body melted away until all that was left was the warmth and comfort of knowing she was, at least for now, safe.

It was a very short-lived relief.

Aidon murmured something in her ear about going away, leaving to rest, but Demi's eyes refocused and glared daggers into his soul. "Don't. You. Dare."

"She's in shock, Demi, what do you want me to do?"

"I want you to leave!" Demi jumped to her feet, and even Aidon took a step back as Prax startled in his arms. "Take your hands off my daughter and go back to Hell where you belong!"

That snapped Prax out of her momentary shock, and she pulled away from Aidon just enough to stand between them. "Mom! Stop it! He never did anything to you—"

Demi barked out a laugh, derision tinged with insanity etched on her face. "You know what? You're right, Prax. He never did anything to *me*."

Aidon growled low and stepped forward, a subtle attempt to shove himself between them. "That's enough."

Both of them stilled when Prax placed a hand on his arm, her own demeanor calm as she stared down her mother. "Mom," she said, firmness and gentleness forming the words on her lips even as she felt herself shake with the strain of the entire day weighing so heavily on her limbs. "I don't know what you're talking about. I don't even know.... What happened?" She swallowed hard, the sudden returning lump in her throat as she cast another glance at the bracelet wrapped around the skeletal wrist. It took some considerable effort to ask what she didn't want the answer to. "What happened to Mya?"

The venom dissipated from her eyes and Demi teetered on her feet, but she vehemently refused Aidon's help when he reached out to assist her. The mercurial professor of biology, the proud woman and mother of two beautiful daughters, crumpled in defeat on top of the wine table. "I swear to you, I don't know." She tucked her knees against her chest like a shield over her fragile, stubborn heart. Her eyes returned to that distant gaze, staring off at nothing, but Prax sensed she was seeing more than anyone would ever care to. Nothing could stop the tears from flowing now, but no one felt compelled to deny this mother her grief. "I called the police, all my friends, and when they couldn't find Jared they figured he'd skipped town and taken Mya with him." Her gaze shifted over to the fireplace, and her skin paled. "And then one day she was back. Standing there, like nothing ever happened. But she was different. And I knew."

Whatever rage or animosity Aidon felt melted away into genuine sympathy. "Why didn't you call us? We could have helped."

Prax furrowed her brow. "Us?" He must have meant Donn and Davidson, or any number of his other friends in Bogarten's underworld.

A shadow of a smile flickered at the corner of Demi's tight lips. "I called her." She looked at Prax. "I called you for help. And you came." Her bottom lip trembled. "And then I almost lost you, too."

The string of curses flowing out of Aidon's mouth was quiet enough that Prax couldn't quite pick up on all of them, just the ones that counted. He sat heavily on the couch and buried his face in his hands, elbows propped on his knees, his thick curls sticking out as he tugged at the roots with his fingers. Prax was at a loss, her whole universe spinning around her as the web of secrets continued to unravel. Finally, *finally*, actual truth and honesty from the woman who hid so much to protect her, and as much as she'd wanted answers, Prax began to feel the full weight of that knowledge.

Aidon was the first to speak, his mouth partially obstructed by his hands. "It was you. You're the reason why I found Prax out there in the mud."

She slowly, oh so slowly, turned to stare at him. *No. Not him. Not…him.* Ice spread inside her veins, a slow drip at first, but rapidly expanded with every passing moment as her mind recounted every tense minute, every dark glare. *Him?*

"Explain."

Both of them quickly looked up at Prax, whose chest rose and fell with trembling, deep breaths. "Mother," she said, the ice now in her own vocal cords as well. "Explain."

"Prax, I—"

"It was my fault." Aidon jumped to his feet in a surprising move to defend Demi. He held his hands out in apology, his eyes pleading for understanding from Prax. "I should have stayed, I should have been there when you woke up. I didn't know what happened, and I panicked—"

She spun on him, ice melting under the heat of her embarrassment—and her pain. "You found me? *You* found me?" Her words barely registered above a whisper, a hiss, laden with disbelief as she gaped at him with a growing sense of horror. Despite the lack of details given when she woke from her coma, even in her checkups, the nagging suspicion over who found her—who *left* her—never fully vanished from her mind. And now, in this cursed room, stood that very person.

The same man who'd given her so much vitriol from the start.

The same man who kept pushing her away.

"You don't understand—"

"You're damn right, I don't understand!" She felt her own venom drip from her tongue, seeping into her words, the only defense she could muster as her heart began to break into a thousand little pieces and her head kept spinning, spinning, *spinning*.

Aidon moved closer, arms outstretched to hold her, but she stepped back from him and the motion itself seemed to wound him in a way a slap across the face never could. From her perch in the corner, Demi softly smirked—and that, as well, stoked Prax's fire.

"*You.*" Somewhere in the back of her mind, Prax was alarmed by the intensity of her own voice. But the burning anger inside her chest, the sudden flash of heat in her eyes and underneath her skin, loved it. She spun on her mother, her own fists clenched, nails digging into her palms. "You knew my sister was dead, this whole time, and you kept that from me? You *lied* to me?" Her voice threatened to break as unbidden tears formed a thicker lump in her throat, but she was still too angry to allow them to take over. "Is there anything else I should know, *Mother*?"

When Demi looked away, Prax felt like anything she did say would be the straw to break her. But nothing prepared her for the words that tumbled, barely audible, from her mother's lips.

"You're his wife."

Shadows deepened inside the room. Had the fireplace been lit, the flames were sure to snuff out under the thick blanket of darkness that settled heavily over the space, where Prax seethed between clenched teeth and fought back the hot tears that now stung her eyes with their own fury...and, damn it all, pain. *So much pain.* Now it was her turn to struggle to speak, because nothing came to mind while everything crashed together in a whirlwind of unanswered questions and seething betrayal.

It was Aidon who broke the silence, who dared to step closer to her despite the fury in her eyes. "I didn't know how to tell you. Not after...not after I realized it was an accident."

His face, his handsome, golden face dusted with just enough shadow to make her weak in the knees, every breath-taking inch was twisted with remorse. That voice in the back of her mind whispered this to her, pointed out all the signs right then and there that clearly indicated he meant every word. Reminded her of the way he'd gradually warmed to her, care for her, rising to her defense at every turn and sheltering her in the safety of his home.

The fury in her chest and the anguish in her heart remembered other words he also, vehemently, meant as well.

"You told me she left you." Prax tilted her head to one side. "You. Told me. That your wife left you." A dark laugh bubbled between her lips. She no longer recognized her own voice—not this molten, rich, so very very dark voice. "Hell, you told *everyone* that your wife left you!"

His shoulders slumped with defeat, and he nodded. "I did. I thought...I honestly thought you *did* leave me."

"Mhm." She pursed her lips in thought and steepled her fingers together. "Okay. Let's just assume, for one moment, you might actually be telling the truth. For once." Prax flicked a scathing glance towards Demi. "So when you found me, naked and bruised and scraped all to heck, lying in the middle of a cornfield after the world's deadliest tornado wiped nearly three thousand other people from the face of the earth, you just, what, thought I'd been out partying or something? On a bender? Forget about the storm, the death, the destruction, obviously I just pranced my naked ass out there to dance in the rain. Is *that* what you thought?" When his cheeks reddened and his own gaze glanced away, she felt the unspoken truth like a backhanded slap across her own face. "You...you son of a bitch."

Demi snorted, and Prax spun back on her with a finger to her face. "*No.*" Demi startled, eyes wide. Prax leaned in closer. "You do not get to snort, or laugh, or cry, or yell, or *anything*. You do not get to tell him what to do, and you sure as hell do not get to tell *me* what to do. *Mother.*"

Demi straightened, opened her mouth to scold her daughter, but quickly thought better of it when she saw the darkness and the flame swirl in the young woman's eyes. She looked to Aidon, who also appeared to make the difficult choice not to poke the beehive of Prax's self-control, despite the very obvious yearning in his eyes to make things right.

Prax stepped back from both of them, edging closer to the nearest exit as she felt the wall of her fury start to crumble under the reality of her pain. Their betrayal. Her grief. The only thing she could think to say, the only thing her body would allow her to say, was the only truth that seemed to exist within these walls.

"I can't believe the only person who never lied to me was a ghost."

The world around her glowed with ethereal brightness as the sky clouded over, and on any other day, she would have marveled at the beauty of it. She loved the way the grass looked so much greener, the lines of houses and barns sharper against the slate-gray sky.

Mya loved storms, too.

Hot tears splashed on her cheeks, the wind flicking them away just as quickly as they emerged from her watery eyes. Prax couldn't focus on anything around her, the storm within her mind and her soul already raging with the ferocity of a hurricane. She didn't even know where she was going, only that her feet carried her far away from the place she once thought of as home but now only felt like a prison of lies.

She couldn't go to the cemetery. Maybe it wasn't a prison, but the memorial park held far too many memories that now clawed against her heart. How could he say that about her? About *them*? Even if he now spoke the truth, even if by some insane possibility Aidon Elrik actually was her husband and she was his "vanishing wife", what the hell kind of husband would do this? How could anyone claim to love her and then turn around and lie to her at every turn?

Despite her earlier statement, Prax doubled over and shook with sobs as she realized even Mya technically lied. Maybe she didn't know at first what she was, or what happened to her, but at some point, the reality of her existence had to have settled in. At some point, Mya knew enough to know Prax's visions could unravel the delicate ties that suspended her between this world and the next.

You weren't supposed to look.

Blades of cornstalks rustled against her legs, slicing at her knees and thighs, but she didn't care. Her skin felt so hot just beneath the surface, her blood racing through her veins as she felt every single emotion course through her, threatening to burst through every pore until nothing of her would be left.

It scared her that it didn't scare her.

The clouds began to swirl overhead, the wind picked up speed, and something deep inside her chest—in her *soul*—leaped with a dark, delicious thrill.

Prax let her arms spread to her sides, just enough to feel the golden tassels lick at her fingertips as she marched deeper into the field. The wind moved with her, walked with her, carried her along as if to say, *I understand.* She didn't feel a need to fight the invisible current, the force only mirroring the pressure inside her chest. In a strange, unexpected way, the stronger the wind blew, the more that pressure against her ribs eased and the heat beneath her skin poured through her fingertips as she slowly lifted them over the corn.

Somewhere in the distance, far away on the glittering edge of the dusky horizon, a sound rang out. She almost didn't hear it amidst the thunder of the wind in her ears, but it was there: a long, hollow, tinny sound rising into the air. It fell, then rose again. And again.

She slowed her steps. Her eyes were clear, now, and she looked up to the sky.

Dark clouds swirled, spiraled into a peak that began to dip low towards the earth—the same earth that now lifted to meet it. Stalks ripped from soil, soil ribboned into the air, and as she raised her hand to the heavens, the two points between earth and sky collided together.

Prax gazed with awe at the pillar before her, the column of earth and wind and water that promised retribution for every ounce of pain and sorrow, every deep slice of betrayal anyone ever dared to give. The pressure within her chest completely eased, poured out into the scream that melted into a laugh as she offered every teardrop to the wind.

And just as it had before, the wind accepted her grief and pain and anger as its own, mingling her teardrops with the rain.

This time, all the sirens worked.

It was the only thing anyone could hear—the deafening cry of Bogarten's storm alert system combined with those of the outlying towns that underwent major updates after the Portund fiasco. Neighbors waved each other towards shelter, mouths wide as they shouted and screamed for everyone to get somewhere safe, but nothing could be heard over the ear-piercing wail of the sirens.

Or the wind.

Aidon gripped the steering wheel until his knuckles turned white, the only things keeping his pickup truck from flipping over were his constant fishtail maneuvers and the dozen or so blank gravestones he loaded in the truck bed before he left the cemetery. The added weight kept the truck's center of gravity much lower to the ground, and his continual lurching of the wheel kept his path in a straight line. People glanced at him like he was crazy, and a small voice in the back of his mind called him an absolute lunatic.

But what could he do? He'd always been crazy for her.

Debris flew across the road and drew more than a few choice words from him as he swerved to avoid the shrapnel that threatened to pop his tires. He skidded up the highway onramp just in time for a blinding sheet of rain to nearly force him off the side rail, but the rapidly changing sky made that moment of terror short-lived.

Aidon wanted so badly to punch his fist against the steering wheel. *Should have told her sooner.*

No.

Should have never, ever left her side to begin with.

His mind raced with a thousand apologies he knew he owed her, a thousand and one explanations as to why this was the way things had gone. But did he have an actual, plausible reason why he simply left her in that hospital after he found her? Something other than his own fickle pride? He resisted a derisive snort he wanted to give to no one but himself, because it wasn't just about leaving her at the hospital, was it? He'd been a downright asshole to her face after she recovered, his bruised ego and terrified heart driving his actions and coating his tongue with words he never truly believed. Every time she managed to wedge her way past his defenses he threw them back up, and then he just suddenly expected her to welcome him with open arms once their secret was out?

He slammed his palm on the horn over and over again.

Dumbass.

Dumbass.

Dumbass.

The horizon before him looked all too familiar, the only difference was that this time, the swirling vortex of darkness descending from the clouds was haloed by the setting sun. And at least this time, the Miskwa River Valley had enough daylight and more than enough post-disaster preparation to withstand the destruction about to come.

But this time, Prax knew exactly what she was doing.

Aidon felt the moment his truck entered the outer rim of the tornado's formation when the wind suddenly stopped, and he hissed a curse when the truck lurched sharply to the left now that the constant resistance was gone. Thankfully the highway was completely clear of other vehicles; surely not even the semis wanted to risk dancing with the dark funnel that was quickly expanding into a solid wall. Neither did he, really, but this was a mess he was at least partly responsible for cleaning up.

Maybe more than partly.

His feet hit the ground and the truck door almost hit him, but he quickly jumped to the side. The furious burst of wind that slammed the door shut nearly bowled him over but he dug his heels into the rich soil and silently thanked the inventor of steel-toed boots. One arm shielded his face while the other shielded his eyes, scanning the horizon for any sign of a wholly pissed-off young woman with curly hair.

That horizon was approaching fast, the darkness widening as the wind picked up more and more debris in its wake. Blades of grass and larger blades of corn leaves whipped at him like a thousand tiny razors trying to shave him clean off the earth, but nothing was going to stop him from finding Prax. Behind him he heard his truck groan. He felt the urge to look back to make sure it was still there and not vaulting through the air towards the city line, but the urge to find Prax was stronger.

Finally he spotted her. Her back was to him, her gaze transfixed on the monstrous twister which swirled impossibly close to her. *"Prax!"*

He might as well have yelled into a black hole, the freight train roar of the winds rendered him mute by comparison. With every step, Aidon was forced to shove his feet harder into the soil just to keep him grounded, quite literally, while he trudged closer and closer to her. She couldn't hear him, and with her back turned she couldn't see him. But damn it all if he was going to go down without telling her the truth.

The sight itself was breathtaking. Golden light spun like thread inside the cyclone, the setting sun shattered and swirled into the darkness of the rich soil, the continuous ribbons of green stalks and leaves, the thunderous clouds that made up the walls of the deadly column. Even the deafening roar was almost like a song, a terrible languish only Prax could understand. And there she stood before it all, serene and splendorous, her long hair swirling around her head and torso like a siren in the deep.

If this was how she felt inside, Aidon's heart broke for her.

"Prax." He knew she still couldn't hear him, but maybe she could sense him approaching, now only just out of arm's reach. He sucked in a breath as his skin was sliced open over and over and over again, blood splattering into the wind.

Slowly, oh so slowly, Prax turned around. The pain in her eyes gave way to surprise, and she screamed something he couldn't hear but sensed it was akin to, "Run!"

He shook his head. No more running. That's what started this whole mess in the first place, and he was done running from her. "If I die, I die, but I'm not leaving you!" He tried to shout, hoping she could at least maybe read his lips.

Maybe she did. Something like recognition, and then sadness, filled her glittering eyes that danced with the light of the golden sun and she shook her head. When he didn't move, she ran to him, arms outstretched...and shoved against his chest.

He grabbed her wrists and pulled her to him. Words were useless, but actions spoke louder, and Aidon was determined to make his actions count. She struggled in his arms for a moment but he could see it was not in anger or bitterness towards him. It was almost like she was afraid. Prax glanced over her shoulder at the approaching column of wind and fury, then swept her gaze to meet Aidon's. He couldn't hear her, but he recognized the curve of her lips form the words, "Please. Run."

"No."

She recognized that word, too. Now she was angry, frustrated with his stubbornness, hot tears splashing her face and spilling into the wind to dance with his blood as she tried so hard to shove him away, to convince him to get to safety. To leave her there.

She gasped when his lips pressed to hers.

He meant for it to only be a kiss of reassurance, to calm her, but the moment he tasted her salty-sweet lips, he was a goner. Aidon felt his arms move on their own, releasing her wrists to wrap around her, hold her close, shelter her in the cocoon of his chest against the raging storm. He felt her move with him, clinging to him, her hands cupping his face as she deepened their kiss.

If he was going to die, this is exactly how he wanted to go.

From the way she felt, the way she melted in his strong embrace and swept her tongue along his, Prax completely agreed.

He broke the kiss only so he could gaze into her eyes, pressing his brow to hers as they both braced for the inevitable. His truck was as good as gone by now, and they were out of time to seek shelter. She couldn't hear the three words he whispered to the wind, to her, but she closed her eyes as they sank in anyways.

And, as the world imploded around them, he almost swore she said them back.

Aidon didn't realize both he and Prax were trembling until the ringing in his ears shifted his focus. The deafening roar was gone. The tornado behind Prax slowly dissipated, debris falling to the ground like muddied, metal rain. The sky above ceased its swirling, the clouds settled into fluffy pink and orange mounds of cotton candy as the sunset neared its final rays.

It was a long, breathless moment before Prax realized she was still very much in the warm embrace of Aidon Elrik, and she blushed bright crimson and tried to pull away.

"Prax, wait." Aidon knew he should let her go, give her space, but dammit, his arms would not obey his mind. "I'm sorry."

She sighed again, this time with more weight. Leaning into him, pressing her brow to his chest, she mumbled, "Me, too."

"What? What do you have to be sorry for?"

Prax almost laughed, casting another glance behind her at the now very torn-up field where the tornado had nearly killed them all. "Aside from that?" She nodded at the crater in the soil before gazing up at him. "I didn't give you a chance to explain. I just ran with my emotions. And then almost destroyed the world."

Aidon's mouth twitched, threatening a smile. "I probably shouldn't feel honored that you would do so on my account." He kissed her blushing cheek and inwardly triumphed at her acceptance, her forgiveness in the way she melted into him.

"My only explanation is that I am a complete and utter idiot."

She giggled, then bit her lip. Worry touched her eyes, and he kissed the corner of one to ease the worry away. "I thought you didn't like me. Actually...for a while I thought you hated me."

"Again, claiming idiocy. And pride." He sighed. "I didn't know what happened, not at first. I woke up one morning and you were gone. Just...gone." His eyes pinched shut, and he held her to him as if the feel of her would chase away the memories which still brought him to his knees. A larger part of him simply marveled at the reality that he could finally, finally hold her in his arms again. "I thought I lost you. And then I found you, but I panicked. And when you didn't come home, didn't even try to reach out to me, I don't know, I just...." Aidon sighed again, rolling his eyes inward at himself. "I don't know if you've noticed, but I put up walls pretty quickly."

"Hmm. You don't say."

"I've heard it makes me all brooding and mysterious."

Prax stifled a chuckle, not wanting to give him the benefit of a boosted ego when she was still grappling with everything thrown at her in less than a day. Her finger absentmindedly traced a pattern on his shirt as she mentally flipped through the past few weeks, the past few days, doing her best to sort it out without losing her absolute shit over it all. Again. "So when you said you'd never be over her, you really meant...."

He tipped her face up to his and stroked her cheek. "I may be a dumbass at times, but I'm a loyal dumbass. It's always been you, Love. Always." He pressed another warm kiss to the corners of her eyes, one for each word.

Prax reached up to caress the side of his face, her eyes memorizing every detail of his golden skin, his dark stubble, his strong features, and his sensual mouth. She wanted to slap him. The urge itched at her palm, to be sure. But she also wanted to kiss him. To be free of the suffocating anxiety of tiptoeing around him. To be…his. "I still don't remember," she whispered, regret heavy on her words. "I wish so much that I could. I feel it…I think I've always felt it, somewhere, deep down…."

Aidon turned his face to press his lips to the palm of her hand and nodded. "I know. It's why I couldn't just sweep you off your feet the moment you woke up. You'd been through enough trauma and didn't need my scary ass stealing you away and staking my territory."

Another sweet blush, then a flash of uncertainty. "So… what do we do now?"

"Whatever you want to do. Anything."

She nodded and thought about it for a moment. "I think…I think I need to go see my mom. She's all alone in that big house and still trying to figure out what happened to Mya. I'm worried about her. Plus, I owe her a serious apology."

Aidon gave her a small, soft smile and tucked a stray curl behind her ear. "Of course."

"But first…."

"Hm?"

Prax quirked her own soft smile. "Can we go home? I'm exhausted."

He chuckled and nodded, his heart pounding in his chest with elation at the sound of "home" on her lips referring to his place. "Absolutely. I don't know about you, but I've had the wind knocked out of me."

She groaned and he laughed, and together they carefully made their way back to where he was overjoyed to find his gleaming black F150 still standing, still intact, just a little worse for wear. Prax didn't even question the pile of gravestones in the back, just shrugged and climbed into the passenger seat. The part of her that felt, rather than remembered, guided her hand to his and threaded her fingers with his. Aidon gave her hand a squeeze and pressed a warm kiss to her fingers as they drove away from the field.

It would be several days of personal leave, then sick leave, before Demi Sadeh felt the energy to sit upright without vomiting or breaking into sobbing fits of grief.

Prax found her asleep in the family room, one hand clutching the bones of her youngest daughter, the other tucked under her head on the hearth. Aidon helped carry the grieving mother to her room, Prax turned down the blankets and both of them eased her into the warmth and safety of her bed.

He texted Ralph, who quickly pulled up in the gravel driveway in his truck, completely unprepared for the ghastly sight in the family room. "You know I'm gonna have to file a report with Sulis," he warned them, unable to look away from the bones.

"There should be one already on file, just under Missing Persons." Prax sank onto the couch, doing her best to remain calm and not lurch every time she glanced over at what remained of her beloved sister. "We found her. Well...part of her."

"Goddamn." Ralph finally tore his gaze away and looked towards Aidon. "You know I mean that. God damn the bastard who did this to her, whoever he is."

Aidon stood behind the couch, hands braced on either side of Prax—giving her space while reassuring her she wasn't alone. "What do you know about Demi's husband?"

"Demi's husband?" Ralph repeated, furrowing his brow as he struggled to remember if he'd ever met the guy. "Can't say I ever met him personally, we didn't exactly run in the same circles."

Prax turned to Aidon. "Jared? What about him?" She remembered what her mother had said about his disappearance coinciding with Mya's, and gasped. "You don't think he had anything to do with this?"

Aidon tried to muster a small smile but only managed a very tight, strained grimace as he tucked a curl behind her ear. "You're not the only one who sees visions, Love." He glanced back up at Ralph, who was watching the pair with no small amount of glee. Aidon ignored the giddy look and pointedly glanced at the bones, which made the city morgue director clear his throat and remember why he was there. "Let Sulis know what we found, and tell her I'll be by to give a statement. Demi, too, when she's ready."

Ralph nodded and went to work taking pictures of the scene, marked any areas that needed further investigation, and carefully set the bones in a box marked for the forensics office. "I don't suppose you have any idea where the rest of her is?" He shot an apologetic glance towards Prax, who hid her face in Aidon's arm.

"We're still looking. We'll let you know if we find anything more. I think we'd just appreciate keeping the police away from here for the time being, if you don't mind."

"You bet." Ralph hesitated, wanting to give Prax some form of sympathy as he carried Mya's remains from the room, but nothing came to mind. So he simply nodded and left the family to grieve in their own way.

The minutes ticked by in silence. Aidon didn't move, no

matter how heavy his arms felt as he braced them on the back of the couch, lest he disturb Prax in her moment. Finally, she blinked and sat up, gestured for him to sit with her, then nestled into his open arms and buried her face in his chest. "I don't want to leave Mom alone, but I hate this house so, so much right now," she mumbled into his shirt.

He stroked a hand over her back, his fingers smoothing her curls away from her face and dancing lightly in her soft tangles. "You tell me where you want to go, and we'll go. You tell me you want my ass outta here, and I'll give you space. Whatever you need."

"I need answers."

The laugh came unbidden, shaking his chest and making her lift her head just enough to peer up at him. Aidon took a breath to regain his Serious Face. "Sorry. It's just, you have no idea how much I've missed your fire. Most women would be bereft or halfway through a pint of ice cream or begging me for grief sex, and all of those are equally valid options." He ignored the Look she gave him at the mention of that last option. "Not you. Not Prax Sadeh, when there are answers to be found and justice to be served."

"I'm too antsy to be bereft. And we're out of ice cream."

He cocked a brow.

Prax laid her head back down on his chest so he wouldn't see her impish smile. "I'll get back to you on the grief sex. Just don't run out, okay?"

"I wouldn't dream of it." And he meant every word.

Despite the lack of police activity at the Sadeh home, the news still spread among the community, especially after Prax paid a discreet visit to the university to speak to the president and explain her mother's impending lengthy absence. With Aidon's help, and—she suspected—Ralph's professional advice, she was able to weave a plausible story that wouldn't be an outright lie, but also wouldn't mention anything about ghosts or dismembered arms decaying inside chimneys. The thought was enough to keep her on the constant edge of sorrow, which helped hasten the necessary conversations as the college arranged to reschedule the upcoming summer midterms. Thankfully, being summer, it wasn't a hefty undertaking for anyone, and the few students Dr. Sadeh currently oversaw were more than happy to accommodate.

Aidon left Prax alone in that big house only long enough to pack a bag and return with Spot, who was all too happy to pad his way through the greenery and stone until he found Prax curled up in the family library, a scrapbook spread across her thighs. She nearly dropped the book when Spot surprised her with a sweet nuzzle, the tears suddenly flowing as she hugged his neck and buried her own nose in his fur. As if he knew what she'd been through, what she still feared lurking in the shadows, he tested the limits of the loveseat and settled in around her. The soft sound of his panting and periodic licks on her arm lifted so much tension she didn't realize she'd been holding until now.

"This is me not being jealous of a dog," Aidon playfully

grumbled when he walked in to find Prax nearly encompassed by the giant mass of black fur. He set a bag of Chinese takeout on the coffee table and offered her a pair of chopsticks. "I got us two orders of steamed dumplings, since you never, ever share."

Prax licked her lips at the delicious smell of chicken and ginger sauce, her stomach reminding her of other senses she'd completely forgotten in the chaos—like hunger. "Is it weird that I don't remember my favorite foods and yet I feel like all of them are in this bag?"

"And this is me not getting my feelings hurt." He squeezed himself onto a papasan chair and handed her a foil tray filled with dumplings and ginger sauce. "I like to think my habit of ordering your favorite foods and drinks would be counted as this thing called 'effort'. As in oh my gosh, Aidon is making an effort to help me remember things!" His girlish impression of Prax made her snort up a lo mein noodle, and he grinned ear to ear. "Plus, if that were to fail, which it did, I could at least impress you with my impeccable taste in alcohol and takeout."

She traded her carton of chicken lo mein for the tray of steamed dumplings on her lap, careful to not drip on the photo album she'd set aside while also careful to not tempt the patient floof who kept eyeing the dumplings imploringly. Prax waited for Aidon to focus his attention on cracking open his can of pop and quietly slipped Spot a dumpling. "Well, now that I know I'm not the Other Woman, it's going to be easier to sort things out. Eventually."

"You're never going to let me live that down, are you?"

"Not a chance."

Aidon stuffed his mouth with sesame chicken just to have an excuse not to respond right away while he scrambled to think of a decent explanation. When it finally came to him, he shrugged and swigged his pop. "Okay, look. Here's what happened. And don't laugh."

"I make no promises."

He narrowed his eyes at her. She wasn't the least bit intimidated, his luscious mouth curved too easily into that smile that always told her he loved her mischief. "Stubborn woman," he muttered. "Anyways, while I was searching heaven and earth for you, out of my mind with worry, it became apparent that my natural state of sexiness was problematic and drew too much attention." He grinned when she rolled her eyes. "No, but seriously—no matter what happened to you, you're my wife. And I'm your husband. Nothing changed that, and nothing will ever change that." A fleeting worry shadowed his face, and he swallowed. "I hope."

Prax realized what he meant, what he worried about, and she wanted to give him words of comfort that just didn't come to mind as easily as she wanted them to. No memories meant no memories from their marriage, good or bad. Aidon Elrik was just some guy she met a few weeks ago.

No. Not just "some guy".

There it was again, a nagging feeling in the deepest part of her being that argued every time she tried to tuck him away in some category other than the one that scared her the most. Not because she felt he wasn't good enough for her.

She worried she wasn't good enough for *him.*

"If it helps," she offered with a coy smile, "I've been crushing pretty hard on you since I saw you in the coffee shop. Grumpy broodiness and all."

That did seem to help, his smile breaking into yet another grin. "I guess I should be relieved that you've seen me at my worst and haven't run away screaming. Anyways, back to my explanation for being a dumbass." He scooped another piece of chicken into his mouth just to make her hang on the dramatic pause. "I didn't actually think that whole thing through. You know, letting everyone know I'm married but not saying to whom. I was so worried about making sure you wouldn't be traumatized that it never occurred to me that my so-called cover story would backfire."

"Traumatized?"

"You're going to make me spell it out for you, aren't you."

Prax nodded, eyes wide with anticipation.

Aidon rubbed the back of his neck and made an effort to look everywhere but directly at her. "Donn wasn't exaggerating, smashed as he was. At the bar. When he called me out for wanting you every waking moment of every day." He mumbled the last part into his carton of sesame chicken, but she heard every word and deeply blushed. "It just didn't feel right pushing marital obligations on you when for all you know, I'm some rando you met in a graveyard. Although it wouldn't be the first time."

"Wait...I meet random guys in graveyards?"

He choked on his fried rice. "No!" He thumped his chest and chugged from the silver can resting on the coffee table, which only made it worse. "Help, I'm dying," he wheezed.

Prax giggled and rushed to his side, thumping his back until he waved his hand and successfully cleared his throat. When he seemed to be breathing properly again, she grabbed his drink and handed it to him to try again. He gave it a careful sip and peered at her over the lid. "Please promise me, if you're ever meeting random guys in graveyards, it's because we're luring them into a trap or something that involves me kicking their ass."

"I promise." She grinned.

No other room felt quite as safe, or as comfortable, so they set up a makeshift camp in the middle of the small library with pillows and blankets from her room and the atrium. Aidon was the one to fetch everything, as the horror Prax experienced in the atrium was still too fresh—and the hall that led to her bedroom also led to the family room with the tainted chimney. It was strange, to Prax, that the house felt a thousand times more haunted by the memory of Mya than it did when her spirit walked and talked within its rooms.

What didn't feel strange at all, despite the logic that dictated it *should* feel strange, was Aidon's closeness as they lay together on the pillows and wrapped up in blankets. At first he suggested he sleep on the floor and she on the loveseat, but something felt...off. She lasted all of two minutes on the couch before she felt the need to tiptoe over his legs and lay down beside him, tucking herself in his warmth as much as she could. He pulled one of the heavier knitted blankets over them, and she held his arm around her until he wrapped it around her waist and pulled her close.

Moonlight bathed the room in soft, silvery light, framed in the velvet sky with glittering stars that promised swift sleep should she begin to count them. Prax felt Aidon's thumb brush back and forth over her wrist where he held her, safe in his arms, the motion soothing even as it gradually slowed. His breath softened into a deep sleep, warm and damp against the nape of her neck. She felt her eyelids grow heavy, her body finally able to completely relax knowing she was safe and protected in the arms of a man who'd already gone to great lengths to ensure her well-being, both of them guarded by the giant mastiff snoring on the couch.

"What was that?"

Greg pressed his hand over her mouth, and Sarah froze.

She wasn't scared of him. She was scared of whatever, whoever, they were running from that made him as terrified as he looked.

"We have to keep moving," he whispered, just audible enough for her to understand and nod. Tears glistened on her face in the moonlight, but he didn't give her time to address what was causing them.

They didn't have time to talk about the patch of freshly dug earth they left behind at the old farmhouse.

Footsteps sounded behind them, only a few yards away, and it was all she could do not to scream. Greg kept his hand clamped over her mouth but gently, silently, urged her to keep quiet, to hold still while they waited behind a tree to see who, or what, would emerge from the brush.

A doe stepped into the small clearing by the stream and dipped her head to drink.

Sarah looked as if she were about to pass out, her breath too quick

as panic and fear really began to set in. She shook her head at him as if to say, "I can't do this anymore, I can't keep going," but he urged her to keep going, just a little further.

It was always just a little further, ever since his white van pulled into Fulton Park and he told them to get in.

They weren't meant to travel by foot, that much she figured out early on. It was when the radio broadcasted the Amber Alert that Greg began to panic. When they stopped at his house for a late lunch and bathroom break, the television news showed pictures of his van driving by Fulton Park. They had his license plate number, and now his address.

Sarah Evans had been walking ever since.

They were supposed to spend at least a day resting in the old farmhouse, far enough away from the city limits and deep enough in the woods to avoid the search, or whoever it was that made Greg sweat between his fingers and glance outside the windows every thirty seconds. Something started to make Sarah think he wasn't the bad guy at all—that he was, in actuality, trying to save them from the bad guy.

But then Rachel panicked.

Sarah hiccuped with an unbidden sob and it made her stumble over a small tree root protruding from the ground. Greg caught her before she fell and he looked as if he wanted to scold her, but one glance at her face made him soften with sympathy. He gave her a small pat on her back and ushered her forward, always casting glances back behind them.

Another branch snapped. This time the sound was too loud to be a deer.

One of the shadows shifted, thickened, drew closer until it became a man, his face stoic and cold as he calmly approached them. "Hand her over," he said, his voice devoid of emotion.

Greg shoved Sarah behind him and edged them back towards the thick of the trees. "I have my orders, just as you," he panted. "You know I can't do that."

The shadowed man stepped closer, the moonlight illuminating his face as he steadily approached the pair. "I'm not going to ask nicely again," said Jared McCready, hand outstretched towards the young girl. "She's coming with me."

Greg slowly turned to Sarah, his hand on her back. Her eyes widened, she shook her head, begged with her tear-streaked face not to surrender her to the darkness fast approaching. For the first time since they met, he gave her the barest hint of a smile.

"Run."

The hand on her back shoved her hard, but didn't knock her to her knees—the wind picked up enough that she gained momentum and distance from that one small advantage. She heard the Shadow Man swear under his breath and Greg struggle fiercely against him.

"Sarah!"

She spun around, her heart threatening to burst through her ribcage.

The Shadow Man gripped Greg by his hair, shoved him to his knees, yanked his head back. Greg tried to yank himself free. "Sarah!" He screamed, no longer caring who heard them. "Don't stop! Never stop!"

His voice cut off with a sickening wet gurgle, the knife in Jared McCready's fist nearly severing his head off completely.

Sarah screamed. She wanted to keep screaming, to collapse in terror, but the wind pushed at her again, picking up speed and whipping through the trees in a way that made her scramble for the safety of the thicker trees, the darker woods, anything that looked like shelter.

Jared wiped the hunting knife on Greg's shirt and tucked it back into his pocket. He wasn't worried about Sarah's head start; he'd seen the direction she ran, seen how tired she was. His hunt was only beginning, but her run was coming to an end.

And soon, so very soon, his debt would finally be paid.

Prax wheezed, the air suddenly returning to her lungs.

She was still in the library, still bathed in silver moonlight. Still safe in the arms of Aidon Elrik, who snored rather loudly into her mass of wild curls with a ferocity that rivaled Spot's canine nostrils.

So very, very carefully, she peeled back the blanket and slipped out from under his wonderfully heavy arm. After a second thought, she replaced herself with a thick throw pillow and watched him hug it to his chest, making her own squeeze with affection that felt unfamiliar and familiar all at once.

Her eyes scanned the darkened room for anything to write with, finding the receipt from their takeout but no pen. *Dammit.* She wanted to text him, but worried the ping would wake him from what looked like a much-needed deep sleep. *Text him in the morning.*

A quick glance at her phone in the kitchen told her it was already morning, 3AM to be exact.

Text him after sunrise.

She slid her feet into her slip-on sneakers and made sure to carefully, slowly, lift the keys from his jacket pocket and wrap her fist around it so they wouldn't jingle. *Note to self: save up for a car.* She hoped he'd be understanding once he found out where she went and why.

Prax nudged the front door open, then tiptoed across the gravel to Aidon's beast of an F-150 parked just along the curve. Thank heavens there was a step and handle to hoist herself up with, otherwise half the morning would be wasted just trying to get into the driver's seat.

It still took a few tries.

She settled into the leather seat that smelled so much like him, for a moment she started to second-guess her plan. But the nightmare came rushing back, far too vivid and tangible to be "just a dream", and she remembered the little girl now alone and running for her life.

Now, if Prax could just figure out how to adjust the seat so her feet could reach the pedals....

Hot, damp breath huffed on her arm and she nearly jumped out of her skin with a shriek. Spot stared back at her in the rearview mirror, tongue lolled out to the side as he made himself comfortable in the backseat of the cab. He, too, seemed to have second thoughts, and it was by some miracle he managed to squeeze his way to the front passenger seat from between the snug space of the armrest.

The front door to the house looked closed, but Prax was admittedly so distracted by her thoughts, her plan, her vision, she probably wouldn't have felt a giant floof climb over her and into the truck.

"Look, it's bad enough I'm stealing his truck," she said to her canine companion. "I don't need to get in trouble for stealing his dog."

Spot gave her a Look, the kind that said on no uncertain terms was she going *anywhere* without him.

Prax sighed. Well, maybe it would be good to have a backup partner with teeth and claws. "Remind me to fuel up before we get back, okay? And grab donuts. He likes donuts, right?" *Note to self: learn Aidon's favorite foods. Use as bribery and tribute.*

The truck was blessedly quiet as she popped it into neutral and guided it down the driveway, constantly glancing in front and behind to make sure the path was clear.

Story of my life.

Once they rolled out onto the pavement, Prax tapped the brake and turned the engine on. It revved to life with a satisfying rumble, and a strong sense of distinct masculinity lanced through her with a thrill. This wasn't just a pickup truck, this was a freaking war chariot. She adjusted the seat once more for good measure and gripped the steering wheel tight in one hand, throwing the shift into gear with the other.

"Hang on, honey. I'm coming."

D ammit!"

The closest Prax could get to the trail that led to where she saw Sarah was one of the small park shelter areas campers frequented during favorable weather. Not that the weather was bad at the moment, just a little windy, but recent meteorological events had most of Bogarten skittish about being caught outside without ample shelter in place, and parks like this defined "shelter" as "planks of wood to keep the rain slightly away".

She parked Aidon's truck as close as she could to the start of the overgrown trail, a part of her aware this might be the only way to leave breadcrumbs for the police to find her should the worst happen.

No. Can't think that way.

Spot whined and looked at her, his eyes barely visible under all that thick fur but still asking her if she was sure she wanted to do this.

"There's a little girl out there," Prax explained, more for herself to bolster her courage. "She's alone, she's scared, and she's being hunted. No one else knows how to find her."

That seemed to be enough for him, and he nosed the passenger door until she hopped out and opened it for him. As his massive bulk plopped down beside her, she was suddenly grateful for his insistent companionship—he was basically a panting bear, dark black fur covering powerful muscles and framing deadly teeth. If push came to shove, Spot was someone Prax definitely wanted in her corner.

The early morning mist clung thick and heavy on the dark emerald leaves of ivy and ferns which wrapped around the trees, and under any other circumstances, this would probably be a mystical, magical place to explore and inspire imagination. It truly looked like an image out of a fairytale, the canopy overhead mirroring the canopy of leaves much closer to the ground where tiny creatures could easily hide.

But it wasn't a fairytale book Prax recognized these woods from. It was a series of pictures taped inside Mya's scrapbook, photographs snapped when her father took her camping out here two summers ago.

Poor Greg probably had no idea he'd steered his charge into the very same woods their pursuer knew like the back of his hand.

The memory of Jared McCready drawing his blade across the man's throat made her steps quicken, and she did her best to run through the trees without causing too much rustling or snapping of twigs. Spot ran beside her, silent and foreboding in the way his fur nearly matched the shadows still clinging to pockets of night. He nudged her side now and then as if to reassure her she wasn't alone, he wasn't going to run off anywhere without her.

Spot stopped in his tracks, sniffing the air with a sudden, low growl. But then he stopped, his ears perked up, and he trotted forward, still careful to keep himself between Prax and whatever—or whoever—he'd just scented.

She saw the blood first, droplets sprayed all around the

leaves and misted on the tree where the knife had flicked on the pull. It was still too dark to see the red hue, but she didn't feel the need for vivid details; she'd had plenty of that in her nightmare, thanks.

"What are you doing way out here?"

The voice was light and friendly, and Prax realized after a beat that it was directed towards Spot, who panted happily and licked the hand that reached for his ears. The man stood from where he crouched over who she assumed to be Greg, and in the faint morning light, she suddenly recognized his face. "Donn?"

"Let me rephrase that. What are *you* doing here?" Donn wiped his hands on his jeans as he gaped at her.

"I could ask you the same thing." She pointedly glanced between him, his bloodied hands, and the body slumped in the damp earth behind him.

Donn's eyes widened. "Oh, Janey Mack," he muttered, "it's not what this looks like, I swear."

She managed a smile, given the circumstances. "I know. I saw what happened."

"You did?" He stepped closer, then rolled his eyes at himself. "You did. Of course, you did."

"So...time for you to answer *my* question."

Donn stole another glance at Greg's body and sighed. "I finally caught a lead on that bastard who killed Jenny's family, led me way out here. Looks like a dead end, though, if you'll forgive the expression." He paused and squinted at her. "Wait. You didn't tell me what you're doing out in the middle of nowhere at this ungodly hour."

Might as well, more backup. "Like I said, I saw what happened here, in a vision. It's Sarah Evans. She's in trouble, and she's all alone now." Her eyes scanned the trees, silently cursing at the darkness of early dawn. "I saw her go that way," she pointed to a thicket across the small clearing, "and he followed her."

"Who?"

"The guy hunting her. The guy who killed Greg." She winced at the ghastly sight of Greg's nearly-beheaded body as she edged her way past. "Mya's father."

Donn sucked in a breath. "That is...all sorts of...."

"Yeah. And Aidon thinks he killed Mya, too."

"Oh! Speaking of his dark lordship," Donn teased as they started into the thicket, Spot giving the body one last sniff before he huffed and trotted after them, "does he have any idea where you are? What you're up to?"

Prax focused her eyes on the path ahead, for any sign of Sarah, but mostly to avoid meeting Donn's curious gaze. "Remind me to text him when it's not the buttcrack of dawn."

Spot bristled, then growled, low and quiet as he pressed to Prax's side and started nudging her behind him. Donn darted his eyes around, looking for whatever made the dog's hackles rise, but he couldn't see anything. There had to be something, because Spot's growling only deepened, his shoulder pressing harder against the woman until she was practically pinned against a tree.

She heard a soft whimper, and looked up.

Sarah Evans straddled a tree branch, knuckles white as she clung for dear life and struggled to keep herself from screaming.

Prax wanted to call up to her, to reassure her help had arrived, but Spot's growl took on an unearthly note of danger and he snapped his teeth, yanking her gaze to the shadows in front of her. At first, she couldn't see anything, but the shadows shifted and swayed, so much like in her dream, until Jared McCready stepped forward from them and gave her the tiniest smile.

"Mya?"

"*You.*" Now it was Donn's voice that held the low, otherworldly tone that made Prax's pulse race and her body suddenly will itself to blend into the tree. His fists clenched, opened, clenched, every muscle in his lean body tensed and poised for the lunge. "*You have a debt to pay.*"

Jared's eyes widened in horror, his steps faltering as he took a sudden step back away from Prax and the giant black canine snarling for an excuse to go for his throat. "Y-y-you're not with them. I don't know you. I d-d-don't owe you anything!"

"*Oh, you know me very well.*"

A moment passed, a breath, a gasp, a tick in the cog of someone's watch, and Prax saw something reflect in Jared's silver-dollar eyes. He screamed, fell back over his own two feet, scrambled to get away from the man who now swaggered towards him with steadfast determination.

Another whimper from overhead reminded Prax of her discovery, and she waited until Donn had Jared McCready's undivided attention before she reached up to the very frightened Sarah Evans. "It's okay, sweetie, I'm here to help you. I'm here to take you home."

Sarah tucked her feet up under herself as much as she could without losing her grip on the branch and violently shook her head. "I can't go home. I can't go back."

Prax hesitated. She was right. From Lacey's yet unsolved case file to Greg's final words, going back sounded like it would be far more dangerous for the young girl than going forward. To where, Prax had no idea, but they'd figure that out once they got away from Jared McCready. "Okay, honey, I'm with you. We'll get you somewhere safe, okay? That's all I want to do, just get you somewhere safe."

Finally, Sarah nodded, and she eased herself down from the limb and into Prax's waiting arms. Spot leaned against the tree to cushion any slips or falls, and his furry presence made Sarah smile for the first time in days.

"No!"

Jared shouted angrily across the woods, struggling against Donn's firm grasp on the man as he dragged him deeper into the trees. Something silver flashed in his hand and before Prax could scream a warning, Jared sank the hunting knife into Donn's side.

"Donn!"

The Shadow Man wrenched himself away from Donn's loosened grip and swiped his silver blade again, landing it with a solid grunt and sickening thud in Donn's chest. He pulled, slashed again, and Prax watched in horror as Donn's head whipped unnaturally to the left.

Sarah screamed.

Jared fisted his knife and beelined towards his prey, who tried her best to scramble back up the tree no matter how much the bark scraped and bloodied her fingers. Prax grabbed the girl and shoved her away into a larger clearing. "Run!"

Spot lunged at the man, barking and snapping ferociously at his throat. Prax screamed for Spot to move away, to back down before the knife sank into him, too, but even as it did and she heard the dog whine in pain, he didn't stop giving the Shadow Man snarling, drooling, razor-sharp hell. His teeth clamped down on the man's slashing arm and ripped hard, making Jared scream with gut-wrenching pain. The knife fell from the man's fingers, and it was all he could do to shove the beast off him just to wriggle away and roll back onto her feet.

Prax ran after Sarah, determined to be the final wall of defense between the little girl and the monster who pursued them. She felt the heat and adrenaline throb under her skin, propelling her forward. "Sarah! Run! *Run!*"

Wind blustered around them, whipping over the tall grass and hissing through the trees as they raced for the next thicket, the next dark patch, the next possibility of a hiding place just long enough to map out their next move. Sarah darted into the treeline and stopped, hesitated, turned to see if Prax was close behind.

She was, in a way, but the wind was growing too strong for her to make a straight path towards the trees. The prairie around her seemed to thicken, reaching higher the further she pushed through, making it difficult to follow Sarah's trail. Prax braced herself against the air current, shielding her eyes with her arm as blades of grass started lashing at her skin. "Sarah!" She saw the girl perk up at her name, and she hoped her voice would carry over the wind and through the grass. "Sarah! Whatever you do, keep running! Don't look back!" She heard Greg's voice in her mind and echoed him from the world beyond. *"Don't stop! Never stop!"*

Something else carried on the wind, a howl, and another... she couldn't be sure if it was Spot or just the sound of hollowed branches groaning under the growing force pressing against them. She didn't stop to ponder, didn't stop at all until her feet touched the tree line and she saw Sarah dart away and far out of sight.

Prax turned around. Braced her feet in the soft earth.

Jared limped through the clearing towards her, his face pale and plastered with a madness that all but distorted his features into something no longer human.

That pressure built inside her chest again, easing away as the wind increased its speed, making weaker trees on the outer line bend under its might. Her skin stung and burned, pulsating in a way that should have hurt—but instead it sharpened her focus.

She closed her eyes and saw Mya's face smiling back at her, heard her laughter and teases, felt her arms wrap around her in a warm, all-too-living hug.

She saw Rachel's sweet face, afraid of the man who took them but trusting her big sister to protect her.

I should have been there to protect you.

Prax's eyes snapped open.

Jared roared and threw himself at her, and while the move took her by surprise, the fury and pain within kept her steady and planted in the fertile soil. She felt her own war cry rip from her chest, from deep in her soul, and she threw her arm over her eyes to shield her face from his impact, ready to tumble and fight until one of them stopped breathing.

The hit never came.

The wind calmed, slowed with the same swift retreat as it had in the cornfield. Prax hesitated to lower her arm. She did, inch by inch, willing her lungs to match her heart in function so she didn't pass out there in the treeline. When she saw the sight in front of her, she almost passed out anyway.

Jared hung in the air, suspended by a thick tree root impaled through his chest. His face was twisted in shock, his limbs limp even as his fingers still curled like claws. Blood and spittle dripped from his open mouth, and the stuff covering the root extending out of his chest did not bear further mentioning. Suffice it to say, Jared McCready was wholly and thoroughly dead.

A figure shifted in the tall prairie grass. Prax whipped her gaze to see who it was, fists poised and ready for a fight. But nothing more than a garter snake slithered by her feet, silent and uncaring about the gruesome sight it passed beneath.

Spot lay on his side in the thicket, and Prax swallowed hard as she slowly approached her sweet canine friend. "Oh god, what have I done?" She groaned, a lump forming in her throat. Her tears didn't get a chance to fall, for the floof lifted his head and panted happily at the sight of her, not without a few complaining whines. "Spot!" She cried, throwing her arms around his furry neck. He let out another whine and she let go, suddenly aware of his injuries, then breathed a sigh of relief. He was injured, for sure, but only in his shoulder. Blood matted his fur but it looked to have congealed and started to scab over enough for them to make it back home and to a vet.

This time the howl she heard ring through the air was most definitely another dog, echoed by yet another. Prax stilled, reaching for anything big enough to fight with to protect her beloved guardian. Her hands found a stick and she poised to strike, hovering as much as she could over Spot's injured bulk. He, for his part, seemed not the least bit concerned about the approaching danger, and instead did his best to roll onto his haunches and...bark.

A head poked around one of the trees, tongue lolled out to one side. A black Tibetan mastiff, identical to Spot, trotted happily over to the pair and gave Prax a long, slobbery lick.

"Spot!"

She froze. She knew *that* voice.

A very exasperated, angry, relieved, confused, horrified, overjoyed Aidon Elrik jogged into the thicket, flanked by yet another black Tibetan mastiff. Before Prax could say a word, he held up his hand, his chest heaving as he caught his breath. She tried to say something but he turned that upheld hand into an upheld finger, his jaw set as he breathed through his nose to either cool down or wind up.

"Okay." Aidon lowered his arm just to fold both across his chest. "Now that I see you're alive and uninjured...where the *hell* have you been?!"

Prax never knew she could be so happy to see someone who was so emotionally unbalanced at that exact moment. Something about everything leading up to this, all the fear and adrenaline and rage, the gut-wrenching horror and heart-pounding madness...pissed-off Aidon Elrik was the most beautiful sight to behold. She didn't care his arms were like steel bands wrapped across his still-heaving chest; Prax stumbled over her own two feet just to fall against him, hold his face in her hands, and kiss his fury-puckered lips.

Those steel bands fell away from his chest to wrap around her, and he held her so tight against him she was pretty sure he would never let her go. And she was, not so surprisingly, totally okay with that.

She felt his hand slide up to tangle in her hair, fisting the curls at the nape of her neck as he deepened the kiss, tasting her as if he'd never get another chance.

To be fair, he almost didn't.

Aidon pulled away only a fraction of an inch, just enough to catch his breath for a whole new reason. "I woke up and you were gone. Again. Do you have any idea how terrified that made me?" His voice rasped with the lump in his throat.

"Sorry." She really was; she'd honestly forgotten in the midst of her determined rush to save Sarah just what sneaking out would mean to him. "How did you find me?"

"Lojack. On my truck. That you *stole*." He grit his teeth and widened his eyes, nose to nose with her as he scolded her. Darn it all, he couldn't help but grin when she blushed and giggled with embarrassment. "We need to talk about your grand theft auto, Miss Carjacker."

Prax snorted. "I think we need to talk about your *three dogs*."

Aidon leaned back and glanced around at the giant mastiffs lumbering around the thicket, licking their wounded brother, sniffing for trouble and panting when it seemed the coast was clear. "What are you talking about? I've always had three dogs."

"What? Since when?"

"Since always?" Crouching low beside the injured canine, Aidon frowned and gently touched his fingers to the wound. "Aw, buddy, what's she gone and got you into?" He leaned into Spot's loving kisses and stroked his fur, careful to mind the bloodied patch that did seem to be doing better already.

Prax gaped at all three dogs, who were now happily licking their master and shoving each other to get their turns hugging

321

and nuzzling him. They were the source of the howls, the beasts who'd been tracking her and Spot while the Shadow Man—Jared, as he once was—hunted Sarah and lost his mind to whatever hellish madness gripped him to the very end. "How...?"

Aidon shrugged mid-belly rub, then cocked a lopsided smile. "I always have one with me, one guarding the grounds, one as a backup in either direction. They take shifts."

"They take shifts." It did serve to explain how she'd been so surprised in the truck—the front door to the house *was* closed. "Okay," she breathed, and she reached down to pet one who whined and nuzzled her side. "What are their names?"

"Spot."

She wished so much to have some form of response to that, but literally nothing came to mind.

One of the Spots sniffed around the leaves bordering the thicket, then let out a loud whine and short bark towards the darker trees a few yards away. Prax's heart dropped into her stomach when she suddenly remembered...*Donn*. She scrambled to her feet to stop Aidon and his canine entourage from stumbling across what was sure to be a gruesome, and traumatic, sight. "Wait! Don't—"

Aidon glanced over his shoulder at her, brow scrunched, and shouldered his way into the trees. She waited for his horrified gasp, a shout, anything. But all she heard was, "All right, drama queen." A grunt, a groan, and she saw him reach down to where Donn lay...and help the man to his feet.

"Donn?" The name choked from her throat, and it was all she could do to stumble through the thicket over to where the not-at-all-dead man stood rubbing his neck and grumbling to Aidon something about "annoying" and "actual pain in the neck". She felt her eyes widen until they felt like they'd bulge from her skull. "I saw...I swear I saw him kill you."

Donn grinned. "What? Me? Nah." He rolled his neck from side to side and stretched his arms, twisting from side to side, working out kinks from his stiff limbs. "Made me need to go schedule a massage, maybe."

"No." Prax frowned. "Donn, I *know* what I saw." It was horrible. The memory too fresh. The pit in her stomach too heavy, too real. "You were...you..." Now it was her turn to choke on the lump in her throat, the tears spilling hot down her dirt-streaked face. Maybe it was watching that man practically gut her friend right in front of her, maybe it was knowing the same had been done to her sister, maybe it was the weight of the entire morning finally lifting from her shoulders. Whatever broke the dam did so full-force and she burst into sobs.

"Hey. Hey," Donn cooed and wrapped his arms around her, gently rocking her as he wiped away her tears. "It was dark, it was intense, there was a lot going on, and you were busy being a total badass. He just cold-cocked me is all. And, speaking of, where is he? I have a few hits to return." He eased her back and peered around the woods, his jaw and fists suddenly clenched.

Prax instantly flushed from neck to brow and turned her attention back to the injured Spot, who managed to limp over to them and lean against her with a small whine. "He's gone."

"Gone."

"Yup."

Donn and Aidon exchanged glances. "It was him," Donn ground out. "This whole time it was Jared goddamned Mc-Cready. That gobshite is not getting away that easily, mark my words." A whispered curse, another scan of the woods surrounding them. "He's got a debt to pay and he will, oh he *will*, pay it. But until then," he glanced back at Aidon, "I think it's time to call Sulis."

By the time Sheriff Brigit Sulis managed to quarantine the woods stretching from the outer edge of Fulton Park all the way to the northern curve of Miska River in Reddon County, national news teams had descended upon the area and swarmed around the yellow tape, shoving to get a good view of each crime scene. "Damned vultures," Sulis muttered to her deputy. She waved her hands at a news team to back away from the service vehicles and make room for Ralph and his team to squeeze in and get to work.

The anonymous tip which led to an abandoned farmhouse just three miles north of Fulton Park also hinted at where to dig—although it wasn't difficult to find the patch of upturned earth underneath the old hickory tree. Ralph knew to expect the small body carefully wrapped in faded gingham sheets under only a foot of soil; it still didn't make it any easier to carry her in his arms to the stretcher waiting to take her home.

What he didn't expect was for his assistant, Phil, to signal him back to the makeshift grave and point at another piece of fabric sticking out of the dirt. They ripped at the sod together, mindful but quick, and Ralph sat on his heels when Phil's fingers brushed over the smooth cranium of another, older body. He didn't have to call Sulis over, she noticed the way he froze and stared at the hole in the ground, and marched over to see what was wrong.

"Shit."

Cameras flashed and footage rolled as reporters scrambled to relay the real-time discovery unfolding before them, and Sulis no longer cared. *Let them.* Let them show the world what kind of monsters haunted these woods.

It would be another three hours before the forensic team—most of them reinforcements from the FBI—finally established the totality of what they were looking at...and standing on. Cadaver dogs sniffed around the twenty-one graves of girls and women surrounding the farmhouse, and Sulis' heart sank every time another howl echoed through the trees.

She needed a break from the ghastly scene, and the irony was not lost on her when she stepped under the police tape of another crime scene several miles north of the farmhouse. The body of Greg Olson was already photographed, outlined, and on the way to the morgue, and judging by the sheer amount of blood covering the leaves and vines and ashwood bark, she was grateful for small favors. The coffee she chugged on her way to respond to the "anonymous tip" threatened to revisit the wrong way.

"It just doesn't make sense." The forensic tech, a recent grad from the university, shook his head as he held a fist to his mouth. "Nothing ever happens here."

"Which is exactly why everything happens here," grumbled Sulis. She scanned the thicket, not really looking for anything in particular, and not sure she wanted to find anything more than the hellscape they already stood in. But dammit, something caught her eye across the clearing—beyond their investigative radius. She glanced around, saw that everyone else was buried in their work, and nodded to the tech. "I need a minute."

He grimaced with a scoff. "Take an hour, no one will blame you."

She made sure her steps were casual, slow, nothing to draw attention from anyone skimming the peripherals of the area. The prairie grass was nowhere near the height of the old days, back before the first covered wagons rolled in and camped along the riverbank, but it was still tall and thick enough to conceal more secrets than she cared to discover. Sometimes the wisest thing to do was to leave well enough alone. Let sleeping snakes lie under their rocks in peace. Only a fool kicked the nest and complained about the bite.

A gentle breeze rustled the grass, parting just enough to allow glimpses at the dark shape she'd seen across the clearing.

No words, not any she'd uttered in ages, dared escape her tongue as she slowly tugged a pack of cigarettes from her pocket and flicked the lighter on. She couldn't look away from the gruesome sight in front of her.

It'd been a very, very long time since she'd seen a warning like this.

A re you ready?"

Demi stared at the tissue twisted between her fingers. Would she ever be ready? Would she ever be able to face the cold, emotionless stone etched with her daughter's name jutting from the earth? It seemed so cruel—to have such a deep connection with everything that grows, everything which relied on the fertile soil in this region...only for her child to be forever encased within it, forever out of reach.

It was strange to feel a thousand times more haunted by the absence of a ghost.

She took a deep breath, straightened her shoulders, and nodded. Her fingers found her eldest daughter's arm and squeezed, trying so hard to offer reassurance when, in reality, she was the one who needed to be reassured.

The smallest details stood out to her as they made their way through the mausoleum out to the memorial park lawn. The way the thick, velvet runner extended along every possible pathway between the folding chairs and the doors so her heels wouldn't echo in the stifling room lined with the dead. The way the sun was too bright, the cloudless sky too blue, the air too warm and fragranced for such a day as this. The way the birds chirped and flowers bloomed with all the vibrancy of Mya's cheerful and loving spirit.

The way she'd never get to see her face again, not even to say goodbye. "Not how you want to remember her," Ralph quietly advised at the morgue. The autopsy confirmed it was her remains they found in the farmhouse graveyard, mere inches away from the far more carefully buried Rachel Evans. It was a detail that they tried to hide from her, but a detail she managed to wrangle from Brigit Sulis in a fury of shrieks and sobs. Out of all the bodies they found out in those woods, it appeared eight-year-old Rachel Evans was the only one buried with care.

The other thirty-eight women and teens were simply disposed of, including what pieces remained of Mya Sadeh.

Demi clenched the soil in her fist while Davidson read aloud the last rites, passages from Scripture to remind them of the better place where their children now danced and played and never had to fear again. That everything had its time, the world its rhythm, even sorrow its place in shaping the soul into a better version of itself.

That vengeance belonged to their Creator.

Authorities were unable to locate their primary suspect, Jared McCready, after their initial suspect was found beheaded in the woods and tracks of the killer matched those they found in the outer perimeter of the farmhouse. The FBI came to Demi, of course, once the connection was made between the former trucker and the professor of biology. She didn't have much to tell them; his missing persons report was already on file from his initial disappearance almost a year ago. All she knew was the man she married, the loving husband and doting father, seemed to have died three years ago when he suddenly came home early from his trucking route. He was never quite the same, shuttering himself away to take phone calls and "discuss business" with someone he started working for shortly after. His new employer replaced his old truck and gave him new routes, longer routes, but paid much more than his previous contract.

And then he was gone.

"Mom, it's okay if you don't want to." Prax wrapped an arm around her waist and laid her head on her shoulder.

Demi blinked. The dirt. She breathed in a shuddering sigh and nodded, forced a smile between her tears, and opened her fist over her youngest daughter's grave. She let it go, let the fertile soil slip through her fingers to tuck her baby girl into eternal sleep.

She just wasn't sure she could let *it* go.

They stood together under the warm summer sun, arm in arm, staring at the swirls in the rich mahogany as other attendees slowly made their way from this grave to the next. Demi was the one who insisted on sharing this day with the other girls, the other women, most of whom were yet to be identified. It didn't feel right to turn a blind eye to these other daughters, not when their mothers still didn't know where they were.

A memorial statue was erected between the Fulton Farm Victims, as the news called them, and the area designated for children—the area where the family of Rachel and Sarah Evans laid the girls to rest. For a while, there'd been hope that Sarah was still alive, but Sheriff Sulis broke the news the same evening they found Rachel that her sister, too, was among the dead. Ralph gave the same gentle advice to Donna Wilkins: remember them happy and healthy and kissed with sunlight. Dental records were confirmation enough.

Happy, healthy, and kissed with sunlight is exactly how Sarah and Rachel appeared in their white marble likeness, forever suspended in a playful spin as their dresses billowed around them. Bright garlands of peonies draped around their necks and framed the base of their statue, spilling soft petals and emerald leaves over the verse which simply declared this "in loving memory". Prax squeezed her mother's hand as they slowly strolled over to admire the work of art commissioned by Mayor Ginnar, who took a moment from the solemn crowd to personally give Dr. Sadeh his deepest condolences. "We'll find whoever did this," he whispered as he clasped Demi's hand between his. "I promise."

Demi could only manage a tight smile. "Thank you."

Ginnar nodded, gave Prax another nod, then parted ways to give the same condolences and promises to the other grieving families.

Among those sharing their sympathies with the service attendees was Aidon Elrik, chatting quietly with Donna Wilkins over the beautiful headstone he'd been able to rush order along with the memorial statue. Prax couldn't hear what they were saying, but she saw the way Donna's face scrunched and her shoulders shook, and Aidon rested his arm around her shoulders until she leaned into him and let out the wail she'd held inside since she first handed Prax that flier. He let her grieve, let her lean on him, and gently hugged her side simply to reassure her she was not alone.

"Mom, do you want to—"

"You go ahead, Baby." Demi stroked her daughter's cheek and kissed the other. She cast a glance over Prax's shoulder to where she saw a figure standing by her car, his chestnut waves tousled in the breeze. "Donn's taking me to lunch, keeping me out of the house for a while. Lord knows I need some fresh air and a good cup of coffee." She actually smiled for the first time in days, and it worked to ease Prax's worry.

Prax watched her mother walk to the car, and only for a moment wondered why Donn and Demi seemed to exchange looks that suggested she should, in fact, be worried.

"Prax." Aidon murmured her name but she heard it as clear as a call, and she carefully approached him as he held the grieving Donna Wilkins, who now only sniffed and hiccuped. as she dabbed at her eyes with his proffered handkerchief. He gestured Prax to his free side and slipped his arm around her waist. "Do you trust me?" He whispered, his lips lightly brushing the skin below her ear.

She didn't know what he meant, but something deep inside, in that part of her being that still lay dormant but somehow knew, made her smile gently and whisper back, "yes".

Aidon took her hand in his, held it to his lips, kissed her fingers. Their eyes met, and she felt a sudden flow of warmth spread through her limbs, swirl in her chest, hum just beneath her skin. He looked reluctant to break their intimate gaze, but he did just so he could turn to Donna and whisper, "Close your eyes." The elderly woman did without hesitation, feeling that same warmth on a much gentler level that encouraged her to trust him. He took her wrist, outstretched her hand.

Donna Wilkins gasped. Then broke into tears anew at the feel of her granddaughter's hair beneath her fingertips.

"Keep them closed," Aidon gently warned, and she did, no matter how much it pained her to only feel without seeing.

Prax felt her own heart break wide open as Mya smiled and walked up to her, glowing with the same golden hue of their mother's skin. She opened her mouth to say something, anything, but all that came out was a choked sob of grief mixed with joy mixed with pain. It was too much and not enough.

Mya lifted her hand and tucked a curl behind her sister's ear. "I didn't get a chance to say goodbye. Not properly, anyway." She bit her lip. "I'm sorry I lied to you. I just wanted to meet you. And I didn't want Mom to be alone."

"She's not alone, not anymore." Finally, her tongue worked. Prax reached to caress her sweet sister's cheek, doing her best to see through the tears that kept stinging her eyes and dampening her own. "I miss you. I love you."

"I love you, too." Mya pressed her brow to Prax's, and that warmth within throbbed with desperation to hold on just a moment longer. "I have to go." With a featherlight kiss to her sister's wet cheek, she stepped away and took Rachel's hand with a gentle squeeze. The little girl gave her grandmother one final kiss of her own, then smiled at Aidon. "Thank you."

Prax blinked back larger tears and swallowed a sob, the warmth in her body slowly fading. She didn't realize her other hand was clinging to Aidon's until he gave it another squeeze, another kiss, and pulled her into his embrace. His closeness was the only thing that kept her from collapsing into the grass, weak as she felt with letting go of...everything.

A sniffled cough brought her back to the present, and she suddenly remembered Donna Wilkins, who looked at them and seemed as if she wanted to thank them for something she couldn't put words to. Finally she nodded, offered a small smile, and turned to walk away. Then stopped. "Where... where is Sarah?"

Prax glanced up at Aidon, who cleared his throat and held her to his side as he guided them down the gravel path, one final reassuring squeeze to Donna Wilkins' hand. Before she could ask any further, he steered them away and towards the path that led to his house.

Prax wanted to ask why she'd never noticed the swing on the porch, but she was enjoying the comfortable silence. If she were honest with herself, there was a strong possibility that he'd never felt comfortable showing her the more intimate areas of his home. Aidon was a very private person concealed by a dark and brooding outer persona no one wanted to be on the wrong side of. It made sense, especially when his defenses were up, that he wouldn't want anyone to discover just how much he loved the simple beauty of life.

She wanted to ask him about this duality, about what carved him into the feared and respected overlord of Bogarten's underworld. She wanted to learn everything about him, from his favorite music to his pettiest fear. No...she wanted to *re-learn* everything about him.

Just...some other time, when her head wasn't so comfortably nestled on his chest and his fingers weren't tracing lazy patterns on her arm. He rocked the swing for them with one foot, her toes too far away from the ground to help.

Spot 2.0 yawned and rested his head on her lap, his eyes peering up with such sweet pleading until she rubbed his ears.

"Are you sure we can't name him Spottacus?" whined Prax, scratching the bear-dog's happy chin.

"I'm sure," Aidon chuckled. "You're lucky if I even let you rename them at all."

"It's confusing!"

"What's confusing? They know their whistles."

"Well...I can't whistle like that." Prax gave him a pout and her best impression of Spot's puppy dog eyes, and Aidon rolled his own with a playful groan. "Fine," he grumbled, "I'll think about it. Or just teach you how to whistle." He didn't need to look directly at her to know she stuck her tongue out at him, and he tugged the ends of her curls with a coy wink. "Careful," he warned, "or I'll insist you show me what else that tongue can do."

Prax's eyes widened and she quickly returned to using him as a pillow, watching the swans paddle across the glassy water. After a long moment, she sighed. "What do you think Mom and Donn are up to?"

"Nothing good."

She peered up at him, and he shrugged. "What? That man is like a dog with a bone, and she's got one to pick. I'd like to say I was surprised to see them suddenly buddying up at the service, but I'm not. Best to just let weird things be weird."

"But shouldn't we at least call them? Or text? Just to check up on them?" Prax sat up and reached for her phone, but Aidon's warm hand stopped her.

"I know you're worried about your mother, but she is a strong, independent woman who's been kicking ass and taking names since long before you were born. And even with Donn's mercurial nature, he won't let anything happen to her." Aidon threaded his fingers with hers and traced each nail with the tips of his own. "Besides, I'm enjoying this time with you. Let me have a few more minutes before I have to share custody again."

Prax snorted. "Oh come on, it's not like that. I'm just staying with her while she works through some things and... so do I."

"I know." His fingers traced the bare patch of skin on her ring finger. "Doesn't make it any easier."

Now it was her turn to kiss his fingers, her guileless eyes gazing up into his with a promise she didn't know how to word. I will *remember you...eventually. Someday. I promise.* She knew there had to be truth to his claim, to her mother's confession, because everything in her basic, most primal instincts completely agreed without question or doubt.

Their lips met, a breathless whisper of a vow between them. Again, that *feeling* was there, sure and strong even though her mind struggled to come up with any shred of memory before the coma. "Promise I get you every other weekend, and Tuesdays for dinner?" he murmured, his mouth curving into a smile as she kissed him again.

"How about I regularly invade your personal space, eat all your food, and drink all your beer?"

"As long as you sleep it off in my bed."

She giggled and shoved at his chest, and Aidon tugged her into his arms just to tickle her sides. Spot, not wanting to be left out of the family fun, nosed between them and slobbered their faces with his broad tongue, making them both squeal.

S ummertime meant no leaves crunched under his feet as he wove between the trees—not that they would, anyways. Whenever it best suited him, whenever he needed, his footfalls were as silent as the grave.

His mouth quirked up in a sardonic smile the deeper he ventured into the woods. How had they missed this? How had such a thorough combing of these woods still allowed him this small favor he was about to thoroughly enjoy?

A hound bayed in the distance. A familiar sound, one that carried the answer on the gentle breeze. *Small favors, indeed.*

"Oh, Janey Mack." He'd seen a lot of interesting situations in his time, but the sight of the upturned root and the man impaled on it still caught him by surprise. Clean through the sternum, although "clean" was not an accurate word he'd use to describe the scene. *Did Aidon see this?* Again his question was immediately answered by the subtle reminder in the back of his mind that under normal circumstances, this gobshite would be on a slab in the morgue awaiting the potter's field.

But these were not normal circumstances, and even the elements refused to touch the monster in their midst.

"Wakey wakey, eggs and bakey!"

The man groaned. His eyes fluttered, then opened, then widened as his mouth stretched into a scream that just wouldn't come out. His chest tried to heave but the root made that impossible, only adding to his terror...and confusion. Hands grabbed him by the front of what was left of his shirt and he fixed his horrified gaze up into the cold, icy glare of the man staring down at him.

Not a normal man.

Donn Morrighan couldn't help himself—his glare shattered into the widest grin, the kind that didn't quite reach his eyes. "What's the matter, boy-o?" The accent seeped thick into his voice, and damn, did it feel good on his tongue. He heaved the man up and off the root without an ounce of effort and pulled him close, holding him several inches off the ground just for good measure. "Didya think I was done with ya?"

Now his chest moved, wet and rasping, the gaping hole in his shattered ribs suddenly throbbing with unearthly pain. He should be dead. He *was* dead.

Donn's smile grew darker. His eyes shadowed with something Jared McCready swore he'd just seen not moments ago, right when he'd launched himself at that nosy bitch and onto—he glanced over at the bloodied tree, at the root still covered with bits of himself. He shuddered, and it wasn't just from the blood loss.

"Oh, don't you worry." Donn's voice rasped with the icy fingers that gripped Jared in more ways than just by his shirt. "We're going to be spending a lot of time together before I'm done with you."

"How...?" Jared's voice returned, just barely, just enough to ask the question he already suspected he knew the answer to. He remembered this man, remembered the feel of metal slicing through flesh.

Not a normal man.

No verbal answer came, not when he was tossed over Donn's shoulder like a sack of potatoes, like a thing, and carried deeper into the woods—deeper and deeper where the vines grew thick and the leaves blocked out the sun. At the odd angle his head hung, it was impossible to clearly make out the figure who stood between the columns of trees that suddenly seemed too thick, too dark, too old. He only caught glimpses of gold-threaded chocolate hair framing an hourglass figure like a veil, topped with leaves that, to his addled mind, looked so much like a crown.

The world spun around him in a way that made him feel like he was no longer in the woods of Miskwa Valley, but instead somewhere else...somewhere he'd rather not be.

Epilogue

"Nature's car alarms", as her grandmother used to describe the cicadas, screamed through the trees with the same blistering agony she felt on her skin. She didn't know how long she'd been walking down the gravel road, only that it was long enough for the summer sun to beat down on the tops of her shoulders now instead of the nape of her neck.

She should have grabbed water before she ran.

She should have done a lot of things before she ran.

The treeline guarding the entrance to a lushly green cornfield slowly faded into the distance behind her, taking the screaming cicadas with it. For a moment, she thought to turn around to gauge the distance, to see how far away everything was now.

No.

No matter how far she went, it didn't matter. So long as she never, ever looked back.

Soon the only sound was the soft panting of her breath and the slight crunching of gravel under her feet. Shuffling was more like it—she'd lost feeling from the ankles down after the throbbing pain faded to numbness. Her lips peeled and blistered, her mouth and throat too dry to muster up any moisture to relieve the stinging pain. Every fiber in her limbs screamed for her to stop.

Can't stop.

Won't stop.

A merciful breeze rustled through the golden tassels, and she glanced over at the ripening corn nestled neatly on the stalks. The barest hint of moisture seeped onto her dry tongue at the mouth-watering memory of roasted sweet corn, fresh off the cob, creamy butter melting over the kernels. Maybe a small ear of corn would be enough to hydrate her tastebuds, just enough to get through. No one would notice.

No.

Can't stop.

Won't stop.

She didn't know why she couldn't allow herself just a few moments to get food, underripe as it may be. Why couldn't she bring herself to rest? The nightmares were behind her, the monsters vanquished and gone in a town she'd never see again.

But something stirred the hairs at the nape of her neck. An unease, a restlessness that drifted over her sunburned skin along with the breeze that now felt more like a gentle shove to her back. As if the wind was saying, *"Keep going...don't stop... you can't stop...."*

The crunching gravel sounded louder, steadier even. It took her several moments before she realized it was a car coming up the road behind her—no, not a car, a pickup truck, dusty and worn but still a newer model, kicking up a cloud of dust as it swiftly approached her. Instinct said to run, to hide, but her aching and numb body protested the very idea.

It pulled up ahead of her and swung around to the side,

cutting off the road to her entirely. She stopped, finally, and very nearly toppled forward from the sudden exhaustion that slammed into her harder than any wind.

She vaguely heard the driver's door creak open and slam shut, someone's steps crunching loudly on the rocks towards her. Arms reached out and caught her before she collapsed, her vision blurry as a kind face appeared. The woman—definitely a woman—crouched down to meet her eye level and quickly scanned her, probably for any sign of injuries.

"Are you alright?" The woman asked, her brow furrowed with concern.

She nodded. Was it true, though? *Was* she alright?

Would she ever, would anything ever, be all right?

The woman moved to rub her arms affectionately but stopped the moment she felt the heat of her burned skin. "Oh, honey, how long have you been out here? Never mind, let's get you inside and cooled off. I have your room ready, and a cold pitcher of lemonade just the way you like it. Does that sound good?"

She frowned and stumbled back. "How do you...?"

"We've been looking everywhere for you, darling."

Panic gripped her heart and squeezed the air from her lungs. "I can't go back!" She had no idea where the sudden ability to shriek with a dry throat came from, but it did, and she used it. "No! You can't make me go back!" She glanced around for anything she could use, anything strong enough to fight with, and when she couldn't find anything fast enough she balled her fists and swung into a stance. "I won't let you take me back!"

The woman quickly held her hands up in surrender and stepped back as well. "Easy, honey! Don't be afraid. I'm not taking you back there. You never, ever have to go anywhere near that town ever again. I promise."

She considered the woman for a long, humid minute. The sun was now lower in the sky, casting a golden glow on the woman's already bronzed skin and illuminated the golden streaks woven into her long braids. For a second, she thought she saw the woman's eyes flash with another kind of golden light, but she blinked and realized just how dry and weary her eyes were— they would probably hallucinate a vending machine at this point. She sighed and lowered her fists. "Promise?"

The woman nodded. "Absolutely. I know where you came from. There's no way in hell I'd make you go back." She carefully stepped around the bed of the truck to open the passenger door, and made sure to give plenty of space to indicate her genuinely good intentions. "Besides," she added as she closed the door, "your father's been worried about you. I promised him I'd make sure you were okay."

She whipped her gaze to the woman, who calmly slid into the driver's seat. Everything smelled like leather, spice, and something distinctly...*home*. "My father? But I don't—"

"You must be exhausted. We'll get you a cold drink, a good meal, and a cool bath the moment we get home." The woman's hand, soothing and cool as it rested on her brow, smoothed back the stray curls that stuck to her sweaty, dust-covered face. "Get some rest, it'll be a few minutes. You're safe now."

She felt, for the first time in ages, a faint smile tug at the corners of her mouth as she rested her head on the leather seat and gazed at the woman. The setting sun looked like a halo of warm light around the woman's head, and that golden flash of...something...flickered in her eyes again....but her own eyes fluttered close, too weary to focus on anything other than much-needed sleep.

The pickup truck kicked rocks and sand onto the road behind, carrying the two well beyond the reach of the monsters who laughed and dined and waited in the light of the setting sun of Bogarten.

About The Author

Nikki Auberkett is a cultural anthropologist, developmental editor, and overall passionate storyteller. With nearly 15 years of research and exploration into global folklore and mythology, biblical archaeology, and all things weird and unusual, she weaves her research and social science expertise into her personal love for fantasy fiction.

When she's not finding ways to vent about human rights via mythological retellings, Nikki can be spotted periodically throughout the city of Chicago testing her limits of coffee intake (she has yet to find one).

Follow Nikki on Instagram: @NikkiAuberkett
and on TikTok: @TalaEditorial

Acknowledgments

First and foremost, I have to give my unending gratitude to my Heavenly Father, who continuously aligns His plans for me in ways that extend beyond my own comprehension.

Simply put: somehow, everything in life lined up seamlessly for me to be able to finally write, finish, and publish this book and that was only possible because of Him!

I also need to give a massive "Thank You!" to my team at Tala Editorial, who knocked this project out of the park and stood by me and cheered me on through the ups and downs of publishing. Yes, even editors go through the same challenges as authors! Tara Cho stepped in as both Developmental Editor and Line Editor, going above and beyond her usual scope to help make Prax an amazing read. Kristy Lynae Moore crushed the typography in ways that still make my head spin - she is a true artist with the fonts and decorations!

Benjamin Richard gets his own paragraph of recognition: not only did he design the stunning cover art, he also acted as my other Developmental Editor and "book coach" from the moment I said, "I'm going to write this dang book."

He's waited over a decade, if not longer, for me to finally publish something! The care and detailed dedication he's given the cover design, the music he wrote (yes, he literally wrote a song for this novel!) and so many other little things to help inspire me through to the end are constant reminders of the amazing friend he truly is.

Special thanks go out to the Prax Launch Team, a group of twenty incredible people who volunteered to join me on the publishing journey, read the Advanced Reader Copy, and gave me constant feedback throughout the process to make this novel the best it can be. Several of these participants are aspiring authors with their own incredible stories debuting soon, and I can't wait to be there for them as well!

I actually have an extensive list of so many people I want to thank individually, but that would be a whole other novel in itself. My family is amazing, my church family is amazing, the staff in my apartment building where I basically holed up and wrote this is amazing…so many people and so few pages to list them all! I must give a special shout out to the barista team at Philz Coffee in Old Town, Chicago, for literally cheering me on and fueling my drive with emotional support and iced mochas.

And of course, I must give an extra-special gesture of gratitude and appreciation to Lincoln Perk in Waterloo, Iowa: the real "Jefferson Java", whose owners and staff were there with Sea Turtle mochas and grilled salmon sandwiches during some of my darkest days, and continue to be there both literally and figuratively for my family during the brightest.